A POEM FOR EVERY NIGHT OF THE YEAR

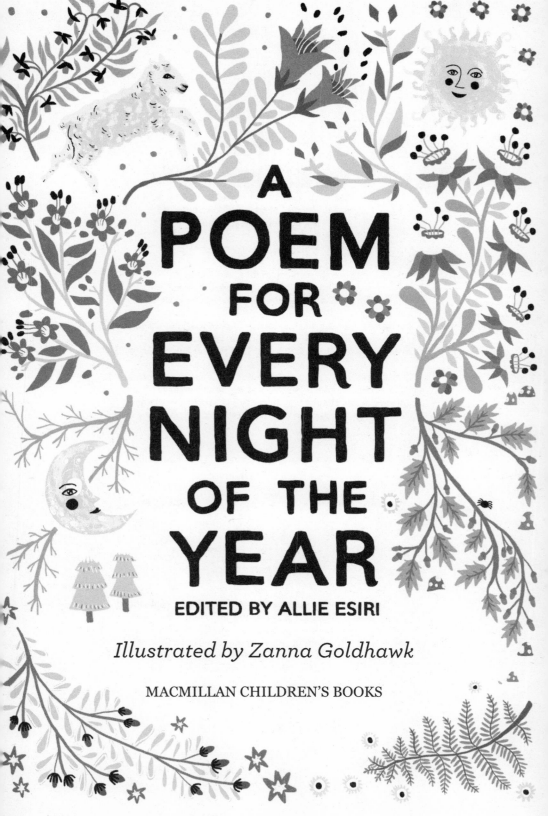

A POEM FOR EVERY NIGHT OF THE YEAR

EDITED BY ALLIE ESIRI

Illustrated by Zanna Goldhawk

MACMILLAN CHILDREN'S BOOKS

First published 2016 by Macmillan Children's Books
an imprint of Pan Macmillan
The Smithson, 6 Briset Street, London EC1M 5NR
Associated companies throughout the world
www.panmacmillan.com

ISBN 978-1-5098-1313-1

25

A CIP catalogue record for this book is available from
the British Library.

Printed and bound by CPI Group (UK) Ltd, Croydon CR0 4YY

To Eliza, Rosie and Jack Esiri

Contents

February

March

April

May

x

August

December

Introduction

William Wordsworth once wrote of beauty 'felt along the heart', like waves beating along a shore. We feel poems along the heart – they wash over us and, though we might not notice the impact they make, they leave the shores of our hearts a little changed. Great poems make us more human. They introduce us to new ways of seeing the world. They force us to imagine what it might be like to be someone completely different – and they show us that someone completely different is just as human as we are.

When I discovered poetry as a child, I remember stumbling over weird and wonderful words whose meaning I felt far from understanding, but I think I knew then that poetry held an extraordinary power. My childhood private passion has become my career: I spend most of my time reading poetry, writing about poetry and banging the metaphorical drum for poetry. Over the past few years I've tried to remind people how remarkable and exhilarating poetry is.

Poetry will stay with you for life. We use it to help us come to terms with the big things in life: love, friendship, loss, nature, beauty and the passing of time. People write and read poems for landmark events – weddings, funerals, political uproars or tragic disasters. But I wanted to share in this collection that poetry can also be for the small things in life, for the everyday. This anthology contains a poem for each and every night of the year. More than being just a sequence of beautiful poems to share at bedtime, however, this is a journey through culture and history and the seasons. Near April Fool's Day are poems that are complete nonsense but huge fun to read aloud, such as Lewis Carroll's bizarre 'Jabberwocky'. And there are poems on certain dates that tell us about the traditions of other cultures and religions. There are poems written about historical events, like the sinking of the *Titanic* or the seminal moment in the Civil Rights Movement in America when Rosa Parks refused to give up her seat on a bus. I hope that there is a poem here for everyone – something for every night and every mood and every person, whose lines never leave you but remain inside the private library of your brain, and whose beauty you feel as Wordsworth did: along the heart.

Allie Esiri

January

1 January ✳ New Every Morning ✳ Susan Coolidge

January takes its name from the Roman two-headed god
Janus, who had one head looking back to the outgoing year
and one facing the year ahead. Here, the American writer of
What Katy Did reflects on new beginnings.

Every day is a fresh beginning,
Listen my soul to the glad refrain.
And, spite of old sorrows
And older sinning,
Troubles forecasted
And possible pain,
Take heart with the day and begin again.

2 January ✻ The Loch Ness Monster's Song ✻ Edwin Morgan

2 January is a public holiday in Scotland. Edwin Morgan's poem celebrates Scotland's legendary monster in an unusual way. Composed of huge strings of wild sounds, this poem seems to make no sense at all — but when you think about it, there really is no reason that Nessie would speak any language that we could understand.

Sssnnnwhufffffll?
Hnwhuffl hhnnwfl hnfl hfl?
Gdroblboblhobngbl gbl gl g g g g glbgl.
Drublhaflablhaflubhafgabhaflhafl fl fl —
gm grawwwww grf grawf awfgm graw gm.
Hovoplodok — doplodovok — plovodokot-doplodokosh?
Splgraw fok fok splgrafhatchgabrlgabrl fok splfok!
Zgra kra gka fok!
Grof grawff gahf?
Gombl mbl bl —
blm plm,
blm plm,
blm plm,
blp.

Sara Coleridge was a writer like her father, the Romantic poet Samuel Taylor Coleridge. In this poem she uses rhyming couplets to guide us through the year.

January brings the snow,
Makes our feet and fingers glow.

February brings the rain,
Thaws the frozen lake again.

March brings breezes, loud and shrill,
To stir the dancing daffodil.

April brings the primrose sweet,
Scatters daisies at our feet.

May brings flocks of pretty lambs
Skipping by their fleecy dams.

June brings tulips, lilies, roses,
Fills the children's hands with posies.

Hot July brings cooling showers,
Apricots and gillyflowers.

August brings the sheaves of corn,
Then the harvest home is borne.

Warm September brings the fruit;
Sportsmen then begin to shoot.

Fresh October brings the pheasant;
Then to gather nuts is pleasant.

4

Dull November brings the blast;
Then the leaves are whirling fast.

Chill December brings the sleet,
Blazing fire, and Christmas treat.

4 January ✳ Stopping by Woods on a Snowy Evening ✳ Robert Frost

Why has the speaker in this poem by Robert Frost pulled up in the middle of a snowy forest? His horse doesn't know, and seems to be worried. The speaker wants to remain here alone; to give up his cold and weary journey homewards.

Whose woods these are I think I know.
His house is in the village though;
He will not see me stopping here
To watch his woods fill up with snow.

My little horse must think it queer
To stop without a farmhouse near
Between the woods and frozen lake
The darkest evening of the year.

He gives his harness bells a shake
To ask if there is some mistake.
The only other sound's the sweep
Of easy wind and downy flake.

The woods are lovely, dark and deep,
But I have promises to keep,
And miles to go before I sleep,
And miles to go before I sleep.

5 January ✷ Explained ✷ A. A. Milne

A. A. Milne is best known as the creator of Winnie the Pooh. Outside of the world of the Hundred Acre Wood, however, he was an accomplished poet.

> Elizabeth Ann
> Said to her Nan:
> 'Please will you tell me how God began?
> *Somebody* must have made Him. So
> Who could it be, cos I want to know?'
> And Nurse said, '*Well!*'
> And Ann said, 'Well?
> I know you know, and I wish you'd tell.'
> And Nurse took pins from her mouth, and said,
> 'Now then, darling, it's time for bed.'
>
> Elizabeth Ann
> Had a wonderful plan:
> She would run round the world till she found a man
> Who knew *exactly* how God began.
>
> She got up early, she dressed, and ran
> Trying to find an Important Man.
> She ran to London and knocked at the door
> Of the Lord High Doodelum's coach-and-four.
> 'Please, sir (if there's anyone in),
> However-and-ever did God begin?'
>
> The Lord High Doodelum lay in bed
> But out of the window, large and red,
> Came the Lord High Coachman's face instead.
> And the Lord High Coachman laughed and said:
> 'Well, what put *that* in your quaint little head?'

7

Elizabeth Ann went home again
And took from the ottoman Jennifer Jane.
'Jenniferjane,' said Elizabeth Ann,
'Tell me at *once* how God began.'
And Jane, who didn't much care for speaking,
Replied in her usual way by squeaking.

What did it mean? Well, to be quite candid,
I don't know, but Elizabeth Ann did.
Elizabeth Ann said softly, 'Oh!
Thank you Jennifer. Now I know.'

6 January * Journey of the Magi * T. S. Eliot

In the Christian calendar, the 6 January is known as the Feast of Epiphany. The date commemorates the visit of three wise men, or kings, to the baby Jesus, who are referred to in this poem as 'Magi' – a word that means 'magicians'. This is one of the most famous stories in the world, but Eliot tells it from the perspective of the Magi themselves, emphasizing the difficulty of the journey.

'A cold coming we had of it,
Just the worst time of the year
For a journey, and such a long journey:
The ways deep and the weather sharp,
The very dead of winter.'
And the camels galled, sore-footed, refractory,
Lying down in the melting snow.
There were times we regretted
The summer palaces on slopes, the terraces,
And the silken girls bringing sherbet.
Then the camel men cursing and grumbling
and running away, and wanting their liquor and women,
And the night-fires going out, and the lack of shelters,
And the cities hostile and the towns unfriendly
And the villages dirty and charging high prices:
A hard time we had of it.
At the end we preferred to travel all night,
Sleeping in snatches,
With the voices singing in our ears, saying
That this was all folly.

Then at dawn we came down to a temperate valley,
Wet, below the snow line, smelling of vegetation,
With a running stream and a water-mill beating the darkness,
And three trees on the low sky.
And an old white horse galloped away in the meadow.
Then we came to a tavern with vine-leaves over the lintel,
Six hands at an open door dicing for pieces of silver,
And feet kicking the empty wine-skins.
But there was no information, and so we continued
And arriving at evening, not a moment too soon
Finding the place; it was (you may say) satisfactory.

All this was a long time ago, I remember,
And I would do it again, but set down
This set down
This: were we led all that way for
Birth or Death? There was a Birth, certainly,
We had evidence and no doubt. I had seen birth and death,
But had thought they were different; this Birth was
Hard and bitter agony for us, like Death, our death.
We returned to our places, these Kingdoms,
But no longer at ease here, in the old dispensation,
With an alien people clutching their gods.
I should be glad of another death.

7 January * Saint Distaff's Day, or The Morrow After Twelfth Day * Robert Herrick

This poem by Robert Herrick describes an old tradition, where men and women used to take the opportunity of 'St Distaff's Day' to play pranks on one another.

Partly work,and partly play
Ye must, on Saint Distaff's day:
From the plough soon free your team;
Then come home, and fodder them:
If the maids a-spinning go;
Burn the flax, and fire the tow,
Scorch their plackets, but beware
That ye singe no maiden hair:
Bring in pails of water, then,
Let the maids bewash the men:
Give Saint Distaff all the right,
Then bid Christmas sport good-night;
And, next morrow, everyone
To his own vocation.

8 January ✴ The more it SNOWS ✴ A. A. Milne

The idea for this poem came to Winnie the Pooh while he was
waiting in a snowstorm for Piglet to answer his knock at the
door. Jumping up and down in the cold, Pooh found that a
'hum' came into his head: 'a Good Hum, such as is Hummed
Hopefully to Others.'

    The more it snows
        (Tiddely-pom)
    The more it goes
        (Tiddely-pom)
    The more it goes
        (Tiddely-pom)
      On snowing.

    And nobody knows
        (Tiddely-pom)
    How cold my toes
        (Tiddely-pom)
    How cold my toes
        (Tiddely-pom)
      Are growing.

9 January * Nobody Knows * Rachel Rooney

The magic of Jonjo, perhaps, is that it doesn't matter whether he is real or not: the important thing is how wonderful the outside world can be.

Nobody knows what Jonjo knows. Nobody knows but he.
So Jonjo took me for a walk and showed his world to me.

I met him by the garden gate when the sun broke fresh and new.
Jonjo knows that fairies sleep on cobwebs laced with dew.

We strolled along the river's edge. It glistened in the light.
Sailing on a leafy boat, we saw a water sprite.

I followed him to forests and sank down to my knees.
Jonjo knows that wood elves meet in the hollow of old trees.

We climbed an icy mountain. Clouds drifted past our eyes.
There we spotted unicorns play chase across the skies.

I joined him at the ocean, where the mist rolled slowly in.
Jonjo knows a silver splash is the glimpse of a mermaid's fin.

He brought me to a stone cave as the sun began to fall,
to watch a dragon's shadow dance across the entrance wall.

We wandered in the starshine. An orange moon glowed bright.
Jonjo knows the man up there will keep us in his sight.

I got back home at midnight. He walked me to my door.
But as I turned to say goodbye, my Jonjo was no more.

Nobody knows what Jonjo knows. Nobody knows it's true.
So let me take you for a walk and I'll show his world to you.

13

10 January ✴ Baby Orang-utan ✴ Helen Dunmore

Although January is a cold, wintry month, it is also the start of
a new year – days are becoming longer, and before we know it
new life will start springing from the earth. This poem is about
the beginning of a life.

> Bold flare of orange –
> a struck match
> against his mother's breast
>
> he listens to her heartbeat
> going yes yes yes

11 January ✳ Escape at Bedtime ✳
Robert Louis Stevenson

Robert Louis Stevenson is now best known as the author of
the adventure novel *Treasure Island*, but he was also a poet.
Despite the lack of pirates and treasure maps, this poem
describes an adventure, as its speaker manages to escape
bedtime.

The lights from the parlour and kitchen shone out
Through the blinds and the windows and bars;
And high overhead and all moving about,
There were thousands of millions of stars.
There ne'er were such thousands of leaves on a tree,
Nor of people in church or the park,
As the crowds of the stars that looked down upon me,
And that glittered and winked in the dark.

The Dog, and the Plough, and the Hunter, and all,
And the star of the sailor, and Mars,
These shone in the sky, and the pail by the wall
Would be half full of water and stars.
They saw me at last, and they chased me with cries,
And they soon had me packed into bed;
But the glory kept shining and bright in my eyes,
And the stars going round in my head.

12 January ✳ A Good Play ✳
Robert Louis Stevenson

This poem continues with the theme of adventure. This time, the narrator is describing 'the very best of plays' that he had with his friend, Tom, when they built a ship on the stairs of the house.

We built a ship upon the stairs
All made of the back-bedroom chairs,
And filled it full of soft pillows
To go a-sailing on the billows.
We took a saw and several nails,
And water in the nursery pails;
And Tom said, 'Let us also take
An apple and a slice of cake;' –
Which was enough for Tom and me
To go a-sailing on, till tea.
We sailed along for days and days,
And had the very best of plays;
But Tom fell out and hurt his knee,
So there was no one left but me.

13 January ✳ The Land of Story Books ✳ Robert Louis Stevenson

This poem celebrates the way the imagination – this time fed by story books – can create a whole world to play in, even in the confines of the house.

At evening when the lamp is lit,
Around the fire my parents sit;
They sit at home and talk and sing,
And do not play at anything.

Now, with my little gun, I crawl
All in the dark along the wall,
And follow round the forest track
Away behind the sofa back.

There, in the night, where none can spy,
All in my hunter's camp I lie,
And play at books that I have read
Till it is time to go to bed.

These are the hills, these are the woods,
These are my starry solitudes;
And there the river by whose brink
The roaring lions come to drink.

I see the others far away
As if in firelit camp they lay,
And I, like an Indian scout,
Around their party prowled about.

So, when my nurse comes in for me,
Home I return across the sea,
And go to bed with backward looks
At my dear land of Story Books.

14 January ✳ Doors ✳ Carl Sandburg

Poetry has the power to change the way we see even the most familiar of objects.

> An open door says, 'Come in.'
> A shut door says, 'Who are you?'
> Shadows and ghosts go through shut doors.
> If a door is shut and you want it shut,
>   why open it?
> If a door is open and you want it open,
>   why shut it?
> Doors forget but only doors know what it is
>   doors forget.

15 January * Dream Variations *
Langston Hughes

Born on 15 January 1929, Martin Luther King, Jr. was an American Baptist minister and leader in the African-American Civil Rights movement. As an activist he led nonviolent protests against racial inequality. He is remembered each year on the third Monday of January – Martin Luther King, Jr. Day. Just as Martin Luther King, Jr. in his often quoted speech, 'I Have a Dream' discussed his vision for a racially equal America in terms of a 'dream', in this poem Hughes depicts freedom as a dream.

> To fling my arms wide
> In some place of the sun,
> To whirl and to dance
> Till the white day is done.
> Then rest at cool evening
> Beneath a tall tree
> While night comes on gently,
>   Dark like me—
> That is my dream!
>
> To fling my arms wide
> In the face of the sun,
> Dance! Whirl! Whirl!
> Till the quick day is done.
> Rest at pale evening . . .
> A tall, slim tree . . .
> Night coming tenderly
>   Black like me.

16 January ✳ I, Too ✳ Langston Hughes

The African-American poet Langston Hughes wrote many
poems on the theme of racial inequality. The table here is a
metaphor for the privileged place of white people in American
society at the time. Yet the poem also contains a message
of hope for the future, where 'the darker brother' will be
acknowledged at the table and recognized as an equal part of
American society.

I, too, sing America.

I am the darker brother.
They send me to eat in the kitchen
When company comes,
But I laugh,
And eat well,
And grow strong.

Tomorrow,
I'll be at the table
When company comes.
Nobody'll dare
Say to me,
'Eat in the kitchen,'
Then.

Besides,
They'll see how beautiful I am
And be ashamed—

I, too, am America.

17 January * Mother to Son * Langston Hughes

In this poem, Hughes likens the struggle of African Americans against oppression to climbing a never-ending staircase. The Civil Rights Movement did not achieve equality overnight: rights were gained incrementally over decades and it is a struggle which is not over, even now in the twenty-first century.

Well, son, I'll tell you:
Life for me ain't been no crystal stair.
It's had tacks in it,
And splinters,
And boards torn up,
And places with no carpet on the floor—
Bare.
But all the time
I'se been a-climbin' on,
And reachin' landin's,
And turnin' corners,
And sometimes goin' in the dark
Where there ain't been no light.
So, boy, don't you turn back.
Don't you set down on the steps.
'Cause you find it kinder hard.
Don't you fall now—
For I'se still goin', honey,
I'se still climbin',
And life for me ain't been no crystal stair.

18 January ✳ Caged Bird ✳ Maya Angelou

Like Langston Hughes, Maya Angelou was a prominent
figure in the American Civil Rights movement. Here Angelou
uses the metaphor of a caged bird to explore the oppression
suffered by African-American citizens. The poem ends
with a message of hope, however, that one day the bird will
experience freedom.

A free bird leaps
on the back of the wind
and floats downstream
till the current ends
and dips his wing
in the orange sun rays
and dares to claim the sky.

But a bird that stalks
down his narrow cage
can seldom see through
his bars of rage
his wings are clipped and
his feet are tied
so he opens his throat to sing.

The caged bird sings
with a fearful trill
of things unknown
but longed for still
and his tune is heard
on the distant hill
for the caged bird
sings of freedom.

The free bird thinks of another breeze
and the trade winds soft through the sighing trees
and the fat worms waiting on a dawn bright lawn
and he names the sky his own

But a caged bird stands on the grave of dreams
his shadow shouts on a nightmare scream
his wings are clipped and his feet are tied
so he opens his throat to sing.

The caged bird sings
with a fearful trill
of things unknown
but longed for still
and his tune is heard
on the distant hill
for the caged bird
sings of freedom.

19 January ✴ To a Snowdrop ✴
William Wordsworth

Snowdrops are the very first flowers to appear each year and they bring the promise of Spring to us in the midst of Winter.

Lone Flower, hemmed in with snows and white as they
But hardier far, once more I see thee bend
Thy forehead, as if fearful to offend,
Like an unbidden guest. Though day by day,
Storms, sallying from the mountain-tops, waylay
The rising sun, and on the plains descend;
Yet art thou welcome, welcome as a friend
Whose zeal outruns his promise! Blue-eyed May
Shall soon behold this border thickly set
With bright jonquils, their odours lavishing
On the soft west-wind and his frolic peers;
Nor will I then thy modest grace forget,
Chaste Snowdrop, venturous harbinger of Spring,
And pensive monitor of fleeting years!

20 January ✶ *from* The Eve of St Agnes ✶
John Keats

'The Eve of St Agnes' was inspired by an ancient superstition surrounding 20 January. It was thought that if a young woman went to bed without eating supper, lay on her back and slept with her hands under the pillow, she would dream of her future husband.

St Agnes' Eve—Ah, bitter chill it was!
The owl, for all his feathers, was a-cold;
The hare limp'd trembling through the frozen grass,
And silent was the flock in woolly fold:
Numb were the Beadsman's fingers, while he told
His rosary, and while his frosted breath,
Like pious incense from a censer old,
Seem'd taking flight for heaven, without a death,
Past the sweet Virgin's picture, while his prayer he saith.

His prayer he saith, this patient, holy man;
Then takes his lamp, and riseth from his knees,
And back returneth, meagre, barefoot, wan,
Along the chapel aisle by slow degrees:
The sculptur'd dead, on each side, seem to freeze,
Emprison'd in black, purgatorial rails:
Knights, ladies, praying in dumb orat'ries,
He passeth by; and his weak spirit fails
To think how they may ache in icy hoods and mails.

Northward he turneth through a little door,
And scarce three steps, ere Music's golden tongue
Flatter'd to tears this aged man and poor;
But no—already had his deathbell rung;
The joys of all his life were said and sung:
His was harsh penance on St Agnes' Eve:
Another way he went, and soon among
Rough ashes sat he for his soul's reprieve,
And all night kept awake, for sinners' sake to grieve.

That ancient Beadsman heard the prelude soft;
And so it chanc'd, for many a door was wide,
From hurry to and fro. Soon, up aloft,
The silver, snarling trumpets 'gan to chide:
The level chambers, ready with their pride,
Were glowing to receive a thousand guests:
The carved angels, ever eager-eyed,
Star'd, where upon their heads the cornice rests,
With hair blown back, and wings put cross-wise on their breasts.

At length burst in the argent revelry,
With plume, tiara, and all rich array,
Numerous as shadows haunting faerily
The brain, new stuff'd, in youth, with triumphs gay
Of old romance. These let us wish away,
And turn, sole-thoughted, to one Lady there,
Whose heart had brooded, all that wintry day,
On love, and wing'd St Agnes' saintly care,
As she had heard old dames full many times declare.

They told her how, upon St Agnes' Eve,
Young virgins might have visions of delight,
And soft adorings from their loves receive
Upon the honey'd middle of the night,
If ceremonies due they did aright;
As, supperless to bed they must retire,
And couch supine their beauties, lily white;
Nor look behind, nor sideways, but require
Of Heaven with upward eyes for all that they desire.

21 January ✴ The Snake and the Apple ✴
Tony Mitton

This poem plays upon a common poetic theme, the Garden of Eden. The garden was the home of the first humans, Adam and Eve, until the snake tricked them into eating apples from the Tree of the Knowledge of Good and Evil. God had forbidden them to do this, and as punishment for this act of disobedience, they were thrown out of the Garden of Eden.

The snake lay up in the apple tree
out of the heat of the day.
'There's nothing to fear from an apple, my dear,'
I heard him slyly say.

He curled his coils around the branch
and looked with a lidless eye.
'It's sweet, for sure, whether eaten raw
or baked in a nice hot pie.'

The snake lay up in the apple tree
out of the light of the sun.
'There's enough in the tree for you and me,
and enough for everyone.'

He licked at a rosy apple
with a smile and a slippery hiss.
'You've nothing to fear from an apple, my dear.
Just take a bite. It's bliss.'

22 January ✳ St Vincent's Day Rhyme ✳ Anon.

22 January is the feast day of St Vincent, the patron saint of wine-makers. In France they say that if it's bright and sunny on January 22nd, the year will bring more wine than water!

> Remember on St Vincent's Day,
> If that the sun his beams display,
> Be sure to mark his transient beam,
> Which through the casement sheds a gleam;
> For 'tis a token bright and clear
> Of prosperous weather all the year.

23 January ✳ Evening Shifts ✳ Graham Denton

A nightwatchman was a kind of police officer who patrolled the streets at night, ringing a bell and calling out the time, as well as keeping lookout for fires and unruly behaviour. In this poem, Graham Denton imagines the moon as a 'nightwatchman of the sky', giving it the task of looking after us.

> As cloak-black clouds
> of evening drift
> across his torch-white eye,
>
> the moon begins
> his evening shift—
> nightwatchman of the sky.

24 January ✷ Moon Child ✷ Sue Hardy-Dawson

Sue Hardy-Dawson's moon is not a policeman but a 'moon child', who creeps across the sky and drops down 'magic beans' that explain why we have dreams during the night.

In the darkness while you sleep
across the sky, Moon Child creeps
around the galaxy of dreams
collecting magic wishing beans.

And where a child sleeps below
he drops a tiny bean to grow
on the countryside or town,
cosy cottage, sleepy farm.

Where the roads and houses meet
on tenements, city streets
in the streetlamp's soft red glow
where only magic beans will grow.

Grey savannas and dry plains
on caravans, midnight trains
under leaves of forest trees
tropical islands, out to sea.

On rowing boats, ocean liners
narrow barges, junks from China
beyond the brown river's flow
where only magic beans will grow.

In houses built on wooden stilts,
tents of canvas, hide or silk,
on shanty shacks made from clay
under thatch or grey blue slate.

On the banks of muddy creaks
high on icy mountain peaks.
Underneath the ice and snow
where only magic beans will grow.

Travelling the desert sands
jungle huts in distant lands
under rooves, beneath the stars
coming home by plane or car.

Here to stay or passing by
under the ground, way up high,
tower block and bungalow
where only magic beans will grow.

Through the night so dark and deep
across the sky Moon Child creeps
dropping magic wishing beans
to fill your head with magic dreams.

25 January ✶ *from* To a Haggis ✶ Robert Burns

Scotland's national poet, Robert Burns, was born on 25 January 1759. In Scotland this date has come to be known as Burns' Night – a night when people gather to feast, drink, and celebrate the life and poetry of Burns. Written in his lowland Scots dialect, this poem is traditionally recited at Burns' Night dinners. Here are the first and last verses in the original Scottish dialect, and below in translation!

Fair fa' your honest, sonsie face,
Great Chieftain o' the Puddin-race!
Aboon them a' ye tak your place,
    Painch, tripe, or thairm:
Weel are ye wordy of a grace
    As lang's my arm.

Ye Pow'rs wha mak mankind your care,
And dish them out their bill o' fare,
Auld Scotland wants nae skinking ware
    That jaups in luggies;
But, if ye wish her gratefu' pray'r,
    Gie her a Haggis!

All hail your honest rounded face,
Great chieftain of the pudding race;
Above them all you take your place,
    Beef, tripe, or lamb:
You're worthy of a grace
    As long as my arm.

You powers that make mankind your care,
And dish them out their bill of fare.
Old Scotland wants no stinking ware,
    That slops in dishes;
But if you grant her grateful prayer,
    Give her a haggis!

26 January ✳ Waltzing Matilda ✳ Banjo Paterson

On 26 January 1788 a fleet of British ships arrived in New South Wales and raised the British flag; this date is now celebrated as the national day of Australia. The bush ballad 'Waltzing Matilda' is so popular in Australia that it is known as the country's unofficial national anthem.

Oh! there once was a swagman camped in the Billabong,
  Under the shade of a Coolabah tree;
And he sang as he looked at his old billy boiling
  'Who'll come a-waltzing Matilda with me.'

  Who'll come a-waltzing Matilda, my darling.
  Who'll come a-waltzing Matilda with me.
Waltzing Matilda and leading a water-bag —
  Who'll come a-waltzing Matilda with me.

Down came a jumbuck to drink at the waterhole,
  Up jumped the swagman and grabbed him in glee;
And he sang as he stowed him away in his tucker-bag,
  'You'll come a-waltzing Matilda with me!'

Down came the Squatter a-riding his thoroughbred;
  Down came Policemen — one, two, and three.
'Whose is the jumbuck you've got in the tucker-bag?
  You'll come a-waltzing Matilda with me.'

But the swagman, he up and he jumped in the waterhole,
  Drowning himself by the Coolabah tree;
And his ghost may be heard as it sings in the Billabong
  'Who'll come a-waltzing Matilda with me?'

27 January ✳ The Shape of Anne Frank's Soul ✳ Louise Greig

Anne Frank, a young Jewish girl from Amsterdam, was only 15 when she died at Bergen-Belsen. Her diary, published posthumously in 1947, offers an extraordinary first-hand account of life under the Nazi occupation. 27 January is now remembered as Holocaust Memorial Day, and commemorates the liberation of Auschwitz, the most notorious of the Nazi concentration camps, on this date in 1945.

What shape does my soul take?
Is it round, like the moon
pale and ghostly, suspended above me
or is it a dark pool at my feet
an ellipse
deep
and infinite

Or is my soul a square?
A bare room
somewhere
left behind.
Or a book lined
in velvet
only to let
rare thoughts fill it

Perhaps my soul is a shape
only fit for a soul,
a blanket, a bed,
an empty bowl
Or not a shape at all
but words on the wind's gust
earth to earth
ashes to ashes
dust to dust

28 January ✳ The Moon ✳ Sappho, translated by
Edwin Arnold

Sappho was an ancient Greek poet. She lived around 600 BC.

> The stars about the lovely moon
> Fade back and vanish very soon,
> When, round and full, her silver face
> Swims into sight, and lights all space.

29 January ✴ Eldorado ✴ Edgar Allan Poe

This poem tells the tale of a knight in search of the city of Eldorado – a mythical city of gold supposedly in South America. In the sixteenth century many explorers went in search of the city, scouring Colombia, Venezuela, Brazil and other areas of the continent.

Gaily bedight,
A gallant knight,
In sunshine and in shadow,
Had journeyed long,
Singing a song,
In search of Eldorado.

But he grew old—
This knight so bold—
And o'er his heart a shadow—
Fell as he found
No spot of ground
That looked like Eldorado.

And, as his strength
Failed him at length,
He met a pilgrim shadow—
'Shadow,' said he,
'Where can it be—
This land of Eldorado?'

'Over the Mountains
Of the Moon,
Down the Valley of the Shadow,
Ride, boldly ride,'
The shade replied,—
'If you seek for Eldorado!'

30 January ✳ On a Quiet Conscience ✳ Charles I

Following his defeat by Oliver Cromwell in the English Civil War, Charles I was convicted of high treason. He was executed on 30 January 1649. Known as a great lover of art, and poetry, it is assumed that he wrote this poem.

Close thine eyes, and sleep secure:
Thy soul is safe, thy body pure.
He that guards thee, He that keeps,
Never slumbers, never sleeps.
A quiet conscience, in a quiet breast
Has only peace, has only rest:
The wisest and the mirth of kings
Are out of tune unless she sings.
Then close thine eyes in peace, and sleep secure,
No sleep so sweet as thine, no rest so sure.

31 January ✳ In the Quiet Night ✳ Li Bai, translated by Vikram Seth

One of the most admired of Chinese poets, Li Bai lived during the Tang Dynasty – a period often called the Golden Age of China. Almost a thousand of his poems remain. Chinese New Year, one of the most important Chinese festivals, marks the turn of the lunar calendar. It is celebrated on the second new moon after the Winter Solstice, which means that it usually falls in late January or early February.

> The floor before my bed is bright:
> Moonlight – like hoarfrost – in my room.
> I lift my head and watch the moon.
> I drop my head and think of home.

February

1 February ✳ Cinquain Prayer, February Night ✳ Fred Sedgwick

This poem takes the form of an American Cinquain, a short type of poem inspired by the compact Japanese haiku, with a set amount of syllables per line: 2, 4, 6, 8, 2.

> On this
> cold night I kneel
> with thanks for catkins, pale
> green under the lamplight by the
> roadside.

2 February ✳ Ceremony upon Candlemas Eve ✳ Robert Herrick

Candlemas, celebrated by Christians on 2 February, is one of the twelve Great Feasts of the church calendar, and commemorates the Presentation of Jesus at the Temple. Herrick's poem reminds the reader to take down their Christmas decorations by this date as it was a tradition that any decorations not taken down by Twelfth Night (5 January) had to stay up until Candlemas.

> Down with the rosemary, and so
> Down with the bays and mistletoe;
> Down with the holly, ivy, all
> Wherewith ye dress'd the Christmas hall;
> That so the superstitious find
> Not one least branch left there behind;
> For look, how many leaves there be
> Neglected, there (maids, trust to me)
> So many goblins you shall see.

Nash wrote this poem for his own daughter, Isabel, who must have been a particularly fearless child.

Isabel met an enormous bear,
Isabel, Isabel, didn't care;
The bear was hungry, the bear was ravenous,
The bear's big mouth was cruel and cavernous.
The bear said, Isabel, glad to meet you,
How do, Isabel, now I'll eat you!
Isabel, Isabel, didn't worry,
Isabel didn't scream or scurry.
She washed her hands and she straightened her hair up,
Then Isabel quietly ate the bear up.

Once in a night as black as pitch
Isabel met a wicked old witch.
The witch's face was cross and wrinkled,
The witch's gums with teeth were sprinkled.
Ho ho, Isabel! The old witch crowed,
I'll turn you into an ugly toad!
Isabel, Isabel, didn't worry,
Isabel didn't scream or scurry.
She showed no rage and she showed no rancor,
But she turned the witch into milk and drank her.

Isabel met a hideous giant,
Isabel continued self-reliant.
The giant was hairy, the giant was horrid,
He had one eye in the middle of his forehead.
Good morning, Isabel, the giant said,
I'll grind your bones to make my bread.
Isabel, Isabel, didn't worry,
Isabel didn't scream or scurry.
She nibbled the zwieback that she always fed off,
And when it was gone, she cut the giant's head off.

Isabel met a troublesome doctor,
He punched and he poked till he really shocked her.
The doctor's talk was of coughs and chills
And the doctor's satchel bulged with pills.
The doctor said unto Isabel,
Swallow this, it will make you well.
Isabel, Isabel, didn't worry,
Isabel didn't scream or scurry.
She took those pills from the pill concocter,
And Isabel calmly cured the doctor.

4 February ✶ There Was an Old Lady ✶ Anon.

The repetition in this poem makes it great fun to read out loud.

There was an old lady who swallowed a fly,
I don't know why she swallowed a fly,
Perhaps she'll die.

There was an old lady who swallowed a spider,
That wriggled and jiggled and tickled inside her,
She swallowed the spider to catch the fly,
I don't know why she swallowed the fly,
Perhaps she'll die.

There was an old lady who swallowed a bird,
How absurd! to swallow a bird,
She swallowed the bird to catch the spider,
That wriggled and jiggled and tickled inside her,
She swallowed the spider to catch the fly,
I don't know why she swallowed the fly,
Perhaps she'll die.

There was an old lady who swallowed a cat,
Imagine that! to swallow a cat,
She swallowed the cat to catch the bird,
She swallowed the bird to catch the spider,
That wriggled and jiggled and tickled inside her,
She swallowed the spider to catch the fly,
I don't know why she swallowed the fly,
Perhaps she'll die.

There was an old lady who swallowed a dog,
What a hog! to swallow a dog,
She swallowed the dog to catch the cat,
She swallowed the cat to catch the bird,
She swallowed the bird to catch the spider,
That wriggled and jiggled and tickled inside her,
She swallowed the spider to catch the fly,
I don't know why she swallowed the fly,
Perhaps she'll die.

There was an old lady who swallowed a goat,
Just opened her throat! to swallow a goat,
She swallowed the goat to catch the dog,
She swallowed the dog to catch the cat,
She swallowed the cat to catch the bird,
She swallowed the bird to catch the spider,
That wriggled and jiggled and tickled inside her,
She swallowed the spider to catch the fly,
I don't know why she swallowed the fly,
Perhaps she'll die.

There was an old lady who swallowed a cow,
I don't know how she swallowed a cow!
She swallowed the cow to catch the goat,
She swallowed the goat to catch the dog,
She swallowed the dog to catch the cat,
She swallowed the cat to catch the bird,
She swallowed the bird to catch the spider,
That wriggled and jiggled and tickled inside her,
She swallowed the spider to catch the fly,
I don't know why she swallowed the fly,
Perhaps she'll die.

There was an old lady who swallowed a horse,
She's dead—of course!

5 February ✳ On the Ning Nang Nong ✳ Spike Milligan

Spike Milligan was a writer, actor, comedian and poet who wrote nonsense poems that combine some phrases that make sense with others that do not.

On the Ning Nang Nong
Where the cows go Bong!
And the monkeys all say BOO!
There's a Nong Nang Ning
Where the trees go Ping!
And the tea pots jibber jabber joo.
On the Nong Ning Nang
All the mice go Clang
And you just can't catch 'em when they do!
So it's Ning Nang Nong
Cows go Bong!
Nong Nang Ning
Trees go Ping!
Nong Ning Nang
The mice go Clang!
What a noisy place to belong
is the Ning Nang
  Ning Nang Nong!!

6 February ✶ The ABC ✶ Spike Milligan

In this poem, Spike Milligan employs personification to allow the different letters to talk to each other, and the poem is full of puns and jokes that focus on the possibilities of spelling, such as 'ill' becoming 'Jill', and also on the relationship between letters and numbers, as V can also be five in Roman numerals.

'Twas midnight in the schoolroom
And every desk was shut
When suddenly from the alphabet
Was heard a loud 'Tut-Tut!'

Said A to B, 'I don't like C;
His manners are a lack.
For all I ever see of C
Is a semi-circular back!'

'I disagree,' said D to B,
'I've never found C so.
From where I stand he seems to be
An uncompleted O.'

C was vexed, 'I'm much perplexed,
You criticize my shape.
I'm made like that, to help spell Cat
And Cow and Cool and Cape.'

'He's right' said E; said F, 'Whoopee!'
Said G, ''Ip, 'Ip, 'ooray!'
'You're dropping me,' roared H to G.
'Don't do it please I pray.'

47

'Out of my way,' LL said to K.
'I'll make poor I look ILL.'
To stop this stunt J stood in front,
And presto! ILL was JILL.

'U know,' said V, 'that W
Is twice the age of me.
For as a Roman V is five
I'm half as young as he.'

X and Y yawned sleepily,
'Look at the time!' they said.
'Let's all get off to beddy byes.'
They did, then 'Z-z-z.'

7 February ✶ Today I Saw a Little Worm ✶
Spike Milligan

This poem by Spike Milligan is very short, but very funny.

> Today I saw a little worm
> Wriggling on its belly.
> Perhaps he'd like to come inside
> And see what's on the Telly.

8 February ✳ Manners ✳ Elizabeth Bishop

The American poet Elizabeth Bishop spent most of her childhood living with her grandparents, and this is reflected in this poem. The contrast between the new cars and the old-fashioned means of transport hints at the changes that are going to come, suggesting that as life speeds up, manners and habits might change.

My grandfather said to me
as we sat on the wagon seat,
'Be sure to remember to always
speak to everyone you meet.'

We met a stranger on foot.
My grandfather's whip tapped his hat.
'Good day, sir. Good day. A fine day.'
And I said it and bowed where I sat.

Then we overtook a boy we knew
with his big pet crow on his shoulder.
'Always offer everyone a ride;
don't forget that when you get older,'

my grandfather said. So Willy
climbed up with us, but the crow
gave a 'Caw!' and flew off. I was worried.
How would he know where to go?

But he flew a little way at a time
from fence post to fence post, ahead;
and when Willy whistled he answered.
'A fine bird,' my grandfather said,

'and he's well brought up. See, he answers
nicely when he's spoken to.
Man or beast, that's good manners.
Be sure that you both always do.'

When automobiles went by,
the dust hid the people's faces,
but we shouted 'Good day! Good day!
Fine day!' at the top of our voices.

When we came to Hustler Hill,
he said that the mare was tired,
so we all got down and walked,
as our good manners required.

9 February ✳ Mix a Pancake ✳ Christina Rossetti

Shrove Tuesday, also known as Pancake Day, is the final day before the beginning of the Christian period of Lent. 'Shrove' comes from the word 'shrive', which means 'to absolve'. For Christians, the forty days of Lent are a time of fasting and penitence in memory of Jesus's forty days in the desert — Shrove Tuesday, however, is a final day of feasting on rich, tasty food. In France the date is even known as Mardi Gras — Fat Tuesday.

Mix a pancake,
Stir a pancake,
  Pop it in the pan;
Fry the pancake,
Toss the pancake,—
  Catch it if you can.

10 February ✳ When the Pancake Bell Rings ✳ Thomas Dekker

Written long before Christina Rossetti's poem about pancakes, Elizabethan dramatist Thomas Dekker referred to Shrove Tuesday as a day of rest in his play *The Shoemaker's Holiday*.

> When the pancake bell rings,
> we are free as my lord Mayor,
> we may shut up our shops,
> and make holiday.

11 February ✳ A Prayer for Lent ✳ David Harmer

For Christians, Lent is a time for thoughtfulness and prayer.

> For all I have said
> and should not have said,
>
> For all I have done
> and should not have done,
>
> For all I have thought
> and should not have thought,
>
> I am sorry.

12 February ✶ Infantry Columns ✶ Rudyard Kipling

This poem by Rudyard Kipling is about the Second Boer War, which the British fought in South Africa. The continuous repetition of 'boots' emphasizes the sheer number of steps the soldiers were taking.

We're foot—slog—slog—slog—sloggin' over Africa—
Foot—foot—foot—foot—sloggin' over Africa—
(Boots—boots—boots—boots—movin' up and down again!)
   There's no discharge in the war!

Seven—six—eleven—five—nine-an'-twenty mile to-day—
Four—eleven—seventeen—thirty-two the day before—
(Boots—boots—boots—boots—movin' up and down again);
   There's no discharge in the war!

Don't—don't—don't—don't—look at what's in front of you.
(Boots—boots—boots—boots—movin' up an' down again);
Men—men—men—men—men go mad with watchin' 'em,
   An' there's no discharge in the war!

Try—try—try—try—to think o' something different—
Oh—my—God—keep—me from goin' lunatic!
(Boots—boots—boots—boots—movin' up an' down again!)
   There's no discharge in the war!

Count—count—count—count—the bullets in the bandoliers.
If—your—eyes—drop—they will get atop o' you!
(Boots—boots—boots—boots—movin' up and down again)—
   There's no discharge in the war!

We—can—stick—out—'unger, thirst, an' weariness,
But—not—not—not—not the chronic sight of 'em—
Boots—boots—boots—boots—movin' up an' down again,
    An' there's no discharge in the war!

'Tain't—so—bad—by—day because o' company,
But night—brings—long—strings—o' forty thousand million
Boots—boots—boots—boots—movin' up an' down again.
    There's no discharge in the war!

I—'ave—marched—six—weeks in 'Ell an' certify
It—is—not—fire—devils, dark, or anything,
But boots—boots—boots—boots—movin' up an' down again,
    An' there's no discharge in the war!

13 February ✶ How Do I Love Thee? ✶ Elizabeth Barrett Browning

This extremely beautiful love sonnet is taken from Elizabeth Barrett Browning's collection *Sonnets from the Portuguese*.

How do I love thee? Let me count the ways.
I love thee to the depth and breadth and height
My soul can reach, when feeling out of sight
For the ends of being and ideal grace.
I love thee to the level of every day's
Most quiet need, by sun and candle-light.
I love thee freely, as men strive for right;
I love thee purely, as they turn from praise.
I love thee with the passion put to use
In my old griefs, and with my childhood's faith.
I love thee with a love I seemed to lose
With my lost saints. I love thee with the breath,
Smiles, tears, of all my life; and, if God choose,
I shall but love thee better after death.

14 February ✶ A Red, Red Rose ✶ Robert Burns

14 February is St Valentine's Day: a day associated with
the celebration of love, and this poem by Robert Burns is
wonderfully romantic. Burns wrote some poems in standard
English but also many, like this one, in a Lowland Scots
dialect – hence the appearance of 'luve' instead of 'love' and
'gang' instead of 'go'.

> O my Luve's like a red, red rose,
>   That's newly sprung in June:
> O my Luve's like the melodie,
>   That's sweetly play'd in tune.
>
> As fair art thou, my bonnie lass,
>   So deep in luve am I;
> And I will luve thee still, my dear,
>   Till a' the seas gang dry.
>
> Till a' the seas gang dry, my dear,
>   And the rocks melt wi' the sun;
> And I will luve thee still, my dear,
>   While the sands o' life shall run.
>
> And fare-thee-weel, my only Luve!
>   And fare-thee-weel, a while!
> And I will come again, my Luve,
>   Tho' 'twere ten thousand mile!

15 February ✶ Cœur, couronne et miroir (Heart, Crown, Mirror) ✶ Guillaume Apollinaire

This poem is a 'calligramme' – a poem where the text is arranged into a picture that expresses the meaning of the language.

Q U M R
L R R
ES OIS I EU ENT
TOUR A TOUR
REANAISSENT AU CŒUR DES POETS

COMME MEURENT LES ROIS (heart shape)

DANS CE MIROIR JE SUIS ENCLOS VIVANT ET VRAI COMME ON IMAGINE LES ANGES ET NON COMME SONT LES REFLETS (mirror oval shape)

My heart is like an inverted flame
The kings who have died one by one
Are reborn in poets' hearts
In this mirror I am captured alive and true
The way you imagine angels
And not only as a reflection

16 February ✳ The Owl and the Pussycat ✳ Edward Lear

The world is full of odd couples, but the title characters of this poem are among the strangest. Of course, in reality an owl and a pussycat would be rather more likely to attack each other than to get married — especially in a ceremony conducted by a turkey, and using a ring from a pig's nose! While Lear's poem can be described as a nonsense poem, it is also, importantly, a love poem.

> The Owl and the Pussy-cat went to sea
>   In a beautiful pea-green boat,
> They took some honey, and plenty of money,
>   Wrapped up in a five-pound note.
> The Owl looked up to the stars above,
>   And sang to a small guitar,
> 'O lovely Pussy! O Pussy, my love,
>   What a beautiful Pussy you are,
>   You are,
>   You are!
> What a beautiful Pussy you are!'

Pussy said to the Owl, 'You elegant fowl!
    How charmingly sweet you sing!
O let us be married! too long we have tarried:
    But what shall we do for a ring?'
They sailed away, for a year and a day,
    To the land where the Bong-tree grows
And there in a wood a Piggy-wig stood
    With a ring at the end of his nose,
            His nose,
            His nose,
    With a ring at the end of his nose.

'Dear Pig, are you willing to sell for one shilling
    Your ring?' Said the Piggy, 'I will.'
So they took it away, and were married next day
    By the Turkey who lives on the hill.
They dined on mince, and slices of quince,
    Which they ate with a runcible spoon;
And hand in hand, on the edge of the sand,
    They danced by the light of the moon,
            The moon,
            The moon,
They danced by the light of the moon.

17 February ✳ Uppity ✳ Eileen Myles

This poem uses the comparison of a mountain to illustrate the difficulty of expressing things in language.

Roads around mountains
'cause we can't drive
through

That's Poetry
to Me.

18 February ✳ Heroes ✳ Benjamin Zephaniah

In this thought-provoking short poem, Benjamin Zephaniah is writing about finding heroism in the everyday.

Heroes are funny people, dey are lost an found
Sum heroes are brainy an sum are muscle-bound
Plenty heroes die poor an are heroes after dying
Sum heroes mek yu smile when yu feel like crying
Sum heroes are made heroes as a political trick
Sum heroes are sensible an sum are very thick!
Sum heroes are not heroes cause dey do not play de game
A hero can be young or old and have a silly name.
Drunks an sober types alike hav heroes of dere kind
Most heroes are heroes out of sight an out of mind,
Sum heroes shine a light upon a place where darkness fell
Yu could be a hero soon, yes, yu can never tell.
So if yu see a hero, better treat dem wid respect
Poets an painters say heroes are a prime subject,
Most people hav heroes even though some don't admit
I say we're all heroes if we do our little bit.

19 February ✳ Mary Had a Little Lamb ✳
Sarah Josepha Hale

On 19 February 1878, Thomas Edison – a prolific American inventor responsible for developing the lightbulb and the motion-picture camera – patented the phonograph: the first device able to reproduce recorded sound. As he was a very serious man, we might assume that Edison would have chosen some very serious poetry to be the first recorded sound in history. Instead he chose this nursery rhyme.

Mary had a little lamb,
   Its fleece was white as snow,
And everywhere that Mary went
   The lamb was sure to go;
He followed her to school one day —
   That was against the rule,
It made the children laugh and play
   To see a lamb at school.

And so the Teacher turned him out,
   But still he lingered near,
And waited patiently about,
   Till Mary did appear.
And then he ran to her and laid
   His head upon her arm,
As if he said — 'I'm not afraid —
   You'll shield me from all harm.'

'What makes the lamb love Mary so,'
   The little children cry;
'O, Mary loves the lamb you know,'
   The Teacher did reply,
'And you each gentle animal
   In confidence may bind,
And make them follow at your call,
   If you are always kind.'

20 February ✶ Don't Be Scared ✶ Carol Ann Duffy

Carol Ann Duffy is currently the Poet Laureate. This poem is full of metaphors for the night.

> The dark is only a blanket
> for the moon to put on her bed.
> The dark is a private cinema
> for the movie dreams in your head.
> The dark is a little black dress
> to show off the sequin stars.
> The dark is the wooden hole
> behind the strings of happy guitars.
> The dark is a jeweller's velvet cloth
> where children sleep like pearls.
> The dark is a spool of film
> to photograph boys and girls,
> so smile in your sleep in the dark.
> Don't be scared.

21 February ✷ How Many Moons! ✷
Graham Denton

This poem makes use of metaphor to compare the moon to different objects.

The top of a tack, the lid off a tin,
A garden path, a lop-sided grin,
A banana wrapped in a silver skin,
How many moons there are!

The sail of a boat afloat on the dark,
The tailfin of a great white shark,
A funny punctuation mark,
How many moons there are!

An elephant's trunk, a pelican's bill,
A slithery snake, a feathery quill,
A frozen lake, a fish's gill,
How many moons there are!

A spiral staircase climbing the sky,
A needle threading through Heaven's eye,
An old grey sock hung out to dry,
How many moons there are!

A butcher's knife, a jungle vine,
A baker's hat, a crooked spine,
A blade of grass, a railway line,
How many moons there are!

A furrowed brow, a stringless kite,
A harvest mouse, a swan in flight,
A farmer ploughing through the night,
How many moons there are!

A boomerang, a trouser zip,
A pocket watch, a rocket ship,
An ancient coin, an apple pip,
How many moons there are!

An ice cream scoop, a pudding spoon,
A bowl of soup, a wrinkled prune,
A ballet shoe, a silk cocoon,
How many moons there are!

A bridal gown, a wedding veil,
An icicle, a rusty nail,
A tidal wave, a squirrel's tail,
How many moons there are!

An oyster's pearl, a caveman's tool,
A skipping rope, a swimming pool,
A wriggling worm, a spinning spool,
How many moons there are!

A scythe, a sickle, a stick of chalk,
A trickle of rain, a flower stalk,
A flicker of flame, a floating cork,
How many moons there are!

A postage stamp, a bony knee,
A shepherd's crook, a cup of tea,
Just take a look and you will see
How very, very, very, very many moons there are!

This poem describes the feeling of lying in bed, as you exist in that strange zone between being asleep and awake.

I've had my supper,
  And *had* my supper,
    And HAD my supper and all;
I've heard the story
  Of Cinderella,
    And how she went to the ball;
I've cleaned my teeth,
  And I've said my prayers,
    And I've cleaned and said them right;
And they've all of them been
  And kissed me lots,
    They've all of them said 'Good-night.'

So – here I am in the dark alone,
  There's nobody here to see;
  I think to myself,
  I play to myself,
  And nobody knows what I say to myself;
Here I am in the dark alone,
  What is it going to be?
I can think whatever I like to think,
I can play whatever I like to play,
I can laugh whatever I like to laugh,
  There's nobody here but me.

I'm talking to a rabbit . . .
  I'm talking to the sun . . .
I think I am a hundred –
  I'm one.
I'm lying in a forest . . .
  I'm lying in a cave . . .
I'm talking to a Dragon . . .
  I'm BRAVE.
I'm lying on my left side . . .
  I'm lying on my right . . .
I'll play a lot to-morrow . . .
. . . .
I'll think a lot tomorrow . . .
. . . .
I'll laugh . . .
        a lot . . .
              to-morrow . . .
        (*Heigh-ho!*)
                    Good-night.

23 February ✳ First Fig ✳ Edna St Vincent Millay

This short poem takes the commonplace phrase 'burning the candle at both ends' and turns it into something positive. Although the expression is usually intended to be a warning to people not to do too much in case they become exhausted, Millay instead chooses to admire the 'lovely light' that this way of life can bring.

> My candle burns at both ends;
> It will not last the night;
> But ah, my foes, and oh, my friends—
> It gives a lovely light!

24 February ✳ The Starlight Night ✳ Gerard Manley Hopkins

Hopkins was a deeply religious man, and his use of the image of Christ and his mother, the Virgin Mary, at the end of the poem illustrates how important the stars and, by extension, the natural world are to him.

Look at the stars! look, look up at the skies!
  O look at all the fire-folk sitting in the air!
  The bright boroughs, the circle-citadels there!
Down in dim woods the diamond delves! the elves'-eyes!
The grey lawns cold where gold, where quickgold lies!
  Wind-beat whitebeam! airy abeles set on a flare!
  Flake-doves sent floating forth at a farmyard scare!
Ah well! it is all a purchase, all is a prize.

Buy then! bid then! — What? — Prayer, patience, alms, vows.
Look, look: a May-mess, like on orchard boughs!
  Look! March-bloom, like on mealed-with-yellow sallows!
These are indeed the barn; withindoors house
The shocks. This piece-bright paling shuts the spouse
  Christ home, Christ and his mother and all his hallows.

25 February ✱ The Night Will Never Stay ✱ Eleanor Farjeon

This beautiful little poem takes as its theme the impossibility of keeping the night in place.

> The night will never stay,
>   The night will still go by,
> Though with a million stars
>   You pin it to the sky,
> Though you bind it with the blowing wind
>   And buckle it with the moon,
> The night will slip away
>   Like sorrow or a tune.

26 February ✳ The Sounds in the Evening ✳ Eleanor Farjeon

This poem speaks of the way sounds seem to be magnified at night. Eventually, however, all the surrounding sounds of night-time disappear into the dreamland of sleep.

The sounds in the evening
Go all through the house,
The click of the clock
And the pick of the mouse,
The footsteps of people
Upon the top floor,
The skirts of my mother
That brush by my door,
The crick in the boards,
And the creak of the chairs,
The fluttering murmurs
Outside on the stairs,
The ring at the bell,
The arrival of guests,
The laugh of my father
At one of his jests,
The clashing of dishes
As dinner goes in,
The babble of voices
That distance makes thin,
The mewing of cats
That seem just by my ear,
The hooting of owls
That can never seem near,
The queer little noises
That no one explains —
Till the moon through the slats

Of my window-blind rains,
And the world of my eyes
And my ears melts like steam
As I find my pillow
The world of my dream.

27 February ✳ Grumbly Moon ✳ Brian Patten

This little poem is an example of a haiku, a form which originated in Japan but has been adopted by many poets writing in English. People often refer to the idea of 'the man in the moon', because from earth some of the moon's craters seem to resemble facial features.

'Turn that music down!'
Shouted the grumbly moon to
The rock 'n' roll stars.

28 February * Thaw * Edward Thomas

This short poem conveys a message of optimism about the approach of Spring.

Over the land freckled with snow half-thawed
The speculating rooks at their nests cawed
And saw from elm-tops, delicate as flower of grass,
What we below could not see, Winter pass.

29 February ✳ Soldier, Soldier, Won't You Marry Me? ✳ Anon.

29 February only occurs once every four years, in a 'leap year'. The reason for this complicated adding of days is that a year is, in fact, not exactly 365 days long, but closer to 365.25 days. If we didn't add leap years, the calendar year would eventually no longer be synchronized with the seasons. It is a tradition in Britain that women are only allowed to propose to men on leap years. This poem tells the story of a young woman deceived by a dishonest soldier, who doesn't seem to have his reasons for not being able to marry her in the correct order.

Soldier, soldier, won't you marry me
With your musket, fife and drum?
O no sweet maid, I cannot marry you
For I have no coat to put on.
So up she went to her grandfather's chest
And she got him a coat of the very, very best
And the soldier put it on.

O soldier, soldier, won't you marry me
With your musket, fife and drum?
O no sweet maid, I cannot marry you
For I have no hat to put on.
So up she went to her grandfather's chest
And she got him a hat of the very, very best
And the soldier put it on.

O soldier, soldier, won't you marry me
With your musket, fife and drum?
O no sweet maid, I cannot marry you
For I have no gloves to put on.
So up she went to her grandfather's chest
And she got him a pair of the very, very best
And the soldier put them on.

O soldier, soldier, won't you marry me
With your musket, fife and drum?
O no sweet maid, I cannot marry you
For I have no boots to put on.
So up she went to her grandfather's chest
And she got him a pair of the very, very best
And the soldier put them on.

O soldier, soldier, won't you marry me
With your musket, fife and drum?
O no sweet maid, I cannot marry you
For I have a wife of my own.

March

1 March ✳ I am Taliesin ✳ Anon.

1 March is St David's Day, the day the Welsh celebrate their patron saint. This poem is about the great Welsh bard and mythological hero Taliesin.

I am Taliesin. I sing perfect metre,
Which will last to the end of the world.
My patron is Elphin . . .

I know why there is an echo in a hollow;
Why silver gleams; why breath is black; why liver is bloody;
Why a cow has horns; why a woman is affectionate;
Why milk is white; why holly is green;
Why a kid is bearded; why the cow-parsnip is hollow;
Why brine is salt; why ale is bitter;
Why the linnet is green and berries red;
Why a cuckoo complains; why it sings;
I know where the cuckoos of summer are in winter.
I know what beasts there are at the bottom of the sea;
How many spears in battle; how may drops in a shower;
Why a river drowned Pharaoh's people;
Why fishes have scales.
Why a white swan has black feet . . .

I have been a blue salmon,
I have been a dog, a stag, a roebuck on the mountain,
A stock, a spade, an axe in the hand,
A stallion, a bull, a buck,
I was reaped and placed in an oven;
I fell to the ground when I was being roasted
And a hen swallowed me.
For nine nights was I in her crop.
I have been dead, I have been alive.
I am Taliesin.

2 **March** ✳ March ✳ Anon.

This traditional and simple rhyme hails originally from
Northumberland. The strange word 'yeans' is from the local
dialect, and means 'gives birth to'. The month of March is here
described as a time in which new life springs forth — lambs
frolic and thorns bloom into roses — but also a period in which
the wind can be bitter and strong enough to blow through to
the core of an ox's horn.

> March yeans the lammie
>   And buds the thorn,
> And blows through the flint
>   Of an ox's horn.

3 March ✳ Dear March – Come In ✳
Emily Dickinson

This poem observes the paradox of the seasons: Emily
Dickinson both blames and praises March for its beauty and
its brevity.

Dear March – Come in –
How glad I am –
I hoped for you before –
Put down your Hat –
You must have walked –
How out of Breath you are –
Dear March, how are you, and the Rest –
Did you leave Nature well –
Oh March, Come right upstairs with me –
I have so much to tell –

I got your Letter, and the Birds –
The Maples never knew that you were coming – till I called
I declare – how Red their Faces grew –
But March, forgive me – and
All those Hills you left for me to Hue –
There was no Purple suitable –
You took it all with you –

Who knocks? That April –
Lock the Door –
I will not be pursued –
He stayed away a Year to call
When I am occupied –
But trifles look so trivial
As soon as you have come

That Blame is just as dear as Praise
And Praise as mere as Blame –

4 March * A Date with Spring * John Agard

This poem is a first-person monologue from the perspective of the tree itself, imagining the end of Winter as a time where the tree prepares to get dressed ready for a 'date' with the new season – Spring.

Got a date with spring
Got to look me best.
Of all the trees
I'll be the smartest dressed.

Perfumed breeze
behind me ear.
Pollen accessories
all in place.

Raindrop moisturizer
for me face.
Sunlight tints
to spruce up the hair.

What's the good of being a tree
if you can't flaunt your beauty?

Winter, I was naked
Exposed as can be.
Me wardrobe took off
with the wind.

Life was a frosty slumber.
Now, spring, here I come.
Can't wait to slip in
to me little green number.

5 March ✶ Spring ✶ Gerard Manley Hopkins

This sonnet begins by describing the beautiful qualities of Spring, before comparing it to the garden of Eden.

Nothing is so beautiful as Spring –
  When weeds, in wheels, shoot long and lovely and lush;
  Thrush's eggs look little low heavens, and thrush
Through the echoing timber does so rinse and wring
The ear, it strikes like lightnings to hear him sing;
  The glassy peartree leaves and blooms, they brush
  The descending blue; that blue is all in a rush
With richness; the racing lambs too have fair their fling.

What is all this juice and all this joy?
  A strain of the earth's sweet being in the beginning
In Eden garden. – Have, get, before it cloy,
  Before it cloud, Christ, lord, and sour with sinning,
Innocent mind and Mayday in girl and boy,
  Most, O maid's child, thy choice and worthy the winning.

6 March ✷ But These Things Also ✷ Edward Thomas

Edward Thomas wrote this poem in 1915, and its message carries memories of the great losses that occurred in the Winter of 1914 during the First World War.

But these things also are Spring's—
On banks by the roadside the grass
Long-dead that is greyer now
Than all the Winter it was;

The shell of a little snail bleached
In the grass; chip of flint, and mite
Of chalk; and the small birds' dung
In splashes of purest white:

All the white things a man mistakes
For earliest violets
Who seeks through Winter's ruins
Something to pay Winter's debts,

While the North blows, and starling flocks
By chattering on and on
Keep their spirits up in the mist,
And Spring's here, Winter's not gone.

7 March ✳ The Sound Collector ✳ Roger McGough

On 7 March 1876 the inventor Alexander Graham Bell patented an object which changed the human experience of sound and communication forever: the telephone. This poem by Roger McGough imagines everyday sounds as objects which might be put into a bag and carried away.

A stranger called this morning
Dressed all in black and grey
Put every sound into a bag
And carried them away

The whistling of the kettle
The turning of the lock
The purring of the kitten
The ticking of the clock

The popping of the toaster
The crunching of the flakes
When you spread the marmalade
The scraping noise it makes

The hissing of the frying pan
The ticking of the grill
The bubbling of the bathtub
As it starts to fill

The drumming of the raindrops
On the windowpane
When you do the washing-up
The gurgle of the drain

86

The crying of the baby
The squeaking of the chair
The swishing of the curtain
The creaking of the stair

A stranger called this morning
He didn't leave his name
Left us only silence
Life will never be the same

8 March ✶ Phenomenal Woman ✶ Maya Angelou

8 March is International Women's Day. This poem celebrates womanhood. Maya Angelou was a pioneering American author, a champion of civil rights, women's rights and by all accounts, a 'phenomenal woman' herself.

Pretty women wonder where my secret lies.
I'm not cute or built to suit a fashion model's size
But when I start to tell them,
They think I'm telling lies.
I say,
It's in the reach of my arms,
The span of my hips,
The stride of my step,
The curl of my lips.
I'm a woman
Phenomenally.
Phenomenal woman,
That's me.

I walk into a room
Just as cool as you please,
And to a man,
The fellows stand or
Fall down on their knees.
Then they swarm around me,
A hive of honey bees.
I say,
It's the fire in my eyes,
And the flash of my teeth,
The swing in my waist,
And the joy in my feet.
I'm a woman

Phenomenally.
Phenomenal woman,
That's me.

Men themselves have wondered
What they see in me.
They try so much
But they can't touch
My inner mystery.
When I try to show them,
They say they still can't see.
I say,
It's in the arch of my back,
The sun of my smile,
The ride of my breasts,
The grace of my style.
I'm a woman
Phenomenally.
Phenomenal woman,
That's me.

Now you understand
Just why my head's not bowed.
I don't shout or jump about
Or have to talk real loud.
When you see me passing,
It ought to make you proud.
I say,
It's in the click of my heels,
The bend of my hair,
the palm of my hand,
The need for my care.
'Cause I'm a woman
Phenomenally.
Phenomenal woman,
That's me.

9 March ✶ 'Hope' is the Thing with Feathers ✶ Emily Dickinson

In this poem, Emily Dickinson imagines Hope to be a bird that lives in the soul, singing eternally. Dickinson's reassuring poem notes with wonder that while Hope has sustained the speaker through the darkest of times, it has never required anything in return.

'Hope' is the thing with feathers –
That perches in the soul –
And sings the tune without the words –
And never stops – at all –

And sweetest – in the Gale – is heard –
And sore must be the storm –
That could abash the little Bird
That kept so many warm –

I've heard it in the chillest land –
And on the strangest Sea –
Yet, never, in Extremity,
It asked a crumb – of Me.

10 March ✳ Knocks on the Door ✳
Maram al-Massri, translated by Khaled Mattawa

Loneliness is here likened to dust. The poem ends with the
suggestion that the emotions we show the world are perhaps
not always those which we truly feel.

> Knocks on the door.
> Who?
> I sweep the dust of my loneliness
> under the rug.
> I arrange a smile
> and open.

11 March ✴ Prior Knowledge ✴ Carol Ann Duffy

Do you think Prior Knowledge is a real boy, or an imaginary friend? Although we all sometimes wish that we could have all the answers, this poem can be interpreted as a warning that knowledge can come at a price.

Prior Knowledge was a strange boy.
He had sad green eyes.
He always seemed to know when I was telling lies.

We were friends for a summer.
Prior got out his knife
and mixed our bloods so we'd be brothers for life.

You'll be rich, he said, and famous;
but I must die.
Then brave, clever Prior began to cry.

He knew so much.
he knew the day before
I'd drop a jamjar full of frogspawn on the kitchen floor.

He knew there were wasps
in the gardening gloves.
He knew the name of the girl I'd grow up to love.

The day he died
he knew there would be
a wind shaking conkers from the horse-chestnut tree;

and an aimless child
singing down Prior's street,
with bright red sandals on her skipping feet.

92

12 March ✴ *from* The Lady of Shalott ✴
Alfred, Lord Tennyson

This poem takes its inspiration from stories of the mythical
King Arthur.

On either side the river lie
Long fields of barley and of rye,
That clothe the wold and meet the sky;
And thro' the field the road runs by
    To many-tower'd Camelot;
And up and down the people go,
Gazing where the lilies blow
Round an island there below,
    The island of Shalott.

Willows whiten, aspens quiver,
Little breezes dusk and shiver
Thro' the wave that runs for ever
By the island in the river
    Flowing down to Camelot.
Four gray walls, and four gray towers,
Overlook a space of flowers,
And the silent isle imbowers
    The Lady of Shalott.

By the margin, willow-veil'd,
Slide the heavy barges trail'd
By slow horses; and unhail'd
The shallop flitteth silken-sail'd
    Skimming down to Camelot:

But who hath seen her wave her hand?
Or at the casement seen her stand?
Or is she known in all the land,
    The Lady of Shalott?

Only reapers, reaping early
In among the bearded barley,
Hear a song that echoes cheerly
From the river winding clearly,
    Down to tower'd Camelot:
And by the moon the reaper weary,
Piling sheaves in uplands airy,
Listening, whispers, ''Tis the fairy
    Lady of Shalott.'

13 March ✳ Lochinvar ✳ Sir Walter Scott

Walter Scott was a nineteenth-century historical novelist
and poet who was very popular during his lifetime. Much of
his work centred upon stories of adventure in the Scottish
countryside and this poem is no different. The poem is
a narrative told in rhyming couplets of the dashing hero
Lochinvar.

O young Lochinvar is come out of the west,
Through all the wide Border his steed was the best;
And save his good broadsword he weapons had none,
He rode all unarm'd, and he rode all alone.
So faithful in love, and so dauntless in war,
There never was knight like the young Lochinvar.

He staid not for brake, and he stopp'd not for stone,
He swam the Eske river where ford there was none;
But ere he alighted at Netherby gate,
The bride had consented, the gallant came late:
For a laggard in love, and a dastard in war,
Was to wed the fair Ellen of brave Lochinvar.

So boldly he enter'd the Netherby Hall,
Among bride's-men, and kinsmen, and brothers and all:
Then spoke the bride's father, his hand on his sword,
(For the poor craven bridegroom said never a word,)
'O come ye in peace here, or come ye in war,
Or to dance at our bridal, young Lord Lochinvar?'

'I long woo'd your daughter, my suit you denied;—
Love swells like the Solway, but ebbs like its tide—
And now I am come, with this lost love of mine,
To lead but one measure, drink one cup of wine.
There are maidens in Scotland more lovely by far,
That would gladly be bride to the young Lochinvar.'

The bride kiss'd the goblet: the knight took it up,
He quaff'd off the wine, and he threw down the cup.
She look'd down to blush, and she look'd up to sigh,
With a smile on her lips and a tear in her eye.
He took her soft hand, ere her mother could bar,—
'Now tread we a measure!' said young Lochinvar.

So stately his form, and so lovely her face,
That never a hall such a galliard did grace;
While her mother did fret, and her father did fume,
And the bridegroom stood dangling his bonnet and plume;
And the bride-maidens whisper'd, ''Twere better by far
To have match'd our fair cousin with young Lochinvar.'

One touch to her hand, and one word in her ear,
When they reach'd the hall-door, and the charger stood near;
So light to the croupe the fair lady he swung,
So light to the saddle before her he sprung!
'She is won! we are gone, over bank, bush, and scaur;
They'll have fleet steeds that follow,' quoth young Lochinvar.

There was mounting 'mong Graemes of the Netherby clan;
Forsters, Fenwicks, and Musgraves, they rode and they ran:
There was racing and chasing on Cannobie Lee,
But the lost bride of Netherby ne'er did they see.
So daring in love, and so dauntless in war,
Have ye e'er heard of gallant like young Lochinvar?

14 March ✶ Tarantella ✶ Hilaire Belloc

A 'tarantella' is a dance in a fast, upbeat tempo. This poem captures the swift rhythm of the dance.

Do you remember an Inn,
Miranda?
Do you remember an Inn?
And the tedding and the spreading
Of the straw for a bedding,
And the fleas that tease in the High Pyrenees,
And the wine that tasted of tar?
And the cheers and the jeers of the young muleteers
(Under the vine of the dark veranda)?
Do you remember an Inn, Miranda,
Do you remember an Inn?
And the cheers and the jeers of the young muleteers
Who hadn't got a penny,
And who weren't paying any,
And the hammer at the doors and the din?
And the hip! hop! hap!
Of the clap
Of the hands to the swirl and the twirl
Of the girl gone chancing,
Glancing,
Dancing,
Backing and advancing,
Snapping of the clapper to the spin
Out and in –
And the ting, tong, tang of the guitar!
Do you remember an Inn,
Miranda?
Do you remember an Inn?

Never more;
Miranda,
Never more.
Only the high peaks hoar;
And Aragon a torrent at the door.
No sound
In the walls of the halls where falls
The tread
Of the feet of the dead to the ground,
No sound:
But the boom
Of the far waterfall like doom.

15 March ✳ *from* Julius Caesar ✳
William Shakespeare

In the Roman calendar the Ides of March is a date which corresponds to 15 March in our calendar — each month had an Ides which signified, roughly, its midpoint. On the Ides of March 44 BC Julius Caesar, the great statesman and general, was assassinated in the Roman senate. These lines come from Shakespeare's play *Julius Caesar*.

CAESAR
    Who is it in the press that calls on me?
    I hear a tongue, shriller than all the music,
    Cry 'Caesar!' Speak; Caesar is turn'd to hear.
SOOTHSAYER
    Beware the Ides of March.
CAESAR
    What man is that?
BRUTUS
    A soothsayer bids you beware the Ides of March.
CAESAR
    Set him before me; let me see his face.
CASSIUS
    Fellow, come from the throng; look upon Caesar.
CAESAR
    What say'st thou to me now? Speak once again.
SOOTHSAYER
    Beware the Ides of March.
CAESAR
    He is a dreamer; let us leave him: pass.

16 March ✳ Toad ✳ Norman MacCaig

The Scottish poet Norman MacCaig often wrote about the natural world and animals, such as the toad in this poem. This poem's positivity is a refreshing way to look at a creature that is often regarded as ugly, or even scary.

Stop looking like a purse. How could a purse
Squeeze under the rickety door and sit,
Full of satisfaction in a man's house?

You clamber towards me on your four corners –
Right hand, left foot, left hand, right foot.

I love you for being a toad,
For crawling like a Japanese wrestler,
And for not being frightened

I put you in my purse hand not shutting it,
And set you down outside directly under
Every star.

A jewel in your head? Toad,
You've put one in mine,
A tiny radiance in a dark place.

17 March ✳ He Wishes for the Cloths of Heaven ✳ W. B. Yeats

17 March is St Patrick's Day, the patron saint of Ireland, and this poem is by one of Ireland's most revered poets, W. B. Yeats.

> Had I the heavens' embroidered cloths,
> Enwrought with golden and silver light,
> The blue and the dim and the dark cloths
> Of night and light and the half-light,
> I would spread the cloths under your feet:
> But I, being poor, have only my dreams;
> I have spread my dreams under your feet;
> Tread softly because you tread on my dreams.

18 March ✳ Spring Snow ✳ John Foster

This cinquain poem concentrates on the fleeting life of snowflakes.

> Snowflakes
> Slip from the sky
> Like soft white butterflies,
> Brush the trees with their flimsy wings,
> Vanish.

19 March ✳ Three Good Things ✳ Jan Dean

This is a perfect poem to put under your pillow and read at day's end.

At day's end I remember
three good things.

Apples maybe – their skinshine smell
and soft froth of juice.

Water maybe – the pond in the park
dark and full of secret fish.

A mountain maybe – that I saw in a film,
or climbed last holiday,
and suddenly today it thundered up
into a playground game.
Or else an owl – I heard an owl today,
and I made bread.
My head is full of all these things,
it's hard to choose just three.

I let remembering fill me up
with all good things
so that good things will overflow
into my sleeping self,

and in the morning
good things will be waiting
when I wake.

20 March ✶ *from* Pippa Passes ✶ Robert Browning

This poem from Browning's verse drama *Pippa Passes* is a
poem about beginnings – about dew-pearled mornings, and
a year about to blossom. Pippa celebrates the simple wonders
of nature, finding a connection between the snail resting on a
thorn and the idea of God in heaven.

> The year's at the spring
> And day's at the morn;
> Morning's at seven;
> The hillside's dew-pearled;
> The lark's on the wing;
> The snail's on the thorn:
> God's in His heaven—
> All's right with the world!

21 March ✶ Flowers and Moonlight on the Spring River ✶ Yang-Ti, translated by Arthur Waley

The emperor Yang-Ti ruled the Sui Dynasty in China from 604 to his death in 618. With its beautiful imagery of springtime colours, this is a perfect poem to read aloud on 21 March – Spring Equinox.

> The evening river is level and motionless —
> The spring colours just open to their full.
> Suddenly a wave carries the moon away
> And the tidal water comes with its freight of stars.

22 March ✶ The Trees ✶ Philip Larkin

Philip Larkin's work was famously melancholy, yet this poem deals with an optimistic subject: the approach of Spring.

> The trees are coming into leaf
> Like something almost being said;
> The recent buds relax and spread,
> Their greenness is a kind of grief.
>
> Is it that they are born again
> And we grow old? No, they die too.
> Their yearly trick of looking new
> Is written down in rings of grain.
>
> Yet still the unresting castles thresh
> In fullgrown thickness every May.
> Last year is dead, they seem to say,
> Begin afresh, afresh, afresh.

23 March ✳ in Just- ✳ E. E. Cummings

E. E. Cummings was an American poet. In his poetry, the layout of the text on the page is crucial in establishing its meaning: in this poem, the differing sentence lengths create a feeling of excitement and change.

in Just-
spring   when the world is mud-
luscious the little
lame balloonman

whistles   far   and wee

and eddieandbill come
running from marbles and
piracies and it's
spring

when the world is puddle-wonderful

the queer
old balloonman whistles
far   and   wee
and bettyandisbel come dancing

from hop-scotch and jump-rope and

it's
spring
and
        the

            goat-footed

balloonMan   whistles
far
and
wee

24 March ✳ The Knight's Tomb ✳
Samuel Taylor Coleridge

Coleridge wrote 'The Knight's Tomb' in 1817, long after the days when valiant knights roamed England wielding swords. The poem is filled with images of England's past and its natural beauty, yet Coleridge was writing during the Industrial Revolution when these natural spaces seemed in great peril.

Where is the grave of Sir Arthur O'Kellyn?
Where may the grave of that good man be?—
By the side of a spring, on the breast of Helvellyn,
Under the twigs of a young birch tree!
The oak that in summer was sweet to hear,
And rustled its leaves in the fall of the year,
And whistled and roared in the winter alone,
Is gone,—and the birch in its stead is grown.—
The Knight's bones are dust,
And his good sword rust;—
His soul is with the saints, I trust.

25 March ✳ In a Station of the Metro ✳ Ezra Pound

For Pound, the visual image of a poem was closely linked to its meaning, and he insisted that this poem was printed in the striking layout shown below. It brings the presence of nature into the urban Parisian station — even here the springtime imagery of rainy woodlands and blossoms is discernible.

The apparition   of these faces   in the crowd :
Petals   on a wet, black   bough .

26 March ✳ A Donkey ✳ Ted Hughes

Ted Hughes, who grew up in rural West Yorkshire, often wrote poems about animals. The repetition of 'I like' conveys an affection for all of the animal's bizarre features.

His face is what I like.
And his head, much too big for his body – a toy head,
A great, rabbit-eared, pantomime head,
And his friendly rabbit face,
His big, friendly, humorous eyes – which can turn wicked,
Long and devilish, when he lays his ears back.

But mostly he's comical – and that's what I like.
I like the joke he seems
Always just about to tell me. And the laugh,
The rusty, pump-house engine that cranks up laughter
From some long-ago, far off, laughter-less desert –

The dry, hideous guffaw
That makes his great teeth nearly fall out.

27 March ✷ The Donkey ✷ G. K. Chesterton

The narrator of this poem is not a human but a donkey, who recounts his history and his moment of glory: the Biblical event of Palm Sunday, when Jesus rode into Jerusalem on a donkey and a jubilant crowd scattered palm branches in his path.

When fishes flew and forests walked
  And figs grew upon thorn,
Some moment when the moon was blood
  Then surely I was born.

With monstrous head and sickening cry
  And ears like errant wings,
The devil's walking parody
  Of all four-footed things.

The tattered outlaw of the earth,
  Of ancient crooked will;
Starve, scourge, deride me: I am dumb,
  I keep my secret still.

Fools! For I also had my hour,
  One far fierce hour and sweet.
There was a shout about my ears,
  And palms before my feet.

28 March ✳ Easter Wings ✳ George Herbert

'Easter Wings' is an example of a shape or pattern poem, and the poem's visual form literally illustrates the wings of the title. Easter commemorates the sacrifice of Jesus on the cross, and his rebirth. The poem echoes this progression from sorrow to joy.

Lord, who createdst man in wealth and store,
Though foolishly he lost the same,
Decaying more and more,
Till he became
Most poor:
With thee
O let me rise
As larks, harmoniously,
And sing this day thy victories:
Then shall the fall further the flight in me.

My tender age in sorrow did begin
And still with sicknesses and shame
Thou didst so punish sin,
That I became
Most thin.
With thee
Let me combine,
And feel this day thy victory:
For, if I imp my wing on thine,
Affliction shall advance the flight in me.

29 March ✳ The Desired Swan-Song ✳ Samuel Taylor Coleridge

This humorous example is based on the ancient belief that, having been silent their entire lives, swans sing a beautiful song in the moment before they die. The term 'swan-song' has come to describe a final performance or achievement just before the death of a creative artist.

> Swans sing before they die – 'twere no bad thing
> Should certain persons die before they sing.

30 March ✶ Against Idleness and Mischief ✶
Isaac Watts

In this poem Watts is trying to argue that there is a moral
purpose to keeping busy.

> How doth the little busy bee
>   Improve each shining hour,
> And gather honey all the day
>   From every opening flower!
>
> How skilfully she builds her cell!
>   How neat she spreads the wax!
> And labours hard to store it well
>   With the sweet food she makes.
>
> In works of labour or of skill,
>   I would be busy too;
> For Satan finds some mischief still
>   For idle hands to do.
>
> In books, or work, or healthful play,
>   Let my first years be passed,
> That I may give for every day
>   Some good account at last.

31 March ✳ How Doth the Little Crocodile ✳ Lewis Carroll

A 'parody' is a way of poking fun at something by imitating its style – in this case, Lewis Carroll is cheekily rewriting the previous poem. This short poem appears in Carroll's 1865 novel *Alice in Wonderland*: it is recited by Alice in Chapter Two.

> How doth the little crocodile
>   Improve his shining tail,
> And pour the waters of the Nile
>   On every golden scale!
>
> How cheerfully he seems to grin,
>   How neatly spread his claws,
> And welcomes little fishes in
>   With gently smiling jaws!

April

1 April ✳ Jabberwocky ✳ Lewis Carroll

April Fool's Day, a day for jokes, pranks and general silliness, is celebrated every year on 1 April – and it's hard to think of a poem sillier than 'Jabberwocky'. Lewis Carroll included 'Jabberwocky' in his novel *Through the Looking Glass, and What Alice Found There*. You might come to the same conclusion as Alice: 'It seems very pretty . . . but it's *rather* hard to understand!' Some of Carroll's nonsense words have since made their way into the dictionary, such as 'chortle', which means 'laugh'.

'Twas brillig, and the slithy toves
　　Did gyre and gimble in the wabe:
All mimsy were the borogoves,
　　And the mome raths outgrabe.

'Beware the Jabberwock, my son!
　　The jaws that bite, the claws that catch!
Beware the Jubjub bird, and shun
　　The frumious Bandersnatch!'

He took his vorpal sword in hand;
　　Long time the manxome foe he sought—
So rested he by the Tumtum tree
　　And stood awhile in thought.

And, as in uffish thought he stood,
　　The Jabberwock, with eyes of flame,
Came whiffling through the tulgey wood,
　　And burbled as it came!

One, two! One, two! And through and through
    The vorpal blade went snicker-snack!
He left it dead, and with its head
    He went galumphing back.

'And hast thou slain the Jabberwock?
    Come to my arms, my beamish boy!
O frabjous day! Callooh! Callay!'
    He chortled in his joy.

'Twas brillig, and the slithy toves
    Did gyre and gimble in the wabe:
All mimsy were the borogoves,
    And the mome raths outgrabe.

2 April ✳ The Mad Gardener's Song ✳ Lewis Carroll

This nonsense poem by Lewis Carroll, with its confusing mixture of animals, people and absolute ridiculousness, was originally published in *Sylvie and Bruno*.

He thought he saw an Elephant
That practised on a fife:
He looked again, and found it was
A letter from his wife.
'At length I realize,' he said,
'The bitterness of Life!'

He thought he saw a Buffalo
Upon the chimney-piece:
He looked again, and found it was
His Sister's Husband's Niece.
'Unless you leave this house,' he said,
'I'll send for the Police!'

He thought he saw a Rattlesnake
That questioned him in Greek:
He looked again, and found it was
The Middle of Next Week.
'The one thing I regret,' he said,
'Is that it cannot speak!'

He thought he saw a Banker's Clerk
Descending from the 'bus:
He looked again, and found it was
A Hippopotamus.
'If this should stay to dine,' he said,
'There won't be much for us!'

He thought he saw a Kangaroo
That worked a coffee-mill:
He looked again, and found it was
A Vegetable-Pill.
'Were I to swallow this,' he said,
'I should be very ill!'

He thought he saw a Coach-and-Four
That stood beside his bed:
He looked again, and found it was
A Bear without a Head.
'Poor thing,' he said, 'poor silly thing!
It's waiting to be fed!'

He thought he saw an Albatross
That fluttered round the lamp:
He looked again, and found it was
A Penny-Postage-Stamp.
'You'd best be getting home,' he said,
'The nights are very damp!'

He thought he saw a Garden-Door
That opened with a key:
He looked again, and found it was
A Double Rule of Three:
'And all its mystery,' he said,
'Is clear as day to me!'

He thought he saw an Argument
That proved he was the Pope:
He looked again, and found it was
A Bar of Mottled Soap.
'A fact so dread,' he faintly said,
'Extinguishes all hope!'

3 April ✴ The Spider and the Fly ✴
Mary Botham Howitt

In this poem, published in 1829, Mary Botham Howitt tells a
cautionary tale . . .

'Will you walk into my parlour?' said the Spider to the Fly,
''Tis the prettiest little parlour that ever you did spy;
The way into my parlour is up a winding stair,
And I've got many curious things to show when you are there.'
'Oh no, no,' said the little Fly, 'to ask me is in vain,
For who goes up your winding stair can ne'er come down
     again.'

'I'm sure you must be weary, dear, with soaring up so high;
Will you rest upon my little bed?' said the Spider to the Fly.
'There are pretty curtains drawn around; the sheets are fine
     and thin,
And if you like to rest awhile, I'll snugly tuck you in!'
'Oh no, no,' said the little Fly, 'for I've often heard it said,
They never, never wake again, who sleep upon your bed!'

Said the cunning Spider to the Fly, 'Dear friend what can I do,
To prove the warm affection I've always felt for you?
I have within my pantry good store of all that's nice;
I'm sure you're very welcome – will you please to take a slice?'
'Oh no, no,' said the little Fly, 'kind sir, that cannot be,
I've heard what's in your pantry, and I do not wish to see!'

'Sweet creature!' said the Spider, 'you're witty and you're wise,
How handsome are your gauzy wings, how brilliant are your
    eyes!
I've a little looking-glass upon my parlour shelf,
If you'll step in one moment, dear, you shall behold yourself.'
'I thank you, gentle sir,' she said, 'for what you're pleased to
    say,
And bidding you good morning now, I'll call another day.'

The Spider turned him round about, and went into his den,
For well he knew the silly Fly would soon come back again:
So he wove a subtle web, in a little corner sly,
And set his table ready, to dine upon the Fly.
Then he came out to his door again, and merrily did sing,
'Come hither, hither, pretty Fly, with the pearl and silver wing;
Your robes are green and purple – there's a crest upon your
    head;
Your eyes are like the diamond bright, but mine are dull as
    lead!'

Alas, alas! how very soon this silly little Fly,
Hearing his wily, flattering words, came slowly flitting by;
With buzzing wings she hung aloft, then near and nearer drew,
Thinking only of her brilliant eyes, and green and purple hue –
Thinking only of her crested head – poor foolish thing! At last,
Up jumped the cunning Spider, and fiercely held her fast.
He dragged her up his winding stair, into his dismal den,
Within his little parlour – but she ne'er came out again!

And now, dear little children, who may this story read,
To idle, silly flattering words, I pray you ne'er give heed:
Unto an evil counsellor, close heart and ear and eye,
And take a lesson from this tale, of the Spider and the Fly.

4 April ✳ The Mock Turtle's Song ✳ Lewis Carroll

In Victorian times, mock turtle soup was a popular dish that used cheap cuts and offal to look like expensive turtle meat. In *Alice in Wonderland*, Alice meets a creature called the Mock Turtle, a pun on the name of this popular soup, as there really was no such creature. 'The Mock Turtle's Song', which he performs for Alice accompanied by a dance, is a parody of the previous poem.

'Will you walk a little faster?' said a whiting to a snail.
'There's a porpoise close behind us, and he's treading on my
    tail.
See how eagerly the lobsters and the turtles all advance!
They are waiting on the shingle— will you come and join the
    dance?
  Will you, won't you, will you, won't you, will you join the
    dance?
  Will you, won't you, will you, won't you, won't you join the
    dance?

'You can really have no notion how delightful it will be
When they take us up and throw us, with the lobsters, out to
    sea!'
But the snail replied 'Too far, too far!' and gave a look
    askance—
Said he thanked the whiting kindly, but he would not join the
    dance.
  Would not, could not, would not, could not, would not join
    the dance.
  Would not, could not, would not, could not, could not join
    the dance.

'What matters it how far we go?' his scaly friend replied.
'There is another shore, you know, upon the other side.
The further off from England the nearer is to France—
Then turn not pale, beloved snail, but come and join the dance?
    Will you, won't you, will you, won't you, won't you join the
        dance?
    Will you, won't you, will you, won't you, won't you join the
        dance?'

5 April ✴ You Are Old, Father William ✴
Lewis Carroll

This poem, also featured in *Alice in Wonderland*, is a mischievous parody of Robert Southey's poem 'The Old Man's Comforts'. In Southey's poem Father William explains that the reason he has found such contentment in his old age is because he led a virtuous, restrained life in his youth, and always 'remembered my God'. Carroll literally turns this poem on its head, as his Father William 'incessantly' stands on his head, as well as arguing the benefits of a life full of pleasure, arguments, extreme physical activity and magical ointment.

'You are old, Father William,' the young man said,
   'And your hair has become very white;
And yet you incessantly stand on your head –
   Do you think, at your age, it is right?'

'In my youth,' Father William replied to his son,
   'I feared it might injure the brain;
But, now that I'm perfectly sure I have none,
   Why, I do it again and again.'

'You are old,' said the youth, 'as I mentioned before,
   And have grown most uncommonly fat;
Yet you turned a back-somersault in at the door –
   Pray, what is the reason of that?'

'In my youth,' said the sage, as he shook his grey locks,
   'I kept all my limbs very supple
By the use of this ointment – one shilling the box –
   Allow me to sell you a couple?'

'You are old,' said the youth, 'and your jaws are too weak
   For anything tougher than suet;
Yet you finished the goose, with the bones and the beak –
   Pray, how did you manage to do it?'

'In my youth,' said his father, 'I took to the law,
   And argued each case with my wife;
And the muscular strength, which it gave to my jaw,
   Has lasted the rest of my life.'

'You are old,' said the youth, 'one would hardly suppose
   That your eye was as steady as ever;
Yet you balanced an eel on the end of your nose –
   What made you so awfully clever?'

'I have answered three questions, and that is enough,'
   Said his father. 'Don't give yourself airs!
Do you think I can listen all day to such stuff?
   Be off, or I'll kick you downstairs!'

6 April ✳ Old Mother Hubbard ✳ Anon.

This popular nursery rhyme was first printed in 1805 although it is thought to date from possibly even centuries before. There is one theory that the poem was written in Tudor times as a mockery of Cardinal Wolsey's failed attempt to obtain an annulment of Henry VIII's marriage to Katherine of Aragon. So 'Mother Hubbard' is Wolsey, the 'bone' is the divorce agreement he was seeking to get for the 'doggie' – the king!

Old Mother Hubbard
Went to the cupboard,
To give the poor dog a bone;
When she came there,
The cupboard was bare,
And so the poor dog got none.

She went to the baker's
To buy him some bread;
But when she got back
The poor dog was dead.

She went to the joiner's
To buy him a coffin;
But when she got back
The doggie was laughing.

She took a clean dish
To get him some tripe;
But when she came back
He was smoking his pipe.

She went to the fishmonger's
To buy him some fish;
And when she came back
He was licking the dish.

She went to the tavern
For white wine and red;
But when she came back
The dog stood on his head.

She went to the hatter's
To buy him a hat;
But when she came back
He was feeding the cat.

She went to the cobbler's
To buy him some shoes;
But when she came back
He was reading the news.

The Dame made a curtsy,
The dog made a bow;
The Dame said, 'Your servant,'
The dog said, 'Bow-wow.'

This wonderful dog
Was Dame Hubbard's delight;
He could sing, he could dance,
He could read, he could write.

She gave him rich dainties
Whenever he fed,
And erected a monument
When he was dead.

7 April * Mrs Darwin * Carol Ann Duffy

In 1859, Charles Darwin published his groundbreaking theory of evolution *The Origin of the Species*, which argues that the human race shares a common ancestor with other primates such as gorillas, chimpanzees, monkeys and bonobos. In dating this poem 7 April 1852, Carol Ann Duffy is making the tongue-in-cheek suggestion that the idea may have come from Mrs Darwin.

7 April 1852.

Went to the Zoo.
I said to Him –
Something about that Chimpanzee over there reminds me
    of you.

8 April ✳ Awakening ✳ Tony Mitton

The poet himself has written this illuminating paragraph
about his poem:

The story has been passed down that the Buddha
(Siddhartha Gautama) achieved a sudden and powerful
experience of understanding after many years of study and
practice. Exhausted by the efforts he had made to get to
grips with the meaning of his life, he gave up and sat down
in meditation under the Bodhi tree, vowing not to get up
until some answer presented itself to him. After sitting all
night in meditation he caught sight of the morning star
rising. The clarity and power of the moment that followed
is sometimes called his Enlightenment (or Awakening). In
spite of his already great learning and wisdom, all he could
say in response to the experience was, 'What is this?'

> The Buddha sat silently
> under a tree.
> He sat and he waited
> determinedly.
>
> He sat like a statue
> and scarcely stirred.
> Out of his lips
> came never a word.
>
> He sat through the hours
> of an Orient night,
> and, just at the edges
> of opening light,

up in the heaven,
so sharp and so far,
glimmered the spark
of a wakening star.

Sitting in stillness,
the sight that he saw
pierced him through
to the innermost core.

And all he could say
in his moment of bliss
was simply and purely,
'What is this?'

9 April ✳ Wynken, Blynken and Nod ✳
Eugene Field

In this poem, which is another example of nonsense verse,
Eugene Field creates a kind of fantastical bedtime story.

Wynken, Blynken, and Nod one night
   Sailed off in a wooden shoe,—
Sailed on a river of crystal light
   Into a sea of dew.
'Where are you going, and what do you wish?'
   The old moon asked the three.
'We have come to fish for the herring-fish
   That live in this beautiful sea;
   Nets of silver and gold have we,'
      Said Wynken,
      Blynken,
      And Nod.

The old moon laughed and sang a song,
   As they rocked in the wooden shoe;
And the wind that sped them all night long
   Ruffled the waves of dew;
The little stars were the herring-fish
   That lived in the beautiful sea.
'Now cast your nets wherever you wish,—
   Never afraid are we!'
   So cried the stars to the fishermen three,
      Wynken,
      Blynken,
      And Nod.

All night long their nets they threw
  To the stars in the twinkling foam,—
Then down from the skies came the wooden shoe,
  Bringing the fishermen home:
'Twas all so pretty a sail, it seemed
  As if it could not be;
And some folk thought 'twas a dream they'd dreamed
  Of sailing that beautiful sea;
  But I shall name you the fishermen three:
    Wynken,
    Blynken,
    And Nod.

Wynken and Blynken are two little eyes,
  And Nod is a little head,
And the wooden shoe that sailed the skies
  Is a wee one's trundle-bed;
So shut your eyes while Mother sings
  Of wonderful sights that be,
And you shall see the beautiful things
  As you rock in the misty sea
  Where the old shoe rocked the fishermen three:—
    Wynken,
    Blynken,
    And Nod.

10 April ✶ The Sugar-Plum Tree ✶ Eugene Field

This next poem by Eugene Field describes a scene just as unusual as Wynken, Blynken and Nod's fishing excursion! Not only is the fruit of this sugar-plum tree 'wondrously sweet', but even the animals that live in it sound delicious: a chocolate cat and a gingerbread dog.

Have you ever heard of the Sugar-Plum Tree?
'Tis a marvel of great renown!
It blooms on the shore of the Lollypop sea
In the garden of Shut-Eye Town;
The fruit that it bears is so wondrously sweet
(As those who have tasted it say)
That good little children have only to eat
Of that fruit to be happy next day.

When you've got to the tree, you would have a hard time
To capture the fruit which I sing;
The tree is so tall that no person could climb
To the boughs where the sugar-plums swing!
But up in that tree sits a chocolate cat,
And a gingerbread dog prowls below –
And this is the way you contrive to get at
Those sugar-plums tempting you so:

You say but the word to that gingerbread dog
And he barks with such terrible zest
That the chocolate cat is at once all agog,
As her swelling proportions attest.
And the chocolate cat goes cavorting around
From this leafy limb unto that,
And the sugar-plums tumble, of course, to the ground –
Hurrah for that chocolate cat!

There are marshmallows, gumdrops, and peppermint canes,
With stripings of scarlet or gold,
And you carry away of the treasure that rains,
As much as your apron can hold!
So come, little child, cuddle closer to me
In your dainty white nightcap and gown,
And I'll rock you away to that Sugar-Plum Tree
In the garden of Shut-Eye Town.

11 April ✶ Casey at the Bat ✶
Ernest Lawrence Thayer

This popular American ballad tells the story of a dramatic game of baseball. Thayer presents Casey as a hero but the story is far from victorious.

The outlook wasn't brilliant for the Mudville nine that day:
The score stood four to two, with but one inning more to play,
And then when Cooney died at first, and Barrows did the
    same,
A pall-like silence fell upon the patrons of the game.

A straggling few got up to go in deep despair. The rest
Clung to the hope which springs eternal in the human breast;
They thought, 'If only Casey could but get a whack at that—
We'd put up even money now, with Casey at the bat.'

But Flynn preceded Casey, as did also Jimmy Blake,
And the former was a hoodoo, while the latter was a cake;
So upon that stricken multitude grim melancholy sat,
For there seemed but little chance of Casey getting to the bat.

But Flynn let drive a single, to the wonderment of all,
And Blake, the much despisèd, tore the cover off the ball;
And when the dust had lifted, and men saw what had
    occurred,
There was Jimmy safe at second and Flynn a-hugging third.

Then from five thousand throats and more there rose a lusty
    yell;
It rumbled through the valley, it rattled in the dell;
It pounded on the mountain and recoiled upon the flat,
For Casey, mighty Casey, was advancing to the bat.

There was ease in Casey's manner as he stepped into his place;
There was pride in Casey's bearing and a smile lit Casey's face.
And when, responding to the cheers, he lightly doffed his hat,
No stranger in the crowd could doubt 'twas Casey at the bat.

Ten thousand eyes were on him as he rubbed his hands with
    dirt;
Five thousand tongues applauded when he wiped them on his
    shirt;
Then while the writhing pitcher ground the ball into his hip,
Defiance flashed in Casey's eye, a sneer curled Casey's lip.

And now the leather-covered sphere came hurtling through
    the air,
And Casey stood a-watching it in haughty grandeur there.
Close by the sturdy batsman the ball unheeded sped—
'That ain't my style,' said Casey. 'Strike one!' the umpire said.

From the benches, black with people, there went up a muffled
    roar,
Like the beating of the storm-waves on a stern and distant shore;
'Kill him! Kill the umpire!' shouted someone on the stand;
And it's likely they'd have killed him had not Casey raised his
    hand.

With a smile of Christian charity great Casey's visage shone;
He stilled the rising tumult; he bade the game go on;
He signaled to the pitcher, and once more the dun sphere flew;
But Casey still ignored it and the umpire said, 'Strike two!'

'Fraud!' cried the maddened thousands, and echo answered
    'Fraud!'
But one scornful look from Casey and the audience was awed.
They saw his face grow stern and cold, they saw his muscles
    strain,
And they knew that Casey wouldn't let that ball go by again.

The sneer is gone from Casey's lip, his teeth are clenched in
    hate,
He pounds with cruel violence his bat upon the plate;
And now the pitcher holds the ball, and now he lets it go,
And now the air is shattered by the force of Casey's blow.

Oh, somewhere in this favoured land the sun is shining bright,
The band is playing somewhere, and somewhere hearts are
    light;
And somewhere men are laughing, and somewhere children
    shout,
But there is no joy in Mudville—mighty Casey has struck out.

12 April * Song in Space * Adrian Mitchell

On 12 April 1961 the Russian pilot and cosmonaut Yuri Gagarin made history as the first human to journey into outer space. Gagarin spent 108 minutes in space before descending back into the atmosphere and parachuting to safety from his capsule. Gagarin said of his experience that he 'could have gone flying through space forever'. This poem about space travel by Adrian Mitchell imagines a conversation between the first man in space and the blue earth which he looks down upon.

When man first flew beyond the sky
He looked back into the world's blue eye.
Man said: What makes your eye so blue?
Earth said: The tears in the ocean do.
Why are the seas so full of tears?
Because I've wept so many thousand years.
Why do you weep as you dance through space?
Because I am the mother of the human race.

13 April ✶ Baisakhi ✶ Anon.

Celebrated on 13 or 14 April, Baisakhi is the festival of Sikh New Year, which commemorates the founding of the Sikh community in 1699 in an event known as the Khalsa. This anonymous poem is filled with names unique to the Sikh religion: Amrit is a syrup sacred to Sikh which is drunk at religious observances such as baptisms, and the Five Beloved Ones were the first men to be baptized into the Sikh faith in 1699. Baisakhi is regarded as the most important festival for Sikhs, though it is celebrated as a harvest festival by people of other faiths in the Punjab region.

> Crystals of sugar
> swirl
> as the sword
> stirs Amrit.
>
> Listening to the tale
> of the Five Beloved Ones,
>
> who dodged death
> by giving their lives
> to God.

14 April ✶ O Captain! My Captain! ✶
Walt Whitman

This poem was written in 1865 by Walt Whitman in response
to the assassination of the American president Abraham
Lincoln. Lincoln was shot on 14 April 1865, by John Wilkes
Booth, an actor. He died the next morning. It is an 'elegy',
meaning a poem of mourning for the dead, and the entire
piece is an extended metaphor, imagining America as a ship,
and Lincoln as the ship's captain.

O Captain! my Captain! our fearful trip is done,
The ship has weather'd every rack, the prize we sought is won,
The port is near, the bells I hear, the people all exulting,
While follow eyes the steady keel, the vessel grim and daring;
        But O heart! heart! heart!
        O the bleeding drops of red,
            Where on the deck my Captain lies,
            Fallen cold and dead.

O Captain! my Captain! rise up and hear the bells;
Rise up—for you the flag is flung—for you the bugle trills,
For you bouquets and ribbon'd wreaths—for you the shores
   a-crowding,
For you they call, the swaying mass, their eager faces turning;
        Here Captain! dear father!
        This arm beneath your head!
            It is some dream that on the deck,
            You've fallen cold and dead.

My Captain does not answer, his lips are pale and still,
My father does not feel my arm, he has no pulse nor will,
The ship is anchor'd safe and sound, its voyage closed and
    done,
From fearful trip the victor ship comes in with object won;
        Exult O shores, and ring O bells!
        But I with mournful tread,
            Walk the deck my Captain lies,
            Fallen cold and dead.

15 April ✷ The Convergence of the Twain ✷ Thomas Hardy

The RMS *Titanic* was a British passenger liner that sank after colliding with an iceberg in the early hours of 15 April 1912. The ship was on its maiden voyage from Southampton to New York. It was lavishly furnished, creating the 'waste of riches' Hardy refers to when it sank. The poem concentrates on the 'Twain' of the title, the ship and the iceberg, and how they came to collide (or 'converge').

I
In a solitude of the sea
Deep from human vanity,
And the Pride of Life that planned her, stilly couches she.

II
Steel chambers, late the pyres
Of her salamandrine fires,
Cold currents thrid, and turn to rhythmic tidal lyres.

III
Over the mirrors meant
To glass the opulent
The sea-worm crawls — grotesque, slimed, dumb, indifferent.

IV
Jewels in joy designed
To ravish the sensuous mind
Lie lightless, all their sparkles bleared and black and blind.

V

Dim moon-eyed fishes near
Gaze at the gilded gear
And query: 'What does this vaingloriousness down here?' . . .

VI

Well: while was fashioning
This creature of cleaving wing,
The Immanent Will that stirs and urges everything

VII

Prepared a sinister mate
For her — so gaily great —
A Shape of Ice, for the time far and dissociate.

VIII

And as the smart ship grew
In stature, grace, and hue,
In shadowy silent distance grew the Iceberg too.

IX

Alien they seemed to be:
No mortal eye could see
The intimate welding of their later history,

X

Or sign that they were bent
By paths coincident
On being anon twin halves of one august event,

XI

Till the Spinner of the Years
Said 'Now!' And each one hears,
And consummation comes, and jars two hemispheres.

16 April ✶ The Skye Boat Song ✶
Sir Harold Boulton

The Battle of Culloden was fought on 16 April 1746, between a British Loyalist army under the command of the Duke of Cumberland and a Scottish force under the command of Charles Edward Stuart ('Bonnie Prince Charlie'). Stuart was the 'Young Pretender' to the British crown, which had been seized from his grandfather King James II in the Glorious Revolution of 1688. 'The Skye Boat Song' paints a romantic image of Charles's flight from Scotland after his army was defeated at Culloden.

Speed, bonnie boat, like a bird on the wing
    Onward, the sailors cry!
Carry the lad that's born to be King
    Over the sea to Skye.

Loud the winds cry, loud the waves roar,
    Thunderclaps rend the air.
Baffled our foes stand by the shore.
    Follow they will not dare

Many's the lad fought on that day
    Well the claymore could wield,
When the night came silently lay
    Dead on Culloden's field.

Burned are our homes, exile and death
    Scatter the loyal men.
Yet ere the sword cool in the sheath
    Scotland will rise again!

17 April ✷ I Wandered Lonely as a Cloud ✷ William Wordsworth

This poem opens with a multitude of natural images: clouds, vales, hills and – most famously – daffodils. While Wordsworth writes at length on the sight of the daffodils, he never mentions their smell. This is unsurprising, as Wordsworth actually suffered from anosmia and had barely any sense of smell at all!

I wandered lonely as a cloud
That floats on high o'er vales and hills,
When all at once I saw a crowd,
A host, of golden daffodils;
Beside the lake, beneath the trees,
Fluttering and dancing in the breeze.

Continuous as the stars that shine
And twinkle on the milky way,
They stretched in never-ending line
Along the margin of a bay:
Ten thousand saw I at a glance,
Tossing their heads in sprightly dance.

The waves beside them danced; but they
Out-did the sparkling waves in glee:
A poet could not but be gay,
In such a jocund company:
I gazed—and gazed—but little thought
What wealth the show to me had brought:

For oft, when on my couch I lie
In vacant or in pensive mood,
They flash upon that inward eye
Which is the bliss of solitude;
And then my heart with pleasure fills,
And dances with the daffodils.

18 April ★ Paul Revere's Ride ★
Henry Wadsworth Longfellow

On 18 April 1775 Paul Revere rode from Boston to Lexington
to warn rebel leaders that British soldiers were on the march
and coming to arrest them. The conflict escalated and by the
next night, the American Revolutionary War (or what we
British call the American War of Independence) had begun.

Listen, my children, and you shall hear
Of the midnight ride of Paul Revere,
On the eighteenth of April, in Seventy-five;
Hardly a man is now alive
Who remembers that famous day and year.

He said to his friend, 'If the British march
By land or sea from the town to-night,
Hang a lantern aloft in the belfry arch
Of the North Church tower as a signal light,—
One, if by land, and two, if by sea;
And I on the opposite shore will be,
Ready to ride and spread the alarm
Through every Middlesex village and farm,
For the country folk to be up and to arm.'

Then he said, 'Good night!' and with muffled oar
Silently rowed to the Charlestown shore,
Just as the moon rose over the bay,
Where swinging wide at her moorings lay
The *Somerset*, British man-of-war;
A phantom ship, with each mast and spar
Across the moon like a prison bar,
And a huge black hulk, that was magnified
By its own reflection in the tide.

Meanwhile, his friend, through alley and street,
Wanders and watches with eager ears,
Till in the silence around him he hears
The muster of men at the barrack door,
The sound of arms, and the tramp of feet,
And the measured tread of the grenadiers,
Marching down to their boats on the shore.

Then he climbed the tower of the old North Church,
By the wooden stairs, with stealthy tread,
To the belfry-chamber overhead,
And startled the pigeons from their perch
On the sombre rafters, that round him made
Masses and moving shapes of shade, —
By the trembling ladder, steep and tall,
To the highest window in the wall,
Where he paused to listen and look down
A moment on the roofs of the town,
And the moonlight flowing over all.

Beneath, in the churchyard, lay the dead,
In their night encampment on the hill,
Wrapped in silence so deep and still
That he could hear, like a sentinel's tread,
The watchful night-wind, as it went
Creeping along from tent to tent,
And seeming to whisper, 'All is well!'
A moment only he feels the spell
Of the place and the hour, and the secret dread
Of the lonely belfry and the dead;
For suddenly all his thoughts are bent
On a shadowy something far away,
Where the river widens to meet the bay, —
A line of black that bends and floats
On the rising tide, like a bridge of boats.

Meanwhile, impatient to mount and ride,
Booted and spurred, with a heavy stride
On the opposite shore walked Paul Revere.
Now he patted his horse's side,
Now gazed at the landscape far and near,
Then, impetuous, stamped the earth,
And turned and tightened his saddle-girth;
But mostly he watched with eager search
The belfry-tower of the old North Church,
As it rose above the graves on the hill,
Lonely and spectral and sombre and still.
And lo! as he looks, on the belfry's height
A glimmer, and then a gleam of light!
He springs to the saddle, the bridle he turns,
But lingers and gazes, till full on his sight
A second lamp in the belfry burns!

A hurry of hoofs in a village street,
A shape in the moonlight, a bulk in the dark,
And beneath, from the pebbles, in passing, a spark
Struck out by a steed flying fearless and fleet:
That was all! And yet, through the gloom and the light,
The fate of a nation was riding that night;
And the spark struck out by that steed, in his flight,
Kindled the land into flame with its heat.

He has left the village and mounted the steep,
And beneath him, tranquil and broad and deep,
Is the Mystic, meeting the ocean tides;
And under the alders, that skirt its edge,
Now soft on the sand, now loud on the ledge,
Is heard the tramp of his steed as he rides.

It was twelve by the village clock,
When he crossed the bridge into Medford town.
He heard the crowing of the cock,
And the barking of the farmer's dog,
And felt the damp of the river fog,
That rises after the sun goes down.

It was one by the village clock,
When he galloped into Lexington.
He saw the gilded weathercock
Swim in the moonlight as he passed,
And the meeting-house windows, blank and bare,
Gaze at him with a spectral glare,
As if they already stood aghast
At the bloody work they would look upon.

It was two by the village clock,
When he came to the bridge in Concord town.
He heard the bleating of the flock,
And the twitter of birds among the trees,
And felt the breath of the morning breeze
Blowing over the meadows brown.
And one was safe and asleep in his bed
Who at the bridge would be first to fall,
Who that day would be lying dead,
Pierced by a British musket-ball.

You know the rest. In the books you have read,
How the British Regulars fired and fled, —
How the farmers gave them ball for ball,
From behind each fence and farm-yard wall,
Chasing the red-coats down the lane,
Then crossing the fields to emerge again
Under the trees at the turn of the road,
And only pausing to fire and load.

So through the night rode Paul Revere;
And so through the night went his cry of alarm
To every Middlesex village and farm, —
A cry of defiance and not of fear,
A voice in the darkness, a knock at the door,
And a word that shall echo for evermore!
For, borne on the night-wind of the Past,
Through all our history, to the last,
In the hour of darkness and peril and need,
The people will waken and listen to hear
The hurrying hoof-beats of that steed,
And the midnight message of Paul Revere.

19 April ✶ Be Like the Bird ✶ Victor Hugo

The great French novelist and poet Victor Hugo was born in France in 1802 and is perhaps best known as the author of *The Hunchback of Notre Dame* and *Les Misérables*.

> Be like the bird, who
> Resting in his flight
> On a twig too slight
> Feels it bend beneath him
> Yet sings,
> Knowing he has wings.

20 April ✳ Cynddylan on a Tractor ✳ R. S. Thomas

In this poem, R. S. Thomas uses the description of the farmer
Cynddylan's first ride on his brand-new tractor to explore
some of the concerns he has about industrialization coming to
the farms of his native Wales.

Ah, you should see Cynddylan on a tractor.
Gone the old look that yoked him to the soil,
He's a new man now, part of the machine,
His nerves of metal and his blood oil.
The clutch curses, but the gears obey
His least bidding, and lo, he's away
Out of the farmyard, scattering hens.
Riding to work now as a great man should,
He is the knight at arms breaking the fields'
Mirror of silence, emptying the wood
Of foxes and squirrels and bright jays.
The sun comes over the tall trees
Kindling all the hedges, but not for him
Who runs his engine on a different fuel.
And all the birds are singing, bills wide in vain,
As Cynddylan passes proudly up the lane.

21 April ✳ In Memoriam (Easter 1915) ✳
Edward Thomas

In these four lines Thomas reminds the reader of the
bloodshed and waste of war. The poem was composed in April
1915, a few months before Thomas decided to enlist in the
Artists' Rifles, which he eventually did in July of that year.

The flowers left thick at nightfall in the wood
This Eastertide call into mind the men,
Now far from home, who, with their sweethearts, should
Have gathered them and will do never again.

22 April ✶ A Dream within a Dream ✶
Edgar Allan Poe

This work by the American poet Edgar Allan Poe takes as its
subject the relationship between reality and fantasy.

Take this kiss upon the brow!
And, in parting from you now,
Thus much let me avow —
You are not wrong, who deem
That my days have been a dream;
Yet if hope has flown away
In a night, or in a day,
In a vision, or in none,
Is it therefore the less gone?
All that we see or seem
Is but a dream within a dream.

I stand amid the roar
Of a surf-tormented shore,
And I hold within my hand
Grains of the golden sand —
How few! yet how they creep
Through my fingers to the deep,
While I weep — while I weep!
O God! Can I not grasp
Them with a tighter clasp?
O God! can I not save
One from the pitiless wave?
Is all that we see or seem
But a dream within a dream?

23 April ✶ Sonnet 18 ✶ William Shakespeare

On 23 April 1564 William Shakespeare was born in Stratford-upon-Avon – and on the same day in 1616 he died. Shakespeare wrote 154 sonnets, but this one is perhaps his most well-known. Traditionally, sonnets have been associated with romantic love, often praising the virtues of the beloved.

Shall I compare thee to a summer's day?
Thou art more lovely and more temperate:
Rough winds do shake the darling buds of May,
And summer's lease hath all too short a date;
Sometime too hot the eye of heaven shines,
And often is his gold complexion dimm'd;
And every fair from fair sometime declines,
By chance, or nature's changing course, untrimm'd:
But thy eternal summer shall not fade,
Nor lose possession of that fair thou ow'st;
Nor shall death brag thou wander'st in his shade
When in eternal lines to time thou grow'st:
  So long as men can breathe or eyes can see,
  So long lives this, and this gives life to thee.

24 April ✶ *from* The Tempest ✶
William Shakespeare

The character of Caliban in Shakespeare's *The Tempest* is one
his most controversial and intriguing creations. While he is
often described as a monster, Shakespeare also gives him lines
which convey a very human, sensitive side.

Be not afeard; the isle is full of noises,
Sounds and sweet airs, that give delight and hurt not.
Sometimes a thousand twangling instruments
Will hum about mine ears, and sometime voices
That, if I then had waked after long sleep,
Will make me sleep again: and then, in dreaming,
The clouds methought would open and show riches
Ready to drop upon me that, when I waked,
I cried to dream again.

25 April ✳ *from* Henry VIII ✳ William Shakespeare

This poem is taken from *Henry VIII*, a history play attributed to Shakespeare and John Fletcher. The poem takes as its subject the mythical figure Orpheus and the power of music. In Greek myth, Orpheus was a musician so talented that even inanimate objects such as stones were charmed by his music.

Orpheus with his lute made trees,
And the mountain tops that freeze,
Bow themselves when he did sing:
To his music plants and flowers
Ever sprung; as sun and showers
There had made a lasting spring.
Every thing that heard him play,
Even the billows of the sea,
Hung their heads, and then lay by.
In sweet music is such art,
Killing care and grief of heart
Fall asleep, or hearing, die.

26 April ✶ Shakespeare ✶ Matthew Arnold

Shakespeare is regarded by many as the most influential writer in the history of English literature. The Bard even fundamentally altered the English language, inventing over 1,700 new words! Matthew Arnold, a well-respected Victorian poet and critic, remembers Shakespeare in his own sonnet, published in 1849. In it, Arnold expresses his awe at Shakespeare's writing, marking him as one of the greatest writers of all time and mourning his death. Shakespeare's astonishing body of work has stood the test of time, and Matthew Arnold's sonnet is one of many love letters to the Bard, written in the form made popular by the man himself.

Others abide our question. Thou art free.
We ask and ask – Thou smilest and art still,
Out-topping knowledge. For the loftiest hill,
Who to the stars uncrowns his majesty,

Planting his steadfast footsteps in the sea,
Making the heaven of heavens his dwelling-place,
Spares but the cloudy border of his base
To the foil'd searching of mortality;

And thou, who didst the stars and sunbeams know,
Self-school'd, self-scann'd, self-honour'd, self-secure,
Didst tread on earth unguess'd at. – Better so!

All pains the immortal spirit must endure,
All weakness which impairs, all griefs which bow,
Find their sole speech in that victorious brow.

27 April ✴ Child's Song in Spring ✴ Edith Nesbit

Edith Nesbit was a poet and an author, and she wrote adventure stories such as *Five Children and It* and *The Railway Children*, but in this poem her inspiration comes from something more familiar – trees in Spring.

The Silver Birch is a dainty lady,
She wears a satin gown;
The elm tree makes the old churchyard shady,
She will not live in town.

The English oak is a sturdy fellow,
He gets his green coat late;
The willow is smart in a suit of yellow
While brown the beech trees wait.

Such a gay green gown God gives the larches –
As green as he is good!
The hazels hold up their arms for arches,
When spring rides through the wood.

The chestnut's proud, and the lilac's pretty,
The poplar's gentle and tall,
But the plane tree's kind to the poor dull city –
I love him best of all!

28 April ✳ The Tickle Rhyme ✳ Ian Serraillier

Walls and caterpillars don't usually speak, but in this rhyme by Ian Serraillier the personification is necessary: without their conversation, the mystery of who it was that was tickling the wall's back may never have been answered!

'Who's that tickling my back?' said the wall.
'Me,' said a small
Caterpillar.
'I'm learning
To crawl.'

29 April * The Emperor's Rhyme * A. A. Milne

This jaunty poem features a fair amount of rhyming, which makes it easy to learn off by heart. Just don't try to do the sums in your head!

The King of Peru
(Who was Emperor too)
    Had a sort of a rhyme
        Which was useful to know,
If he felt very shy
When a stranger came by,
    Or they asked him the time
        When his watch didn't go;
or supposing he fell
(By mistake) down the well,
    Or he tumbled when skating
        And sat on his hat,
Or perhaps wasn't told,
    Till his porridge was cold,
        That his breakfast was waiting –
Or something like that;

Oh, whenever the Emperor
got into a temper, or
    Felt himself sulky or sad,
He would murmur and murmur,
Until he felt firmer,
    This curious rhyme which he had:

'Eight eights are sixty-four;
    Multiply by seven.
When it's done,
Carry one,
    And take away eleven.
Nine nines are eighty-one;
    Multiply by three.

If it's more,
Carry four,
   And then it's time for tea.'

So whenever the Queen
Took his armour to clean,
   And didn't remember
      To use any starch;
Or his birthday (in May)
Was a horrible day,
   Being wet as November
      And windy as March;
Or, if sitting in state
With the Wise and the Great
   He happened to hiccup
      While signing his name,
Or The Queen gave a cough,
When his crown tumbled off
   As he bent down to pick up
      A pen for the same;

Oh, whenever the Emperor
Got into a temper, or
   Felt himself awkward or shy,
He would whisper and whisper,
Until he felt crisper,
   This odd little rhyme to the sky.

'Eight eights are eighty-one;
   Multiply by seven.
When it's done,
Carry one,
   And take away eleven.
Nine nines are sixty-four;
   Multiply by three.
When it's done,
Carry one,
   And then it's time for tea.'

30 April ✶ The Hippopotamus's Birthday ✶ E. V. Rieu

Although E. V. Rieu was well-known for his hugely successful translation of *The Odyssey*, his humorous poetry for children suggests that he didn't spend all of his time on the classics.

He has opened all his parcels
  but the largest and the last;
His hopes are at their highest
  and his heart is beating fast.
O happy Hippopotamus,
  what lovely gift is here?
He cuts the string. The world stands still.
  A pair of boots appear!

O little Hippopotamus,
  the sorrows of the small!
He dropped two tears to mingle
  with the flowing Senegal;
And the 'Thank you' that he uttered
  was the saddest ever heard
In the Senegambian jungle
  from the mouth of beast or bird.

May

1 May ✶ May Day ✶ Sara Teasdale

1 May, known as May Day, marks an ancient festival dating
back to the pre-Christian era, and is often regarded as the
first day of Summer in the northern hemisphere. Traditional
English activities associated with the day include Morris
dancing, the crowning of a May Queen to lead the festival
celebrations, and dancing around a maypole. This poem by the
American poet Sara Teasdale celebrates the beauty of nature
on May Day.

> The shining line of motors,
> The swaying motor-bus,
> The prancing dancing horses
> Are passing by for us.
>
> The sunlight on the steeple,
> The toys we stop to see,
> The smiling passing people
> Are all for you and me.
>
> 'I love you and I love you!'—
> 'And oh, I love you, too!'
> 'All of the flower girl's lilies
> Were only grown for you!'
>
> Fifth Avenue and April
> And love and lack of care—
> The world is mad with music
> Too beautiful to bear.

2 May   *   Leisure   *   W. H. Davies

Sometimes we are so busy that we forget to look up and notice the glories of nature.

> What is this life if, full of care,
> We have no time to stand and stare?
>
> No time to stand beneath the boughs
> And stare as long as sheep or cows.
>
> No time to see, when woods we pass,
> Where squirrels hide their nuts in grass.
>
> No time to see, in broad daylight,
> Streams full of stars, like skies at night.
>
> No time to turn at Beauty's glance,
> And watch her feet, how they can dance.
>
> No time to wait till her mouth can
> Enrich that smile her eyes began.
>
> A poor life this is if, full of care,
> We have no time to stand and stare.

3 May ✶ The Fawn ✶ Edna St Vincent Millay

Millay often wrote about nature, and in this poem she describes a moment in which she came upon a fawn on a 'forest day'.

There it was I saw what I shall never forget
And never retrieve.
Monstrous and beautiful to human eyes, hard to believe,
He lay, yet there he lay,
Asleep on the moss, his head on his polished cleft small
    ebony hooves,
The child of the doe, the dappled child of the deer.

Surely his mother had never said, 'Lie here
Till I return,' so spotty and plain to see
On the green moss lay he.
His eyes had opened; he considered me.
I would have given more than I care to say
To thrifty ears, might I have had him for my friend
One moment only of that forest day:

Might I have had the acceptance, not the love
Of those clear eyes;
Might I have been for him in the bough above
Or the root beneath his forest bed,
A part of the forest, seen without surprise.

Was it alarm, or was it the wind of my fear lest he depart
That jerked him to his jointy knees,
And sent him crashing off, leaping and stumbling
On his new legs, between the stems of the white trees?

4 May ✳ Old Pond ✳ Matsuo Bashō, translated by
Robert Hass

In Japan, 4 May is known as Greenery Day or *Midori no hi* – a
day for the celebration of natural beauty. Traditional Japanese
haikus often took nature as their subject. This haiku is by the
most revered poet Matsuo Bashō.

The old pond –
a frog jumps in,
sound of water.

5 May ✶ Clouds ✶ Matsuo Bashō, translated by Robert Hass

This is another haiku by Bashō, and like 'Old Pond' it uses very simple imagery to great effect.

> From time to time
> The clouds give rest
> To the moon-beholders.

6 May ✳ To a Squirrel at Kyle-Na-No ✳ W. B. Yeats

'To a Squirrel' was inspired by a visit to the wood of Kyle-na-no in Coole Park, County Galway. W. B. Yeats lived just three miles away from the park, and several of his poems were inspired by experiences in the beautiful nature reserve.

Come play with me;
Why should you run
Through the shaking tree
As though I'd a gun
To strike you dead?
When all I would do
Is to scratch your head
And let you go.

7 May ✶ You Ain't Nothing but a Hedgehog ✶
John Cooper Clarke

The performance poet John Cooper Clarke's witty poem is a
rewriting of a blues song, 'Hound Dog', famously recorded in
1956 by Elvis Presley, the 'King of Rock and Roll'.

You ain't nothing but a hedgehog
Foragin' all the time
You ain't nothing but a hedgehog
Foragin' all the time
You ain't never pricked a predator
You ain't no porcupine.

8 May ∗ Why the Bat Flies at Night ∗
Roger Stevens

Like John Cooper Clarke's reimagining of a hedgehog as a rock
'n' roll figure, this work by the contemporary poet Roger Stevens
gives us a completely new perspective on a familiar animal.

Once, when the moon was as bright as the sun
And the stars lit up the sky
And the day and the night were both as one,
The bat came flying by

The bat flew by fast and furious
And attached to his back with string
Was a basket. The animals were curious
They said, Bat, what is in that thing?

Ah, said the bat, well, this afternoon
I was given a task to do
To take this basket up to the moon
But what's in it? I haven't a clue.

But the bat was no long-distance flyer
And he had to lie down for a sleep
So, due to the others' insistence,
The lion opened the basket to peep

Then all at once from the basket
There came a most terrible sight
A shadow that fell like a dark net
Bringing the blackness of night

And that is why bats rise at twilight
And they sleep through the bright hours of day
Why they chivvy and chase the dark slivers of night
The darkness they let get away

174

9 May ✳ Mayfly ✳ Mary Ann Hoberman

People have always been fascinated by the brief lives of mayflies. Hatching in vast numbers on warm Spring days, these insects often live only for a single day! We might find in the poem a message about the fragility and preciousness of all life.

Think how fast a year flies by
A month flies by
A week flies by
Think how fast a day flies by
A Mayfly's life lasts but a day
A single day
To live and die
A single day
How fast it goes
The day
The Mayfly
Both of those.
A Mayfly flies a single day
The daylight dies and darkness grows
A single day
How fast it flies
A Mayfly's life
How fast it goes.

10 May ✳ Brother ✳ Mary Ann Hoberman

This poem by Mary Ann Hoberman feels almost like a tongue twister in its repetitions of 'bother' and 'brother' so close together.

I had a little brother
And I brought him to my mother
And I said I want another
Little brother for a change.
But she said don't be a bother
So I took him to my father
And I said this little bother
Of a brother's very strange.
But he said one little brother
Is exactly like another
And every little brother
Misbehaves a bit he said.
So I took the little bother
From my mother and my father
And I put the little bother
Of a brother back to bed.

The subject of this poem is the mythological selkie – a creature
that resembles a seal in the water but a human on land.
Legends involving the selkie can be found in Scottish, Irish,
and Icelandic folklore. Tony Mitton's poem tells the story of
young Donallan who falls in love with a selkie.

Young Donallan lived alone
with the sound of the sea and the wind's wild moan,
and the hiss of the kettle, the sigh of the peat,
with a cat in his lap and a dog at his feet.

Young Donallan spread his net.
He landed the fish that he could get.
He grew his cabbage in a scant croft patch,
and he caulked his boat and he roped his thatch.

On the seventh day of the high Spring tide
His heart grew full and he stretched and sighed.
So he walked the length of the lonely strand
To the chafe of the surf on the soft sea sand.

Young Donallan tuned his ear
to the cry of the gulls on the salt sea air.
But above the birds and the fall of the flood
there rose a sound that swelled his blood.

Down on the rocks a selkie sang,
And he drank the song till his senses rang.
He gazed at the sight of her glimmering there
With her graceful form and her winnowing hair.

He knew the lore and the ways of old
From the talk, and the tales his father told.

So he seized the skin that lay by her side,
Crying, 'Selkie, I take you to be my bride.'

She begged for the skin, on her bended knee,
for without it she could not return to the sea.
But her eyes were dark and her skin was soft,
and Donallan led her back to his croft.

Young Donallan and his selkie bride
lived in the croft to the tune of the tide,
She stitched his shirt and she baked his bread
And she lay by his side in the old box bed.

She bore him children, one, two, three.
Their eyes were as soft as the seals' of the sea.
They loved their mother with her gentle ways
But they knew her sigh and her sad sea gaze.

And they felt in their hearts there was something wrong
for her voice was sweet but she sang no song.
Whenever she soothed them to sleep at night
Her eyes were kind but her lips pressed tight.

It was on a day when the wind was wild
and Donallan was out with the eldest child,
that the Selkie Bride was baking bread
when all of a sudden the youngest said,

'Early this morning while the family slept
I followed our father out where he crept.
He loosened a stone in the old croft wall
And he took from the hollow a sleek grey caul.

'He oiled and smoothed that supple skin,
Then he folded it tight and put it back in.

Now tell me, Mother, oh spell to me
the meaning of this mystery.'

But his mother, never a word she said.
She found the skin and she left her bread.
Then she led the children to the edge of the land
where the waters lap at the silver sand.

'Now, listen, my dears, oh listen to me.
Your mother's home is here in the sea.
It was here in Spring, at the height of the tide,
Your father took me to be his bride.

'And though it tear at your mother's heart,
it's here on the shore that we must part.'
She shook her skin and she put it on.
Then she fell to the waves and she was gone.

When they told their father, he scarcely stirred.
He gave a sigh, but he spoke no word.
For he knew that a selkie, such as she,
must come at last to her home in the sea.

So Donallan lived in the small thatched croft,
with his children three and their eyes so soft.
But whenever in Spring the tides rose high
And a round moon rode in the cool night sky,

they would hear the music, clear and strong,
the sound of their mother's selkie song,
and they knew she was near, in the swing of the sea,
where the waters roll and the seal swim free.

And from that time, in the midst of the storm,
they were safe from the waves that spoil and harm.
And whoever was of their selkie brood,
their boats stayed sound and their catch was good.

12 May ✶ Silkie ✶ Dave Calder

This poem by Dave Calder also takes the mythological selkie, spelt here as 'silkie', as its subject. The poet here pairs the transformation between human and selkie form with the transition between being awake and falling asleep.

The gulls had quietened on the chimneypots
and in the unending dusk of the summer night
he could hear the sea pushing and pulling at pebbles, in and
    out, rise and fall,
and when he slid into the sheets they felt
as smooth and cool as slipping into water
down down
until only his head only his nose and eyes
bobbed above water and then
his body losing all sense of weight so
sleek skinned sinking deeper
into the pulse of the sea breathing
rise and fall, in and out, down down
deep and far the song of whales sounding

When he woke, the sheets were a tangle
of breakers, he lay beached on the bed, his head resting on
    the small white sandbank, the gulls wheeling against the
    sunlight

180

13 May ✳ Swan and Shadow ✳ John Hollander

With its beautiful and startlingly symmetrical appearance, this poem is one of the most famous examples of a picture poem.

```
                        Dusk
                     Above the
              water  hang the
                          loud
                         flies
                         Here
                         O so
                         gray
                         then
                      What              A pale signal will appear
                      When          Soon before its shadow fades
                      Where        Here in this pool of opened eye
                      In us     No Upon us As at the very edges
                      of where we take shape in the dark air
                       this object bares its image awakening
                          ripples of recognition that will
                             brush darkness up into light
   even after this bird this hour both drift by atop the perfect sad instant now
                            already passing out of sight
                          toward yet-untroubled reflection
                         this image bears its object darkening
                      into memorial shades Scattered bits of
                      Light       No of water Or something across
                      water       Breaking up No Being regathered
                      Soon          Yet by then a swan will have
                       gone              Yes Out of mind into what
                       vast
                       pale
                       hush
                       of a
                       place
                       past
              sudden dark as
                 if a swan
                    sang
```

14 May ✶ Love You More ✶ James Carter

It is difficult to tell somebody how much you love them,
and in this poem James Carter uses increasingly enormous
metaphors to try and measure his emotions.

Do I love you
to the moon and back?
No I love you
more than that
I love you to the desert sands
the mountains, stars
the planets and
I love you to the deepest sea
and deeper still
through history
Before beyond I love you then
I love you now
I'll love you when
The sun's gone out
the moon's gone home
and all the stars are fully grown
When I no longer say these words
I'll give them to the wind, the birds
so that they will still be heard
I love you

15 May ✳ I Found a Ball of Grass among the Hay ✳
John Clare

John Clare was the son of a farm labourer, and he is noted for
his poems that celebrate the English countryside.

I found a ball of grass among the hay
And progged it as I passed and went away;
And when I looked I fancied something stirred,
And turned again and hoped to catch the bird—
When out an old mouse bolted in the wheats
With all her young ones hanging at her teats;
She looked so odd and so grotesque to me,
I ran and wondered what the thing could be,
And pushed the knapweed bunches where I stood;
Then the mouse hurried from the craking brood.
The young ones squeaked, and as I went away
She found her nest again among the hay.
The water o'er the pebbles scarce could run
And broad old cesspools glittered in the sun.

16 May ✳ Apple Blossom ✳ Louis MacNeice

In this poem, Louis MacNeice travels back to the Garden of
Eden, and imagines Adam's first taste of the fruit which God
had told him not to eat. These were the first apples anyone had
ever tasted, and the best, MacNeice says, because they were
new, exciting and full of possibilities.

The first blossom was the best blossom
For the child who never had seen an orchard;
For the youth whom whiskey had led astray
The morning after was the first day.

The first apple was the best apple
For Adam before he heard the sentence;
When the flaming sword endorsed the Fall
The trees were his to plant for all.

The first ocean was the best ocean
For the child from streets of doubt and litter;
For the youth for whom the skies unfurled
His first love was his first world.

But the first verdict seemed the worst verdict
When Adam and Eve were expelled from Eden,
Yet when the bitter gates clanged to
The sky beyond was just as blue.

For the next ocean is the first ocean
And the last ocean is the first ocean
And, however often the sun may rise,
A new thing dawns upon our eyes.

For the last blossom is the first blossom
And the first blossom is the last blossom
And when from Eden we take our way
The morning after is the first day.

17 May ✳ Aunt Julia ✳ Norman MacCaig

In this poem, the Scottish poet Norman MacCaig is writing
about his aunt. His Aunt Julia worked as a crofter, which is a
small-scale farmer. She only spoke Gaelic, a Celtic language
native to Scotland, and MacCaig's poem is full of the regret he
feels that he only learned the language after she had died.

Aunt Julia spoke Gaelic
very loud and very fast.
I could not answer her —
I could not understand her.

She wore men's boots
when she wore any.
— I can see her strong foot,
stained with peat,
paddling with the treadle of the spinningwheel
while her right hand drew yarn
marvellously out of the air.

Hers was the only house
where I've lain at night
in the absolute darkness
of a box bed, listening to
crickets being friendly.

She was buckets
and water flouncing into them.
She was winds pouring wetly
round house-ends.
She was brown eggs, black skirts
and a keeper of threepennybits
in a teapot.

Aunt Julia spoke Gaelic
very loud and very fast.
By the time I had learned
a little, she lay
silenced in the absolute black
of a sandy grave
at Luskentyre. But I hear her still, welcoming me
with a seagull's voice
across a hundred yards
of peatscrapes and lazybeds
and getting angry, getting angry
with so many questions
unanswered.

18 May ✳ The Moment ✳ Margaret Atwood

Although we often seem to link the idea of being 'at home'
somewhere with owning it, this poem looks at the matter a
different way.

The moment when, after many years
of hard work and a long voyage
you stand in the centre of your room,
house, half-acre, square mile, island, country,
knowing at last how you got there,
and say, I own this,

is the same moment when the trees unloose
their soft arms from around you,
the birds take back their language,
the cliffs fissure and collapse,
the air moves back from you like a wave
and you can't breathe.

No, they whisper. You own nothing.
You were a visitor, time after time
climbing the hill, planting the flag, proclaiming.
We never belonged to you.
You never found us.
It was always the other way round.

19 May ✷ One Art ✷ Elizabeth Bishop

At the beginning of this poem, Bishop half-jokingly suggests that you should practise 'the art of losing' by losing small, material things like house keys and watches, so you're prepared for the larger, more difficult losses to come.

The art of losing isn't hard to master;
so many things seem filled with the intent
to be lost that their loss is no disaster.

Lose something every day. Accept the fluster
of lost door keys, the hour badly spent.
The art of losing isn't hard to master.

Then practise losing farther, losing faster:
places, and names, and where it was you meant
to travel. None of these will bring disaster.

I lost my mother's watch. And look! my last, or
next-to-last, of three loved houses went.
The art of losing isn't hard to master.

I lost two cities, lovely ones. And, vaster,
some realms I owned, two rivers, a continent.
I miss them, but it wasn't a disaster.

—Even losing you (the joking voice, a gesture
I love) I shan't have lied. It's evident
the art of losing's not too hard to master
though it may look like (Write it!) like disaster.

20 May ✳ Courage ✳ Amelia Earhart

On 20 May 1932 Amelia Earhart made history as the first
female to complete a transatlantic flight. Departing from
Harbour Grace, Newfoundland, in the morning, Earhart flew
for 14 hours and 56 minutes before landing just north of Derry
in Northern Ireland. Famed for her daring and ambition, it is
perhaps no surprise that this poem by Earhart takes courage
as its topic.

Courage is the price that Life exacts for granting peace.

The soul that knows it not knows no release
From little things:

Knows not the livid loneliness of fear,
Nor mountain heights where bitter joy can hear
The sound of wings.

How can life grant us boon of living, compensate
For dull gray ugliness and pregnant hate
Unless we dare

The soul's dominion? Each time we make a choice, we pay
With courage to behold the resistless day,
And count it fair.

21 May * Little Orphant Annie *
James Whitcomb Riley

This poem, which was first published in 1885, is based in part on an orphan who lived with the poet's family, and told stories about children being snatched away by goblins and elves if they didn't behave well. It is written in 'Hoosier dialect', which originates from Indiana in America.

Little Orphant Annie's come to our house to stay,
An' wash the cups an' saucers up, an' brush the crumbs away,
An' shoo the chickens off the porch, an' dust the hearth, an'
    sweep,
An' make the fire, an' bake the bread, an' earn her board-an'-
    keep;
An' all us other childern, when the supper things is done,
We set around the kitchen fire an' has the mostest fun
A-list'nin' to the witch-tales 'at Annie tells about,
An' the Gobble-uns 'at gits you
       Ef you
      Don't
       Watch
       Out!

Onc't they was a little boy wouldn't say his prayers,—
So when he went to bed at night, away up stairs,
His Mammy heerd him holler, an' his Daddy heerd him bawl,
An' when they turn't the kivvers down, he wasn't there at all!
An' they seeked him in the rafter-room, an' cubby-hole, an'
    press,
An' seeked him up the chimbly-flue, an' ever'wheres, I guess;
But all they ever found was thist his pants an' roundabout—
An' the Gobble-uns'll git you

       Ef you
          Don't
             Watch
                Out!

An' one time a little girl 'ud allus laugh an' grin,
An' make fun of ever'one, an' all her blood an' kin;
An' onc't, when they was 'company', an' ole folks was there,
She mocked 'em an' shocked 'em, an' said she didn't care!
An' thist as she kicked her heels, an' turn't to run an' hide,
They was two great big Black Things a-standin' by her side,
An' they snatched her through the ceilin' 'fore she knowed
    what she's about!
An' the Gobble-uns'll git you
          Ef you
             Don't
                Watch
                   Out!

An' little Orphant Annie says when the blaze is blue,
An' the lamp-wick sputters, an' the wind goes woo-oo!
An' you hear the crickets quit, an' the moon is gray,
An' the lightnin'-bugs in dew is all squenched away,—
You better mind yer parents, an' yer teachers fond an' dear,
An' churish them 'at loves you, an' dry the orphant's tear,
An' he'p the pore an' needy ones 'at clusters all about,
Er the Gobble-uns'll git you
          Ef you
             Don't
                Watch
                   Out!

22 May ✳ Jim, Who Ran Away from his Nurse and Was Eaten by a Lion ✳ Hilaire Belloc

A 'nurse' is a word that was used for the women who looked after small children, just as nannies and childminders do nowadays. In this poem, Hilaire Belloc tells the cautionary tale of Jim, who ran away from his nurse. Although the subject of the poem is a scary one, the rhyming couplets and the humorous tone make it very funny.

There was a Boy whose name was Jim;
His Friends were very good to him.
They gave him Tea, and Cakes, and Jam,
And slices of delicious Ham,
And Chocolate with pink inside
And little Tricycles to ride,
And read him Stories through and through,
And even took him to the Zoo—
But there it was the dreadful Fate
Befell him, which I now relate.

You know—or at least you ought to know,
For I have often told you so—
That Children never are allowed
To leave their Nurses in a Crowd;
Now this was Jim's especial Foible,
He ran away when he was able,
And on this inauspicious day
He slipped his hand and ran away!

He hadn't gone a yard when—Bang!
With open Jaws, a lion sprang,
And hungrily began to eat
The Boy: beginning at his feet.

Now, just imagine how it feels
When first your toes and then your heels,
And then by gradual degrees,
Your shins and ankles, calves and knees,
Are slowly eaten, bit by bit.
No wonder Jim detested it!
No wonder that he shouted 'Hi!'

The Honest Keeper heard his cry,
Though very fat he almost ran
To help the little gentleman.
'Ponto!' he ordered as he came
(For Ponto was the Lion's name),
'Ponto!' he cried, with angry Frown,
'Let go, Sir! Down, Sir! Put it down!'
The Lion made a sudden stop,
He let the Dainty Morsel drop,
And slunk reluctant to his Cage,
Snarling with Disappointed Rage.
But when he bent him over Jim,
The Honest Keeper's Eyes were dim.
The Lion having reached his Head,
The Miserable Boy was dead!

When Nurse informed his Parents, they
Were more Concerned than I can say:—
His Mother, as She dried her eyes,
Said, 'Well—it gives me no surprise,
He would not do as he was told!'
His Father, who was self-controlled,
Bade all the children round attend
To James's miserable end,
And always keep a-hold of Nurse
For fear of finding something worse.

194

23 May ✳ Bookworm ✳ Anon., translated by Michael Alexander

When we use the term 'bookworm' we generally mean a person who loves to read. Here, however, an anonymous medieval poet is playing on the double-meaning of the term: a bookworm can also be an actual worm, or maggot, that feeds on paper.

A worm ate words. I thought that wonderfully
Strange – a miracle – when they told me a crawling
Insect had swallowed noble songs,
A night-time thief had stolen writing
So famous, so weighty. But the bug was foolish
Still, though its belly was full of thought.

24 May ✳ A Riddle ✳ Christina Rossetti

Can you guess the answer to this riddle by Christina Rossetti?
(Answer underneath!)

> There is one that has a head without an eye,
>   And there is one that has an eye without a head.
> You may find the answer if you try;
>   And when all is said,
>   Half the answer hangs upon a thread.

The answer to this riddle is 'a pin and a needle'.

25 May ✶ The Riddle Song ✶ Anon.

'The Riddle Song' contains four riddles in one poem. In the final verse, the poem surprisingly supplies all the answers to its own questions.

My love gave me a chicken, but it had no bone.
My love gave me a cherry, but it had no stone.
My love gave me a scare, without a single shiver.
My love showed me a bridge without a running river.

How can there be a chicken, without a bone?
How can there be a cherry, without a stone?
How can there be a scare, without a single shiver?
How can there be a bridge, without a running river?

When the chicken is in the egg, there is no bone.
When the cherry is in the blossom, there is no stone.
When the scare is in the field, to frighten off the crows.
When the bridge is on the face and runs across the nose.

26 May ✳ One Fine Day in the Middle of the Night ✳
Anon.

This poem is a nonsense rhyme; even the title makes no sense.
You're right not to believe a word of it, and in fact the poet
does not really expect you to believe them. They are playing
a game: how many impossible things can they fit into a short
rhyming poem?

One fine day in the middle of the night,
Two dead boys got up to fight,
Back to back they faced each other,
Drew their swords and shot each other,
One was blind and the other couldn't see
So they chose a dummy for a referee.
A blind man went to see fair play,
A dumb man went to shout 'hooray!'
A paralysed donkey passing by,
Kicked the blind man in the eye,
Knocked him through a nine inch wall,
Into a dry ditch and drowned them all,
A deaf policeman heard the noise,
And came to arrest the two dead boys.
If you don't believe this story's true,
Ask the blind man he saw it too!

27 May ✶ M.O.R.E.R.A.P.S. ✶ Joseph Coelho

When we discuss poetry, we often use many complex words, such as 'onomatopoeia', 'metaphor' and 'alliteration'. This poem by the prize-winning performance poet and playwright Joseph Coelho is particularly useful for helping you to remember all the different definitions.

The M.O.R.E.R.A.P.S are a trick
to help with your writing.
They add a kick to language,
Make writing more exciting.

M is for Metaphor —
saying one thing is another.
'The sun is an oven.'
'The Earth is everyone's mother.'

O is for Onomatopoeia —
words that are also sounds.
'Whoosh went the wind.'
'Howl went the hound.'

R is for Rhyme —
words that sound the same.
You can put a cat in a hat.
Or simply try rhyming your name.

E is for Emotion —
happy, worried and sad.
Great writing shares a feeling
from the good to the bad.

R is for Repetition —
But don't repeat any old word!
Find a phrase with a musical rhythm
that sounds like a song from a bird.

A is for Alliteration —
words sharing the same starting letter,
used in the tongue-twister
that made Betty's bitter batter better.

P is for Personification —
human features ascribed to a thing.
I looked to the sky and saw
the sun's bright shining grin.

S is for Simile —
using 'as' and 'like' to compare.
For instance, 'When Mother gets angry
she snarls like a rampaging bear.'

The M.O.R.E.R.A.P.S are a wonderful way
to add a punch to your writing.
Master them like a juggler.
make your words ripe for the biting.

28 May ✱ Yes ✱ Adrian Mitchell

In this poem different things speak to illustrate what they can mean to us. While some of the things 'spoken' in this poem are funny, like the kangaroo saying 'trampoline', others have deeper meanings, such as the bus saying 'us' while the car says 'me'.

A smile says: Yes.
A heart says: Blood.
When the rain says: Drink.
The earth says: Mud.

The kangaroo says: Trampoline.
Giraffes say: Tree.
A bus says: Us.
While a car says: Me.

Lemon trees say: Lemons.
A jug says: Lemonade.
The villain says: You're wonderful.
The hero: I'm afraid.

The forest says: Hide and Seek.
The grass says: Green and Grow.
The railway says: Maybe.
The prison says: No.

The millionaire says: Take.
The beggar says: Give.
The soldier cries: Mother!
The baby sings: Live.

The river says: Come with me.
The moon says: Bless.
The stars say: Enjoy the light.
The sun says: Yes.

29 May ✳ There was a Young Lady whose Chin ✳
Edward Lear

A limerick is a silly, funny, often rather rude poem of five lines.
This limerick by Edward Lear creates the comical picture of
the Young Lady of the title playing the harp using only her
exceedingly pointy chin.

There was a Young Lady whose chin
Resembled the point of a pin;
So she had it made sharp,
And purchased a harp,
And played several tunes with her chin.

30 May ✶ Joan of Arc ✶ Florence Earle Coates

On 30 May 1431 the French military leader Joan of Arc, a famous figure in the Hundred Years War between France and England, was burnt at the stake. It is thought that she was only 19 years old at the time. This poem by Florence Earle Coates was written in 1916, and praises Joan's extraordinary life.

Her spirit is to France a living spring
   From which to draw deep draughts of life. To-day,—
   As when a peasant girl she led the way
Victorious to Rheims and crowned the King,—
High and heroic thoughts about her cling,
   And sacrificial faiths as pure as they,
   Moving the land she loved, with gentle sway,
To be, for love of her, a better thing!
Was she unhappy? No: her radiant youth
   Burned, like a meteor, on to swift eclipse;
   But where it passed, there lingers still a light.
She waited, wistful, for the word of truth
   That breathed in blessing from immortal lips
   When earthly comfort failed, and all around was night.

31 May ✳ This is Just to Say ✳ William Carlos Williams

This poem resembles the kind of apologetic note you might leave on the fridge door.

I have eaten
the plums
that were in
the icebox

and which
you were probably
saving
for breakfast

Forgive me
they were delicious
so sweet
and so cold

June

1 June ✷ Sumer is i-cumen in ✷ Anon.

This thirteenth-century medieval poem is written in Middle English. It would have been sung as a 'round' – which means at least three voices singing in unison, but beginning at different times. It has been set to music many times and it is still popular today.

Sumer is i-cumen in,
Loude sing cuckow!
Groweth seed and bloweth meed
And spryngeth the wode now.
Syng cuckow!
Ewe bleteth after lamb,
Loweth after calve cow;
Bullock sterteth, bukke farteth, –
Myrie syng cuckow!
Cuckow! Cuckow!
Wel syngest thou cuckow:
Ne swik thou nevere now!
   Syng cuckow, now, syng cuckow!
   Syng cuckow, syng cuckow, now!

2 June ✶ Summer ✶ Christina Rossetti

Here Christina Rossetti uses the technique of listing to make
a persuasive case for why Summer, for her, beats all the other
seasons.

Winter is cold-hearted,
　Spring is yea and nay,
Autumn is a weathercock
　Blown every way:
Summer days for me
　When every leaf is on its tree;

When Robin's not a beggar,
　And Jenny Wren's a bride,
And larks hang singing, singing, singing,
　Over the wheat-fields wide,
　And anchored lilies ride,
And the pendulum spider
　Swings from side to side,

And blue-black beetles transact business,
　And gnats fly in a host,
And furry caterpillars hasten
　That no time be lost,
And moths grow fat and thrive,
And ladybirds arrive.

Before green apples blush,
　Before green nuts embrown,
Why, one day in the country
　Is worth a month in town;
　Is worth a day and a year
Of the dusty, musty, lag-last fashion
　That days drone elsewhere.

3 June ✳ Just One ✳ Laura Mucha

In this poem, Laura Mucha uses a list and the repetition of
the phrase 'one more' to illustrate just how many things the
speaker of the poem enjoys.

One more mountain, just the one, one more trip away
     with Mum, one more apple rhubarb pie,
one more amber-lilac sky.

One more chocolate – plain and dark,
a peacock and a national park,
Arctic iceberg, Shetland sheep
and one more really good night's sleep. One more day of
     blazing heat,

one more friend I'd like to meet,
one more bike ride, one more hike, I'd talk to every bird
     and bee,
I'd soak them up, I'd set them free
with paint, with words, perhaps a song. Life is short and
     life is long,
so quickly please, before it's gone,

just one more poem.

4 June ✳ Wiegenlied (Lullaby) ✳ Anon.

In 1868 the German composer Johannes Brahms took the
first verse of the famous Wiegenlied (a German word meaning
'lullaby') from a collection of German folk poetry, and set it to
a gentle, rocking melody which is now instantly recognizable.
Nowadays, every night across the world parents sing the
Brahms Lullaby to soothe their children into a peaceful night
of sleep.

> Lullaby and good night,
> With roses bedight,
> With lilies o'er spread
> Is baby's wee bed.
> Lay thee down now and rest,
> May thy slumber be blessed.
>
> Lullaby and good night,
> Thy mother's delight,
> Bright angels beside
> My darling abide.
> They will guard thee at rest,
> Thou shalt wake on my breast.

5 June ✶ Cradle Song ✶ Thomas Dekker

This short lullaby by the Elizabethan writer Thomas Dekker was first published in 1603 – over 250 years before Johannes Brahms composed his Wiegenlied. Yet in spite of its early origins, Dekker's poem already contains many of the phrases which we associate with lullabies.

Golden slumbers kiss your eyes,
Smiles awake you when you rise;
Sleep, pretty wantons, do not cry,
And I will sing a lullaby:
Rock them, rock them, lullaby.

Care is heavy, therefore sleep you;
You are care, and care must keep you.
Sleep, pretty wantons, do not cry,
And I will sing a lullaby:
Rock them, rock them, lullaby.

6 June ✶ Golden Slumbers ✶ Paul McCartney

Paul McCartney, who is most famous as a member of The Beatles, adapted the lyrics to 'Golden Slumbers' from a poem by the Elizabethan playwright Thomas Dekker, which he found by chance in a book of sheet music in 1969. Like Dekker's poem, the song McCartney wrote is a kind of lullaby, though he made many changes to the lyrics; the 'golden slumbers' of the title 'fill your eyes' in McCartney's song, rather than, as Dekker wrote, 'kiss your eyes'.

> Once there was a way to get back homeward
> Once there was a way to get back home
> Sleep pretty darling do not cry
> And I will sing a lullaby
>
> Golden slumbers fill your eyes
> Smiles awake you when you rise
> Sleep pretty darling do not cry
> And I will sing a lullaby
>
> Once there was a way to get back homeward
> Once there was a way to get back home
> Sleep pretty darling do not cry
> And I will sing a lullaby

7 June ✶ Swing Low, Sweet Chariot ✶ Wallis Willis

Though in Britain 'Swing Low, Sweet Chariot' is best known as the England Rugby Team anthem, the song, or 'spiritual', was originally sung in the nineteenth century, by black slaves, longing for freedom in the American South. Spirituals are a type of religious folksong, and this one is inspired by the Old Testament tale of Elijah who was taken to heaven in a chariot. With its rocking rhythm and its promise of rest, this is also a perfect poem for the evening.

> Swing low, sweet chariot
> Coming for to carry me home,
> Swing low, sweet chariot,
> Coming for to carry me home.
>
> I looked over Jordan, and what did I see
> Coming for to carry me home?
> A band of angels coming after me,
> Coming for to carry me home.
>
> Sometimes I'm up, and sometimes I'm down,
> (Coming for to carry me home)
> But still my soul feels heavenly bound.
> (Coming for to carry me home)
>
> The brightest day that I can say,
> (Coming for to carry me home)
> When Jesus washed my sins away.
> (Coming for to carry me home)
>
> If you get there before I do,
> (Coming for to carry me home)
> Tell all my friends I'm coming there too.
> (Coming for to carry me home)

8 June ✳ Auto-Lullaby ✳ Franz Wright

The title of this poem suggests both a lullaby that you sing
to yourself, and a lullaby that is automatically generated
by a machine rather than composed by a human – and this
definition might explain the strange and unrelated pieces of
advice that the poem gives.

Think of a sheep
knitting a sweater;
think of your life
getting better and better.

Think of your cat
asleep in a tree;
think of that spot
where you once skinned your knee.

Think of a bird
that stands in your palm.
Try to remember
the Twenty-first Psalm.

Think of a big pink horse
galloping south;
think of a fly, and
close your mouth.

If you feel thirsty, then
drink from your cup.
The birds will keep singing
until they wake up.

9 June ✶ Hush, Little Baby ✶ Anon.

You may already know the lullaby 'Hush, Little Baby'. If you do, you will probably find it very hard to read it without humming along in your head.

Hush, little baby, don't say a word,
Mama's gonna buy you a mockingbird.
If that mockingbird don't sing,
Mama's gonna buy you a diamond ring.
If that diamond ring gets broke,
Mama's gonna buy you a billy goat.
If that billy goat won't pull,
Mama's gonna buy you a cart and bull.
If that cart and bull turn over,
Mama's gonna buy you a dog named Rover.
If that dog named Rover won't bark.
Mama's gonna buy you a horse and cart.
If that horse and cart fall down,
You'll still be the sweetest little baby in town.
So hush little baby don't you cry,
'Cause Daddy loves you and so do I.

10 June * Sweet and Low (*from* The Princess) *
Alfred, Lord Tennyson

This poem is also a lullaby. If you read carefully it is clear that the poem is only partly about the child. The speaker of the poem is a lonely mother who is wishing for the return of the baby's father.

Sweet and low, sweet and low,
    Wind of the western sea,
Low, low, breathe and blow,
    Wind of the western sea!
Over the rolling waters go,
Come from the dying moon, and blow,
    Blow him again to me;
While my little one, while my pretty one, sleeps.

Sleep and rest, sleep and rest,
    Father will come to thee soon;
Rest, rest, on mother's breast,
    Father will come to thee soon;
Father will come to his babe in the nest,
Silver sails all out of the west
    Under the silver moon:
Sleep, my little one, sleep, my pretty one, sleep.

11 June ✳ The Eagle ✳ Alfred, Lord Tennyson

This is one of Tennyson's shortest poems and is, quite simply, a portrait of an eagle. We don't actually see the prey, but we can anticipate the inevitable swoop.

He clasps the crag with crooked hands;
Close to the sun in lonely lands,
Ring'd with the azure world, he stands.

The wrinkled sea beneath him crawls;
He watches from his mountain walls,
And like a thunderbolt he falls.

12 June ✶ Sloth ✶ Theodore Roethke

Sloths are mammals that live in trees in the jungles of Central and South America. They move very slowly, and only when it is absolutely necessary!

In moving slow he has no Peer.
You ask him something in his Ear,
He thinks about it for a Year;

And, then, before he says a Word
There, upside down (unlike a Bird),
He will assume that you have Heard

A most Ex-as-per-at-ing Lug.
But should you call his manner Smug,
He'll sigh and give his Branch a Hug;

Then off again to Sleep he goes,
Still swaying gently by his Toes,
And you just know he knows he knows.

13 June ✶ The Way Through the Woods ✶
Rudyard Kipling

In this poem, Rudyard Kipling describes the scene of a tussle between human land-use and the wild, unordered forces of nature.

They shut the road through the woods
    Seventy years ago.
Weather and rain have undone it again,
    And now you would never know
There was once a road through the woods
    Before they planted the trees.
It is underneath the coppice and heath,
    And the thin anemones.
Only the keeper sees
    That, where the ring-dove broods,
And the badgers roll at ease,
    There was once a road through the woods.

Yet, if you enter the woods
    Of a summer evening late,
When the night-air cools on the trout-ringed pools
    Where the otter whistles his mate,
(They fear not men in the woods,
    Because they see so few)
You will hear the beat of a horse's feet
    And the swish of a skirt in the dew,
    Steadily cantering through
The misty solitudes,
    As though they perfectly knew
The old lost road through the woods . . .
    But there is no road through the woods.

14 June ✷ The Star-Spangled Banner ✷
Francis Scott Key

In America, 14 June is Flag Day, the annual celebration of the day on which the American flag was adopted in 1777. This poem commemorates an early use of the American flag on the battlefield. Key wrote the poem after witnessing the Battle of Fort McHenry in 1814. Though he was being held captive on a British ship, Key watched through the night and was heartened to see the American flag still flying over the fort in the morning. The poem was set to music in the nineteenth century but it did not become the official American national anthem until 1931.

O say, can you see, by the dawn's early light,
What so proudly we hailed at the twilight's last gleaming?
Whose broad stripes and bright stars through the perilous
    fight,
O'er the ramparts we watched were so gallantly streaming;
And the rocket's red glare, the bombs bursting in air,
Gave proof through the night that our flag was still there;
O say, does that star-spangled banner yet wave
O'er the land of the free, and the home of the brave?

On the shore dimly seen through the mists of the deep,
Where the foe's haughty host in dread silence reposes,
What is that which the breeze, o'er the towering steep,
As it fitfully blows, now conceals, now discloses?
Now it catches the gleam of the morning's first beam,
In full glory reflected now shines on the stream;
'Tis the star-spangled banner; O long may it wave
O'er the land of the free, and the home of the brave!

And where is that band who so vauntingly swore
That the havoc of war and the battle's confusion
A home and a country should leave us no more?
Their blood has washed out their foul footsteps' pollution.
No refuge could save the hireling and slave,
From the terror of flight and the gloom of the grave;
And the star-spangled banner in triumph doth wave
O'er the land of the free, and the home of the brave!

O! thus be it ever, when freemen shall stand
Between their loved homes and the war's desolation!
Blest with victory and peace, may the heav'n-rescued land
Praise the power that hath made and preserved us a nation.
Then conquer we must, for our cause it is just.
And this be our motto — 'In God is our trust';
And the star-spangled banner in triumph shall wave
O'er the land of the free, and the home of the brave.

15 June ✳ The Reeds of Runnymede ✳
Rudyard Kipling

Runnymede is a water-meadow on the banks of the River
Thames, west of London, where – on 15 June 1215 – King
John signed the document that came to be known as Magna
Carta, 'the great charter'. The charter set limits on the power
of the king.

At Runnymede, at Runnymede,
    What say the reeds at Runnymede?
The lissom reeds that give and take,
That bend so far, but never break.
They keep the sleepy Thames awake
    With tales of John at Runnymede.

At Runnymede, at Runnymede,
    Oh, hear the reeds at Runnymede: –
'You mustn't sell, delay, deny,
A freeman's right or liberty.
It makes the stubborn Englishry,
    We saw 'em roused at Runnymede!

'When through our ranks the Barons came,
With little thought of praise or blame,
But resolute to play the game,
    They lumbered up to Runnymede;
And there they launched in solid line
The first attack on Right Divine –
The curt, uncompromising "Sign!"
    That settled John at Runnymede.

'At Runnymede, at Runnymede,
Your rights were won at Runnymede!
No freeman shall be fined or bound,
    Or dispossessed of freehold ground,
Except by lawful judgment found
And passed upon him by his peers.
Forget not, after all these years,
    The Charter Signed at Runnymede.'

And still when mob or monarch lays
Too rude a hand on English ways,
The whisper wakes, the shudder plays,
    Across the reeds at Runnymede.
And Thames, that knows the moods of kings,
And crowds and priests and suchlike things,
Rolls deep and dreadful as he brings
    Their warning down from Runnymede!

16 June ✳ The Lake Isle of Innisfree ✳ W. B. Yeats

W. B. Yeats claimed that the inspiration for 'The Lake Isle of Innisfree' came when he was walking down Fleet Street, London, in 1888 and was struck suddenly by a memory of his childhood. As a city boy he loved and longed for his Summers in the countryside, especially the little island of Innisfree, on Lough Gill, an Irish lake in County Sligo.

I will arise and go now, and go to Innisfree,
And a small cabin build there, of clay and wattles made:
Nine bean-rows will I have there, a hive for the honey-bee,
And live alone in the bee-loud glade.

And I shall have some peace there, for peace comes
    dropping slow,
Dropping from the veils of the morning to where the cricket
    sings;
There midnight's all a glimmer, and noon a purple glow,
And evening full of the linnet's wings.

I will arise and go now, for always night and day
I hear lake water lapping with low sounds by the shore;
While I stand on the roadway, or on the pavements grey,
I hear it in the deep heart's core.

17 June ✳ *from* Childe Harold's Pilgrimage ✳ George Gordon, Lord Byron

The English Romantic poet Lord Byron was notoriously eccentric, even keeping a bear in his rooms while he was a student at Trinity College, Cambridge. These stanzas are taken from his lengthy narrative poem, *Childe Harold's Pilgrimage*, which tells the story of a melancholic young man who, tired by a life of pleasure and excess, searches for distraction in foreign lands. The extract given here describes Europe on the eve of the Battle of Waterloo, which was fought on 18 June 1815.

> There was a sound of revelry by night,
> And Belgium's Capital had gathered then
> Her Beauty and her Chivalry, and bright
> The lamps shone o'er fair women and brave men;
> A thousand hearts beat happily; and when
> Music arose with its voluptuous swell,
> Soft eyes looked love to eyes which spake again,
> And all went merry as a marriage bell;
> But hush! hark! a deep sound strikes like a rising knell!

> Did ye not hear it? — No; 'twas but the wind,
> Or the car rattling o'er the stony street;
> On with the dance! let joy be unconfined;
> No sleep till morn, when Youth and Pleasure meet
> To chase the glowing Hours with flying feet —
> But hark! — that heavy sound breaks in once more,
> As if the clouds its echo would repeat;
> And nearer, clearer, deadlier than before!
> Arm! Arm! it is – it is – the cannon's opening roar!

Within a windowed niche of that high hall
Sat Brunswick's fated chieftain; he did hear
That sound the first amidst the festival,
And caught its tone with Death's prophetic ear;
And when they smiled because he deemed it near,
His heart more truly knew that peal too well
Which stretched his father on a bloody bier,
And roused the vengeance blood alone could quell;
He rushed into the field, and, foremost fighting, fell.

18 June ✳ The Sun Has Long Been Set ✳ William Wordsworth

The Battle of Waterloo, fought on this date in 1815, saw the final defeat of Napoleon Bonaparte – the French military leader and emperor – who had conquered much of mainland Europe in the first years of the nineteenth century. The French army found itself facing the massed forces of the British (led by the Duke of Wellington), Prussia, and several other states. Wellington reportedly said that the battle was 'the nearest-run thing you ever saw in your life'. This poem by William Wordsworth describes a night in June, questioning why any military parade would occur when there is such beauty in nature.

The sun has long been set,
  The stars are out by twos and threes,
The little birds are piping yet
  Among the bushes and trees;
There's a cuckoo, and one or two thrushes,
And a far-off wind that rushes,
And a sound of water that gushes,
And the cuckoo's sovereign cry
Fills all the hollow of the sky.
  Who would go 'parading'
In London, and 'masquerading',
On such a night of June
With that beautiful soft half-moon,
And all these innocent blisses?
On such a night as this is!

19 June ✶ On Liberty and Slavery ✶
George Moses Horton

On 19 June 1865 African-American slaves were told that
slavery was abolished and they were finally free. 19 June is
known as 'Juneteenth' and is celebrated and recognized today
in most American states. This powerful poem was written
by George Moses Horton, who was born a slave in 1798 on
William Horton's plantation. He taught himself to read and
even managed to sell poems during his 68 years of being
a slave, but he was not allowed to buy his freedom. He is
thought to have had at least 17 years at the end of his life as a
free man, as he died around 1883.

Alas! and am I born for this,
To wear this slavish chain?
Deprived of all created bliss,
Through hardship, toil and pain!

How long have I in bondage lain,
And languished to be free!
Alas! and must I still complain—
Deprived of liberty.

Oh, Heaven! and is there no relief
This side the silent grave—
To soothe the pain—to quell the grief
And anguish of a slave?

Come Liberty, thou cheerful sound,
Roll through my ravished ears!
Come, let my grief in joys be drowned,
And drive away my fears.

227

Say unto foul oppression, Cease:
Ye tyrants rage no more,
And let the joyful trump of peace,
Now bid the vassal soar.

Soar on the pinions of that dove
Which long has cooed for thee,
And breathed her notes from Afric's grove,
The sound of Liberty.

Oh, Liberty! thou golden prize,
So often sought by blood—
We crave thy sacred sun to rise,
The gift of nature's God!

Bid Slavery hide her haggard face,
And barbarism fly:
I scorn to see the sad disgrace
In which enslaved I lie.

Dear Liberty! upon thy breast,
I languish to respire;
And like the Swan unto her nest,
I'd like to thy smiles retire.

Oh, blest asylum—heavenly balm!
Unto thy boughs I flee—
And in thy shades the storm shall calm,
With songs of Liberty!

20 June * Midsummer, Tobago * Derek Walcott

At the start of this poem Derek Walcott describes the type of lazy Summer day that feels as if it will go on forever. What is surprising is the contrast between the first seven lines and the four that follow. Despite the sleepiness of the Summer's day, the poet says time is racing by.

Broad sun-stoned beaches.

White heat.
A green river.

A bridge,
scorched yellow palms

from the summer-sleeping house
drowsing through August.

Days I have held,
days I have lost,

days that outgrow, like daughters,
my harbouring arms.

21 June ✳ *from* A Midsummer Night's Dream ✳ William Shakespeare

21 June is the Summer Solstice – the longest day of the year in the Northern hemisphere. Also known as Midsummer, the date has been celebrated since ancient times as an important pagan festival. Traditionally bonfires were lit to protect against evil spirits which pagans believed were free to wander the earth on this auspicious date. Shakespeare's comedy *A Midsummer Night's Dream*, with its cast of fairies and plot filled with magic, taps into the tradition of Midsummer as a date on which remarkable things can happen.

> I know a bank where the wild thyme blows,
> Where oxlips and the nodding violet grows,
> Quite over-canopied with luscious woodbine,
> With sweet musk-roses and with eglantine:
> There sleeps Titania sometime of the night,
> Lull'd in these flowers with dances and delight;
> And there the snake throws her enamell'd skin,
> Weed wide enough to wrap a fairy in:
> And with the juice of this I'll streak her eyes,
> And make her full of hateful fantasies.
> Take thou some of it, and seek through this grove:
> A sweet Athenian lady is in love
> With a disdainful youth: anoint his eyes;
> But do it when the next thing he espies
> May be the lady: thou shalt know the man
> By the Athenian garments he hath on.
> Effect it with some care, that he may prove
> More fond on her than she upon her love:
> And look thou meet me ere the first cock crow.

22 June ✴ *from* As You Like It ✴ William Shakespeare

This speech from *As You Like It* is given by the character
Jaques. As a comedy, *As You Like It* is for the most part a
light-hearted play. Jaques, however, is notably melancholic,
and his speeches are reflective and philosophical in tone.

> All the world's a stage,
> And all the men and women merely players;
> They have their exits and their entrances;
> And one man in his time plays many parts,
> His acts being seven ages. At first the infant,
> Mewling and puking in the nurse's arms;
> And then the whining school-boy, with his satchel
> And shining morning face, creeping like snail
> Unwillingly to school. And then the lover,
> Sighing like furnace, with a woeful ballad
> Made to his mistress' eyebrow. Then a soldier,
> Full of strange oaths, and bearded like the pard,
> Jealous in honour, sudden and quick in quarrel,
> Seeking the bubble reputation
> Even in the cannon's mouth. And then the justice,
> In fair round belly with good capon lin'd,
> With eyes severe and beard of formal cut,
> Full of wise saws and modern instances;
> And so he plays his part. The sixth age shifts
> Into the lean and slipper'd pantaloon,
> With spectacles on nose and pouch on side;
> His youthful hose, well sav'd, a world too wide
> For his shrunk shank; and his big manly voice,
> Turning again toward childish treble, pipes
> And whistles in his sound. Last scene of all,
> That ends this strange eventful history,
> Is second childishness and mere oblivion;
> Sans teeth, sans eyes, sans taste, sans everything.

23 June * The Summer Day * Mary Oliver

This wonderful poem is by the Pulitzer Prize-winning poet
Mary Oliver, who was born in Ohio, America, in 1935.

Who made the world?
Who made the swan, and the black bear?
Who made the grasshopper?
This grasshopper, I mean –
the one who has flung herself out of the grass,
the one who is eating sugar out of my hand,
who is moving her jaws back and forth instead of up and
    down –
who is gazing around with her enormous and complicated eyes.
Now she lifts her pale forearms and thoroughly washes her
    face.
Now she snaps her wings open, and floats away.
I don't know exactly what a prayer is.
I do know how to pay attention, how to fall down
into the grass, how to kneel down in the grass,
how to be idle and blessed, how to stroll through the fields,
which is what I have been doing all day.
Tell me, what else should I have done?
Doesn't everything die at last, and too soon?
Tell me, what is it you plan to do
with your one wild and precious life?

232

24 June ✶ Adlestrop ✶ Edward Thomas

On 24 June 1914, the poet Edward Thomas was travelling
from London to his friend and fellow poet Robert Frost's
house near Ledbury when the steam train he was on made
an unscheduled stop at a Gloucestershire hamlet called
Adlestrop. This brief visit provided the inspiration for this
poem. Thomas was greatly inspired by nature, and in his
notebook, writing about the stop in Adelstrop, he scribbled:
'. . . thro the willows cd be heard a chain of blackbird songs at
12.45, and one thrush and no man seen, only a hiss of engine
letting off steam.'

Yes. I remember Adlestrop—
The name—because one afternoon
Of heat the express-train drew up there
Unwontedly. It was late June.

The steam hissed. Someone cleared his throat.
No one left and no one came
On the bare platform. What I saw
Was Adlestrop—only the name—

And willows, willow-herb, and grass,
And meadowsweet, and haycocks dry;
No whit less still and lonely fair
Than the high cloudlets in the sky.

And for that minute a blackbird sang
Close by, and round him, mistier,
Farther and farther, all the birds
Of Oxfordshire and Gloucestershire.

25 June ✱ Skimbleshanks: The Railway Cat ✱
T. S. Eliot

'Skimbleshanks' is part of a larger collection of cat-poems by T. S. Eliot titled *Old Possum's Book of Practical Cats*. Like other children's books – A. A. Milne's *Winnie-the-Pooh*, for instance – Eliot's collection began as an attempt to entertain children the writer actually knew. The poems were sent in a series of letters to the poet's godchildren.

There's a whisper down the line at 11:39
When the Night Mail's ready to depart,
Saying 'Skimble where is Skimble has he gone to hunt the
    thimble?
We must find him or the train can't start.'
All the guards and all the porters and the stationmaster's
    daughters
They are searching high and low,
Saying 'Skimble where is Skimble for unless he's very nimble
Then the Night Mail just can't go.'
At 11:42 then the signal's nearly due
And the passengers are frantic to a man –
Then Skimble will appear and he'll saunter to the rear:
He's been busy in the luggage van!
    He gives one flash of his glass-green eyes
        And the signal goes 'All Clear!'
    And we're off at last for the northern part
        Of the Northern Hemisphere!

You may say that by and large it is Skimble who's in charge
Of the Sleeping Car Express.
From the driver and the guards to the bagmen playing cards
He will supervise them all, more or less.
Down the corridor he paces and examines all the faces
Of the travellers in the First and in the Third;
He establishes control by a regular patrol
And he'd know at once if anything occurred.
He will watch you without winking and he sees what you are
   thinking
And it's certain that he doesn't approve
Of hilarity and riot, so the folk are very quiet
When Skimble is about and on the move.
   You can play no pranks with Skimbleshanks!
     He's a Cat that cannot be ignored;
  So nothing goes wrong on the Northern Mail
    When Skimbleshanks is aboard.

Oh it's very pleasant when you have found your little den
With your name written up on the door.
And the berth is very neat with a newly folded sheet
And there's not a speck of dust on the floor.
There is every sort of light – you can make it dark or bright;
There's a button that you turn to make a breeze.
There's a funny little basin you're supposed to wash your face in
And a crank to shut the window if you sneeze.
Then the guard looks in politely and will ask you very brightly
'Do you like your morning tea weak or strong?'
But Skimble's just behind him and was ready to remind him,
For Skimble won't let anything go wrong.
   And when you creep into your cosy berth
     And pull up the counterpane,
  You are bound to admit that it's very nice
  To know that you won't be bothered by mice –
  You can leave all that to the Railway Cat,
    The Cat of the Railway Train!

In the middle of the night he is always fresh and bright;
Every now and then he has a cup of tea
With perhaps a drop of Scotch while he's keeping on the
   watch,
Only stopping here and there to catch a flea.
You were fast asleep at Crewe and so you never knew
That he was walking up and down the station;
You were sleeping all the while he was busy at Carlisle,
Where he greets the stationmaster with elation.
But you saw him at Dumfries, where he summons the police
If there's anything they ought to know about:
When you get to Gallowgate there you do not have to wait –
For Skimbleshanks will help you to get out!
   He gives you a wave of his long brown tail
      Which says: 'I'll see you again!
   You'll meet without fail on the Midnight Mail
      The Cat of the Railway Train.'

26 June ✶ At the Railway Station, Upway ✶ Thomas Hardy

Thomas Hardy was one of the most celebrated novelists of the nineteenth and twentieth centuries, but he saw himself primarily as a poet. In both his fiction and his verse, he sought to create realistic depictions of life in Victorian England, including the controversial topics of poverty and crime. Upway is a railway station in Dorset, where Hardy spent most of his life, and where many of his literary works were set.

'There is not much that I can do,
For I've no money that's quite my own!'
Spoke up the pitying child –
A little boy with a violin
At the station before the train came in, –
'But I can play my fiddle to you,
And a nice one 'tis, and good in tone!'

The man in the handcuffs smiled;
The constable looked, and he smiled, too,
As the fiddle began to twang;
And the man in the handcuffs suddenly sang
With grimful glee:
'This life so free
Is the thing for me!'
And the constable smiled, and said no word,
As if unconscious of what he heard;
And so they went on till the train came in –
The convict, and boy with the violin.

237

27 June ✶ The Car Trip ✶ Michael Rosen

This poem tells a story that might be all too familiar to you –
and to your parents – if you've ever been on a long car journey
with your family.

Mum says:
'Right, you two,
this is a very long car journey.
I want you two to be good.
I'm driving and I can't drive properly
if you two are going mad in the back.
Do you understand?'

So we say,
'OK, Mum, OK. Don't worry,'
and off we go.

And we start The Moaning:
Can I have a drink?
I want some crisps.
Can I open my window?
He's got my book.
Get off me.
Ow, that's my ear!

And Mum tries to be exciting:
'Look out the window
there's a lamp-post.'

And we go on with The Moaning:
Can I have a sweet?
He's sitting on me.
Are we nearly there?
Don't scratch.
You never tell him off.
Now he's biting his nails.

I want a drink. I want a drink.
And Mum tries to be exciting again:
'Look out the window.
There's a tree.'

And we go on:
My hands are sticky.
He's playing with the doorhandle now.
I feel sick.
Your nose is all runny.
Don't pull my hair.

He's touching me, Mum.
That's really dangerous, you know.
Mum, he's spitting.

And Mum says:
'Right I'm stopping the car.
I AM STOPPING THE CAR.'

She stops the car.

'Now, if you two don't stop it
I'm going to put you out of the car
and leave you by the side of the road.'

He started it.
I didn't. He started it.

'I don't care who started it
I can't drive properly
if you two go mad in the back.
Do you understand?'

And we say:
OK, Mum, OK, don't worry.

Can I have a drink?

28 June ✳ June ✳ John Updike

This poem, 'June', is taken from the Pulitzer Prize-winning author John Updike's little-known book of children's poems, *A Child's Calendar*. In it Updike writes a poem for every month of the year.

The sun is rich
And gladly pays
In golden hours,
Silver days,

And long green weeks
That never end.
School's out. The time
Is ours to spend.

There's Little League,
Hopscotch, the creek,
And, after supper,
Hide-and-seek.

The live-long light
Is like a dream,
and freckles come
Like flies to cream.

29 June ✳ Joys of Ramzan ✳ Sitara Khan

This poem details the various rituals and customs observed
during Ramzan. Ramzan is the Urdu name for Ramadan – the
ninth month of the Islamic calendar, during which Muslims
observe the tradition of fasting each day from dawn until
sunset. Ramadan is intended to teach the values of patience
and spirituality, and it is a time to focus on prayer and charity.

> In Ramzan we please Allah,
> We please Allah.
> Offer Namaz and Jummah.
>
> Shaitan is chained
> Blessings gained
> Vices forbidden
> Sins forgiven.
>
> Wings spread
> Angels descend
> Enfold us under
> Realms of wonder:
>
> They join us in daily routine
> Rise early for Sehri cuisine
> Five prayers and breaking the fast
> Late to bed, midnight past.
>
> In Ramzan we please Allah,
> We please Allah.
> Offer Namaz and Jummah.

To forget hunger,
We do Zikker, think of others:
Friends and neighbours.

Feasts are shared —
All our favourites: tikka masala
Spring rolls and potato phulkah

In Ramzan we please Allah,
We please Allah.
Offer Namaz and Jummah.

Good will ignites
Everyone unites
Invitations ring for breaking fast
Doors are opened to the outcast

We feel proud at having fasted
Made sacrifices, and having lasted
Made our lives a little harder
Seeking peace for the here and the hereafter

Radio voices, charity appeals,
Making gifts is no big deal.
Daddies empty their pockets
And hand over wallets
Mummies, their gold bracelets

Children caress their favourite toys
As they say goodbye for strangers' joys.
With bodies leaner,
the spirit's cleaner.

In caring, sharing we please Allah,
Please Allah
Offer Namaz and Jummah.

30 June * Einstein's Brain * Kenn Nesbitt

On 30 June 1905, the theoretical physicist Albert Einstein published the 'Theory of Special Relativity', which included his most famous equation, $E = mc^2$, which means that energy and mass are the same thing. Albert Einstein's theories related to light, matter, gravity, space and time, and he is one of the most influential scientists the world has ever known.

I heard that they've got Einstein's brain
just sitting in a jar.
I don't know where they keep it,
but I hope it isn't far.

I need to go and borrow it
to help me with this test.
I've answered twenty questions
but on every one I guessed.

If someone asks you where I've gone,
then kindly please explain
I'll be right back; I've just gone out
to look for Einstein's brain.

July

1 July ✶ Alfred, Lord Tennyson ✶ E. C. Bentley

The invention of Edmund Clerihew Bentley, a 'clerihew' is a short comic poem which provides some form of comment on a famous figure's name and biography. This one rests on the pun that venison is both dear – that is, expensive – and deer. The 1st of July is the start of the deer-stalking season in Scotland.

> Alfred, Lord Tennyson
> Lived upon venison;
> Not cheap, I fear,
> Because venison's deer.

2 July ✶ Wolfgang Amadeus Mozart ✶ E. C. Bentley

This clerihew takes as its subject one of the most celebrated composers of Western Classical music, Wolfgang Amadeus Mozart. Although he died at the age of only 36, he was hugely prolific in his lifetime, composing 41 symphonies, 27 piano concertos and 22 operas. The unusual word 'otophagic' means 'painful to the ear', and the poem puns on the title of one of Mozart's most popular operas: *The Magic Flute*.

Wolfgang Amadeus Mozart
Whose very name connotes art
Thought flutes untunable and otophagic
Till he made one that was magic.

3 July ✷ *from* An Essay on Criticism ✷
Alexander Pope

The eighteenth-century English poet and master of wit Alexander
Pope wrote much that is memorable: 'To err is human; to forgive,
divine,' 'A little learning is a dang'rous thing,' and 'For fools rush
in where angels fear to tread' are just some of his most quoted
lines. He was best-known for his satirical heroic couplets. Here
he launches an attack on bad, predictable writing.

And ten low Words oft creep in one dull Line,
While they ring round the same *unvary'd Chimes*,
With sure *Returns* of still *expected Rhymes*.
Where-e'er you find *the cooling Western Breeze*,
In the next Line, it *whispers thro' the Trees*;
If *Chrystal Streams with pleasing Murmurs creep*,
The Reader's threaten'd (not in vain) with *Sleep*.

4 July ✳ I Hear America Singing ✳ Walt Whitman

For Americans, 4 July is Independence Day, a federal holiday celebrating the day in 1776 on which representatives of the thirteen American states declared themselves independent of the British Empire. This was the beginning of the United States of America, and so it is fitting on this day to read a poem by Walt Whitman, who wrote extensively about what it meant to be American.

I hear America singing, the varied carols I hear,
Those of mechanics, each one singing his as it should be
    blithe and strong,
The carpenter singing his as he measures his plank or
    beam,
The mason singing his as he makes ready for work, or
    leaves off work,
The boatman singing what belongs to him in his boat, the
    deckhand singing on the steamboat deck,
The shoemaker singing as he sits on his bench, the hatter
    singing as he stands,
The wood-cutter's song, the ploughboy's on his way in the
    morning, or at noon intermission or at sundown,
The delicious singing of the mother, or of the young wife at
    work, or of the girl sewing or washing,
Each singing what belongs to him or her and to none else,
The day what belongs to the day—at night the party of
    young fellows, robust, friendly,
Singing with open mouths their strong melodious songs.

5 July ✱ Epitaph on Sir Isaac Newton ✱
Alexander Pope

On 5 July 1687 Sir Isaac Newton's *Philosophiae Naturalis Principia Mathematica* ('Mathematical Principles of Natural Philosophy') – regarded as one of the most important works in the history of science – was first published. The work outlines Newton's laws of motion and gravity, which are regarded as the foundation for the science of mechanics. Alexander Pope's epitaph for Newton powerfully summarizes his extraordinary contribution to science, but was not allowed to be carved into Newton's monument in Westminster Abbey.

> Nature and Nature's Laws lay hid in Night.
> God said, 'Let Newton be!' and All was *Light*.

6 July * Sir Isaac Newton Told Us Why * Anon.

This is another poem about Isaac Newton's theory of gravity.
This comic piece comes from – of all things strange – a public
information programme broadcast in the 1970s, which warned
people to take care at work and to wear appropriate safety gear.

Sir Isaac Newton told us why
An apple falls down from the sky,
And from this fact, it's very plain,
All other objects do the same.
A brick, a bolt, a bar, a cup
Invariably fall down, not up,
And every common working tool
Is governed by the self-same rule.
So when you handle tools up there,
Let your watchword be 'Take Care'.
If at work you drop a spanner,
It travels in a downward manner.
At work, a fifth of accidents or more
Illustrate old Newton's law,
But one thing he forgot to add,
The damage won't be half as bad
If you are wearing proper clothes,
Especially on your head and toes.
These hats and shoes are there to save
The wearer from an early grave.
So best feet forward and take care
About the kind of shoes you wear,
It's better to be sure than dead,
So get a hat and keep your head.
Don't think to go without is brave:
The effects of gravity can be grave . . .

7 July ✳ *from* The Pied Piper of Hamelin ✳ Robert Browning

'The Pied Piper of Hamelin' tells the story of a mysterious man who arrived in the German city of Hamelin some time during the Middle Ages carrying a magic pipe. The city was overrun with rats, and the piper made a deal with the mayor: for a fee, he agreed to enchant the rats with his pipe and lead them into a nearby river. The piper carried out his half of the bargain, but the mayor refused to pay, whereupon the piper used his magic pipe to abduct the children of the town. The moral of the story is simple: if you've made a promise, keep it.

Into the street the Piper stept,
   Smiling first a little smile,
As if he knew what magic slept
   In his quiet pipe the while;
Then, like a musical adept,
To blow the pipe his lips he wrinkled,
And green and blue his sharp eyes twinkled,
Like a candle-flame were salt is sprinkled;
And ere three shrill notes the pipe uttered,
You heard as if an army muttered;
And the muttering grew to a grumbling;
And the grumbling grew to a mighty rumbling;
And out of the houses the rats came tumbling.
Great rats, small rats, lean rats, brawny rats,
Brown rats, black rats, grey rats, tawny rats,
Grave old plodders, gay young friskers,
   Fathers, mothers, uncles, cousins,
Cocking tails and pricking whiskers,
   Families by tens and dozens,
Brothers, sisters, husbands, wives –
Followed the Piper for their lives.

From street to street he piped advancing,
And step for step they followed dancing,
Until they came to the river Weser,
    Wherein all plunged and perished!
– Save one who, stout as Julius Caesar,
Swam across and lived to carry
    (As he, the manuscript he cherished)
To Rat-land home his commentary:
Which was, 'At the first shrill notes of the pipe,
I heard a sound as of scraping tripe,
And putting apples, wondrous ripe,
Into a cider-press's gripe:
And a moving away of pickle-tub-boards,
And a leaving ajar of conserve-cupboards,
And a drawing the corks of train-oil-flasks,
And a breaking the hoops of butter-casks;
And it seemed as if a voice
    (Sweeter far than by harp or by psaltery
Is breathed) called out, 'Oh rats, rejoice!
    The world is grown to one vast drysaltery!
So munch on, crunch on, take your nuncheon,
Breakfast, supper, dunner, luncheon!'
And just as a bulky sugar-puncheon,
All ready staved, like a great sun shone
Glorious scarce an inch before me,
Just as methought it said, "Come, bore me!"
– I found the Weser rolling o'er me.'

8 July ✳ *from* Endymion ✳ John Keats

While John Keats is now remembered as one of the greatest
of English poets, when his long poem *Endymion* was first
published in 1818 it was met with scathing reviews. Keats
reacted in a letter to a friend: 'I was never afraid of failure;
for I would sooner fail than not be among the greatest.' The
elegant opening lines of the poem, with their comforting
message of the immortal nature of beauty, are some of Keats's
most famous words.

A thing of beauty is a joy for ever:
Its loveliness increases; it will never
Pass into nothingness; but still will keep
A bower quiet for us, and a sleep
Full of sweet dreams, and health, and quiet breathing.
Therefore, on every morrow, are we wreathing
A flowery band to bind us to the earth,
Spite of despondence, of the inhuman dearth
Of noble natures, of the gloomy days,
Of all the unhealthy and o'er-darkened ways
Made for our searching: yes, in spite of all,
Some shape of beauty moves away the pall
From our dark spirits. Such the sun, the moon,
Trees old, and young, sprouting a shady boon
For simple sheep; and such are daffodils
With the green world they live in; and clear rills
That for themselves a cooling covert make
'Gainst the hot season; the mid forest brake,
Rich with a sprinkling of fair musk-rose blooms:
And such too is the grandeur of the dooms
We have imagined for the mighty dead;
All lovely tales that we have heard or read:
An endless fountain of immortal drink,
Pouring unto us from the heaven's brink.

9 July ✳ A Boat, Beneath a Sunny Sky ✳
Lewis Carroll

Lewis Carroll is best known for his wonderful and surreal
children's book *Alice in Wonderland*, which came about
after he was asked to tell a story to a young girl called Alice
Pleasance Liddell. This poem was also inspired by Alice, and
takes the form of an 'acrostic' – read vertically, the first letters
of each line combine to spell her name. The final lines echo the
strange, ethereal nature of Carroll's books set in Wonderland.

> A boat, beneath a sunny sky,
> Lingering onward dreamily
> In an evening of July —
>
> Children three that nestle near,
> Eager eye and willing ear,
> Pleased a simple tale to hear —
>
> Long has paled that sunny sky:
> Echoes fade and memories die:
> Autumn frosts have slain July.
>
> Still she haunts me, phantomwise,
> Alice moving under skies
> Never seen by waking eyes.
>
> Children yet, the tale to hear,
> Eager eye and willing ear,
> Lovingly shall nestle near.

In a Wonderland they lie,
Dreaming as the days go by,
Dreaming as the summers die:

Ever drifting down the stream —
Lingering in the golden gleam —
Life, what is it but a dream?

10 July ✳ The Puzzler and the Stolen Jewels ✳ Ros Palmer

What would you do if you suspected that someone you completely trusted had stolen one of your most prized possessions?

The Puzzler was summoned by a Queen from far away . . .
He set off as the moon came up, and journeyed night and day.
Then after seven suns had set, and stars lit up the sky,
He spied the golden palace on a mountainside nearby.

His advent being heralded by trumpet and by drum,
The Queen swept from her bedchamber to see just who had
    come.
The Puzzler then learned about the reason for her grief . . .
That somewhere in the palace lurked a liar and a thief.

The Queen explained some time ago she'd started to prepare
For a banquet in the palace grounds – a truly grand affair;
She'd put her gown out on the chair, then looked for jewels to
    match,
But when she'd fetched her silver box she'd seen the broken
    catch . . .
And opening the casket lid she'd found, to her dismay,
The necklace she had hoped to wear had clearly gone astray.

The Puzzler assured The Queen that he would do his best –
Until he'd found the wrongdoer, he swore he wouldn't rest.
And so he asked Her Majesty just where the jewels were
    kept . . .
She whispered that she hid them in the bed in which she slept.
The only other people who had known this hiding place?
Her two devoted maid servants, Penelope and Grace.

The loyalty of both these maids had won them great acclaim,
Her Majesty was sure though, one of them *must* be to blame.
But each proclaimed her innocence, and so, as he'd foreseen,
His task was to establish *who* had stolen from The Queen.

The Puzzler delved in his bag, and found his box of tricks.
He rummaged deep inside it then pulled out his magic sticks . . .
Explained the sticks had powers to detect when lies were told,
And thus by daybreak he was sure the story would unfold.
The maidservants, escorted by The Puzzler and guard,
Were then dismissed to spend the night in two rooms off the
    yard,
Each girl received a magic stick, identical in size,
And each was told the stick would grow if they'd been telling
    lies . . .

And when the sun rose in the sky, the maids were both
    brought out –
The Puzzler had advised The Queen that soon, without a
    doubt,
They'd know for sure *which* girl it was who'd whisked the
    jewels away . . .
He asked the girls to lay their sticks together on the clay.
And so at once Penelope put *her* stick on the ground
And as Grace placed hers next to it you couldn't hear a sound.
The Puzzler just pointed and declared he'd solved the case:
'I think you'll find, Your Majesty, the culprit here is Grace.'

Well, Grace at once began to wail and said it wasn't true –
Her stick was not the *longer*, but the *shorter* of the two!
The Puzzler just smiled as he put the sticks away
And everybody craned their necks to catch what he would
    say . . .

'I told each maid their stick would grow if they'd not told the
    truth,
But they're not really *magic*, they are just bits of wood,
    forsooth.
Well, as young Grace has pointed out, her stick *is* shorter now,
But this can only mean that it has been cut down somehow . . .
For thinking that her stick would grow, Grace panicked and
    took fright
And found a knife to shorten it at some time in the night,
By doing this she hoped her friend would therefore get the
    blame . . .
But we all here are witnesses to her deceit and shame.'

The Queen turned to The Puzzler and thanked him from her
    heart –
He'd used his ingenuity and talent from the start,
And as he bowed and turned away to face the rising sun,
He said, 'It's time to take my leave, my puzzling is done.'

11 July ∗ The Pig ∗ Roald Dahl

In this rather gruesome poem, Roald Dahl turns the tables on
bacon-chomping humans, as the clever pig of the title decides
to take defensive action against being turned into sausages.
Dahl doesn't shy away from detailed descriptions, whether
they're funny, like the pig leaping up 'like a ballet dancer', or
sinister, as the pig enjoys his unusual meal.

In England once there lived a big
And wonderfully clever pig.
To everybody it was plain
That Piggy had a massive brain.
He worked out sums inside his head,
There was no book he hadn't read.
He knew what made an airplane fly,
He knew how engines worked and why.
He knew all this, but in the end
One question drove him round the bend: He simply
   couldn't puzzle out
What LIFE was really all about.
What was the reason for his birth?
Why was he placed upon this earth?
His giant brain went round and round.
Alas, no answer could be found,
Till suddenly one wondrous night
All in a flash he saw the light.
He jumped up like a ballet dancer
And yelled, 'By gum, I've got the answer!
They want my bacon, slice by slice,
To sell at a tremendous price!
They want my tender juicy chops
To put in all the butchers' shops!

They want my pork to make a roast
And that's the part'll cost the most!
They want my sausages in strings!
They even want my chitterlings!
The butcher's shop! The carving knife!
That is the reason for my life!'
Such thoughts as these are not designed
To give a pig great peace of mind.
Next morning, in comes Farmer Bland,
A pail of pigswill in his hand,
And Piggy, with a mighty roar,
Bashes the farmer to the floor. . .
Now comes the rather grizzly bit
So let's not make too much of it,
Except that you must understand
That Piggy did eat Farmer Bland.
He ate him up from head to toe,
Chewing the pieces nice and slow.
It took an hour to reach the feet,
Because there was so much to eat,
And when he finished,
Pig, of course,
Felt absolutely no remorse.
Slowly he scratched his brainy head
And, with a little smile, he said,
'I had a fairly powerful hunch
That he might have me for his lunch.
And so, because I feared the worst,
I thought I'd better eat *him* first.'

12 July ✷ The Cruel Moon ✷ Robert Graves

In this poem Robert Graves uses a technique almost like that of a dialogue to personify the moon.

The cruel Moon hangs out of reach
Up above the shadowy beech.
Her face is stupid, but her eye
Is small and sharp and very sly.
Nurse says the Moon can drive you mad?
No, that's a silly story, lad!
Though she be angry, though she would
Destroy all England if she could,
Yet think, what damage can she do
Hanging there so far from you?
Don't heed what frightened nurses say:
Moons hang much too far away.

13 July ✳ The Cat and the Moon ✳ W. B. Yeats

This mysterious, deceptively simple poem plays with the
similarity between a cat's eyes and the changing shapes of
the moon.

> The cat went here and there
> And the moon spun round like a top,
> And the nearest kin of the moon,
> The creeping cat, looked up.
> Black Minnaloushe stared at the moon,
> For, wander and wail as he would,
> The pure cold light in the sky
> Troubled his animal blood.
> Minnaloushe runs in the grass
> Lifting his delicate feet.
> Do you dance, Minnaloushe, do you dance?
> When two close kindred meet,
> What better than call a dance?
> Maybe the moon may learn,
> Tired of that courtly fashion,
> A new dance turn.
> Minnaloushe creeps through the grass
> From moonlit place to place,
> The sacred moon overhead
> Has taken a new phase.
> Does Minnaloushe know that his pupils
> Will pass from change to change,
> And that from round to crescent,
> From crescent to round they range?
> Minnaloushe creeps through the grass
> Alone, important and wise,
> And lifts to the changing moon
> His changing eyes.

14 July ✳ *from* La Marseillaise ✳
Claude-Joseph Rouget de Lisle

14 July is Bastille Day, commemorating the storming of the Bastille fortress in Paris on this date in 1789 – one of the most significant events of the French Revolution. 'La Marseillaise' is the French national anthem. Nowadays, the anthem is sung at international sporting events and other occasions, expressing the enduring national pride of France.

> Allons, enfants de la Patrie
> Le jour de gloire est arrivé!
> Contre nous, de la tyrannie
> L'étendard sanglant est levé
> Entendez-vous dans les campagnes
> Mugir ces féroces soldats?
> Ils viennent jusque dans nos bras
> Égorger nos fils, nos compagnes!
>
> Aux armes, citoyens!
> Formez vos bataillons
> Marchons, marchons!
> Qu'un sang impur
> Abreuve nos sillons!

Arise, children of the Fatherland
The day of glory has arrived
Against us tyranny's
Bloody banner is raised
Do you hear, in the countryside
The roar of those ferocious soldiers?
They're coming right into your arms
To cut the throats of your sons, your women!

To arms, citizens!
Form your battalions
Let's march, let's march
Let an impure blood
Water our furrows!

15 July ✳ Come to the Edge ✳ Christopher Logue

In 1969, Christopher Logue created this as a 'poster poem',
which was displayed to advertise a show on the innovative
French poet Apollinaire (see 15 February), a man he admired
for his daring.

Come to the edge.
We might fall.
Come to the edge.
It's too high!
COME TO THE EDGE!
And they came,
And he pushed,
And they flew.

16 July ✴ *from* Njal's Saga ✴ Anon.

This extract from the ancient Norse *Njal's Saga* makes use
of a very old form of poetic language: the kenning. A kenning
is usually comprised of two seemingly unrelated words
connected to form a new idea – or to discuss an old idea in
a new way! For instance, a very ancient kenning is 'world-
candle', meaning sun. We still use some kennings in modern
language, however, such as describing a toddler as a 'rug-rat',
or someone who loves nature as a 'tree-hugger'.

> The killer of the giant's offspring
> broke the strong bison of the gull's meadow.
> So the gods, while the keeper of the bell despaired,
>   destroyed the seashore's hawk.
> The horse that rides the reefs
> found no help in the King of the Greeks.
>
> *Meaning:*
> Thor
> broke the ship.
> So the gods, while the Christian priest despaired,
>   destroyed the ship.
> The ship
> found no help in Jesus.

17 July ✷ She Walks in Beauty ✷
George Gordon, Lord Byron

In this poem Byron compares his beloved to aspects of the
natural world.

> She walks in beauty, like the night
>   Of cloudless climes and starry skies;
> And all that's best of dark and bright
>   Meet in her aspect and her eyes:
> Thus mellowed to that tender light
>   Which heaven to gaudy day denies.
>
> One shade the more, one ray the less,
>   Had half impaired the nameless grace
> Which waves in every raven tress,
>   Or softly lightens o'er her face;
> Where thoughts serenely sweet express,
>   How pure, how dear their dwelling-place.
>
> And on that cheek, and o'er that brow,
>   So soft, so calm, yet eloquent,
> The smiles that win, the tints that glow,
>   But tell of days in goodness spent,
> A mind at peace with all below,
>   A heart whose love is innocent!

18 July ✳ Invictus ✳ W. E. Henley

This poem, written in 1875, has been quoted in speeches
by Winston Churchill in 1941, and Barack Obama in 2013.
Nelson Mandela, the South African freedom fighter and
later President of his country, whose birthday was 18 July,
allegedly found this poem a great comfort during the twenty-
seven years he spent in prison. 'Invictus' is the Latin word for
'unconquered'.

Out of the night that covers me,
    Black as the pit from pole to pole,
I thank whatever gods may be
    For my unconquerable soul.

In the fell clutch of circumstance
    I have not winced nor cried aloud.
Under the bludgeonings of chance
    My head is bloody, but unbowed.

Beyond this place of wrath and tears
    Looms but the Horror of the shade,
And yet the menace of the years
    Finds and shall find me unafraid.

It matters not how strait the gate,
    How charged with punishments the scroll,
I am the master of my fate,
    I am the captain of my soul.

19 July ✳ *from* Julius Caesar ✳
William Shakespeare

During his incarceration Nelson Mandela found solace in the words of one of the greatest of writers: William Shakespeare. These lines from Shakespeare's tragedy *Julius Caesar* are among those that Mandela marked as particularly significant in a copy of the Collected Works secretly kept in his prison on Robben Island.

> Cowards die many times before their deaths;
> The valiant never taste of death but once.
> Of all the wonders that I yet have heard,
> It seems to me most strange that men should fear,
> Seeing that death, a necessary end,
> Will come when it will come.

20 July ✶ The First Men on the Moon ✶
J. Patrick Lewis

The two epigraphs shown below are from Neil Armstrong and Buzz Aldrin, who were on board the American spaceship *Apollo 11* when it landed on the moon on 20 July, 1969. This was the first time mankind had ever reached the moon, and Neil Armstrong's declaration, 'One small step for man, one giant leap for mankind', has become one of the most famous remarks in history.

> *'The Eagle has landed!' —Apollo 11 Commander*
> *Neil A. Armstrong*
> *'A magnificent desolation!' — Air Force Colonel*
> *Edwin E. 'Buzz' Aldrin, Jr.*
> *July 20, 1969*

That afternoon in mid-July,
Two pilgrims watched from distant space
The moon ballooning in the sky.
They rose to meet it face-to-face.

Their spidery spaceship, Eagle, dropped
Down gently on the lunar sand.
And when the module's engines stopped,
Rapt silence fell across the land.

The first man down the ladder, Neil,
Spoke words that we remember now—
'One small step . . .' It made us feel
As if we were there too, somehow.

When Neil planted the flag and Buzz
Collected lunar rocks and dust,
They hopped like kangaroos because
Of gravity. Or wanderlust?

A quarter million miles away,
One small blue planet watched in awe.
And no one who was there that day
Will soon forget the sight they saw.

21 July ✳ Apples ✳ Laurie Lee

Laurie Lee's autobiographical account of growing up in rural Gloucestershire is called *Cider with Rosie*, and in this poem the 'cidery bite' of the apples makes a vivid appearance.

Behold the apples' rounded worlds:
juice-green of July rain,
the black polestar of flowers, the rind
mapped with its crimson stain.

The russet, crab and cottage red
burn to the sun's hot brass,
then drop like sweat from every branch
and bubble in the grass.

They lie as wanton as they fall,
and where they fall and break,
the stallion clamps his crunching jaws,
the starling stabs his beak.

In each plump gourd the cidery bite
of boys' teeth tears the skin;
the waltzing wasp consumes his share,
the bent worm enters in.

I, with as easy hunger, take
entire my season's dole;
welcome the ripe, the sweet, the sour,
the hollow and the whole.

22 July ✶ Walking Across the Atlantic ✶
Billy Collins

Billy Collins is a much admired American poet. This free verse poem is purposefully ambiguous, as Collins describes 'walking across' the Atlantic Ocean. It is unclear whether the poem's speaker is actually walking across the water, or just using their imagination, just as they are when they picture what their feet must look like from the perspective of the fish.

I wait for the holiday crowd to clear the beach
before stepping onto the first wave.

Soon I am walking across the Atlantic
thinking about Spain,
checking for whales, waterspouts.
I feel the water holding up my shifting weight.
Tonight I will sleep on its rocking surface.

But for now I try to imagine what
this must look like to the fish below,
the bottoms of my feet appearing, disappearing.

23 July ✶ The Shark ✶ Lord Alfred Douglas

Lord Alfred Douglas was an English poet, author and translator. In this poem, the 'warning' that comes at the end of the shark's 'dangerous bite' contrasts with the jaunty rhythm of the piece as a whole.

A treacherous monster is the Shark
He never makes the least remark.

And when he sees you on the sand,
He doesn't seem to want to land.

He watches you take off your clothes,
And not the least excitement shows.

His eyes do not grow bright or roll,
He has astonishing self-control.

He waits till you are quite undressed,
And seems to take no interest.

And when towards the sea you leap,
He looks as if he were asleep.

But when you once get in his range,
His whole demeanour seems to change.

He throws his body right about,
And his true character comes out.

274

It's no use crying or appealing,
He seems to lose all decent feeling.

After this warning you will wish
To keep clear of this treacherous fish.

His back is black, his stomach white,
He has a very dangerous bite.

24 July ✶ maggie and milly and molly and may ✶ E. E. Cummings

E. E. Cummings wrote a great deal of very unusual-looking poetry: he used punctuation and capital letters in unexpected ways, or sometimes no punctuation or capitalization at all! With its lack of capitalized names and strange punctuation, this poem is an example of visual verse – a type of visually striking poetry that Cummings developed.

maggie and milly and molly and may
went down to the beach (to play one day)

and maggie discovered a shell that sang
so sweetly she couldn't remember her troubles,and

milly befriended a stranded star
whose rays five languid fingers were;

and molly was chased by a horrible thing
which raced sideways while blowing bubbles:and

may came home with a smooth round stone
as small as a world and as large as alone.

For whatever we lose (like a you or a me)
it's always ourselves we find in the sea

25 July ✶ The Night Mail ✶ W. H. Auden

On 25 July 1814, George Stephenson demonstrated the first
fully effective steam train, a milestone which was to transform
travel in the nineteenth century. Auden wrote 'The Night
Mail' for the 1936 documentary film of the same name, which
followed the Postal Special train as it brought mail up from
London as far as Aberdeen.

This is the Night Mail crossing the border,
Bringing the cheque and the postal order,
Letters for the rich, letters for the poor,
The shop at the corner and the girl next door.
Pulling up Beattock, a steady climb—
The gradient's against her, but she's on time.

Past cotton-grass and moorland boulder
Shovelling white steam over her shoulder,
Snorting noisily as she passes
Silent miles of wind-bent grasses;
Birds turn their heads as she approaches,
Stare from the bushes at her blank-faced coaches;
Sheepdogs cannot turn her course;
They slumber on with paws across,
In the farm she passes no one wakes,
But a jug in the bedroom gently shakes.

Dawn freshens, the climb is done.
Down towards Glasgow she descends
Towards the steam tugs, yelping down the glade of cranes
Towards the fields of apparatus, the furnaces
Set on the dark plain like gigantic chessmen.
All Scotland waits for her;
In the dark glens, beside the pale-green sea lochs
Men long for news.

Letters of thanks, letters from banks,
Letters of joy from the girl and boy,
Receipted bills and invitations
To inspect new stock or visit relations,
And applications for situations
And timid lovers' declarations
And gossip, gossip from all the nations;
News circumstantial, news financial,
Letters with holiday snaps to enlarge in,
Letters with faces scrawled in the margin.
Letters from uncles, cousins, and aunts,
Letters to Scotland from the South of France,
Letters of condolence to Highlands and Lowlands
Notes from overseas to Hebrides;
Written on paper of every hue,
The pink, the violet, the white and the blue
The chatty, the catty, the boring, adoring,
The cold and official and the heart's outpouring,
Clever, stupid, short and long,
The typed and the printed and the spelt all wrong.

Thousands are still asleep
Dreaming of terrifying monsters
Or friendly tea beside the band at Cranston's or Crawford's;
Asleep in working Glasgow, asleep in well-set Edinburgh;
Asleep in granite Aberdeen,
They continue their dreams
But shall wake soon and long for letters.
And none will hear the postman's knock
Without a quickening of the heart,
For who can bear to feel himself forgotten?

26 July ✷ Fern Hill ✷ Dylan Thomas

'Fern Hill' is a reminiscence of a rural childhood which tackles common poetic subjects – the passing of time, the loss of youth and innocence, and the blurring of memory.

Now as I was young and easy under the apple boughs
About the lilting house and happy as the grass was green,
   The night above the dingle starry,
     Time let me hail and climb
   Golden in the heydays of his eyes,
And honoured among wagons I was prince of the apple towns
And once below a time I lordly had the trees and leaves
     Trail with daisies and barley
   Down the rivers of the windfall light.

And as I was green and carefree, famous among the barns
About the happy yard and singing as the farm was home,
   In the sun that is young once only,
     Time let me play and be
   Golden in the mercy of his means,
And green and golden I was huntsman and herdsman, the calves
Sang to my horn, the foxes on the hills barked clear and cold,
     And the sabbath rang slowly
   In the pebbles of the holy streams.

All the sun long it was running, it was lovely, the hay—
Fields high as the house, the tunes from the chimneys, it was air
   And playing, lovely and watery
     And fire green as grass.
   And nightly under the simple stars
As I rode to sleep the owls were bearing the farm away,
All the moon long I heard, blessed among stables, the nightjars
   Flying with the ricks, and the horses
     Flashing into the dark.

And then to awake, and the farm, like a wanderer white
With the dew, come back, the cock on his shoulder: it was all
   Shining, it was Adam and maiden,
     The sky gathered again
   And the sun grew round that very day.
So it must have been after the birth of the simple light
In the first, spinning place, the spellbound horses walking warm
   Out of the whinnying green stable
     On to the fields of praise.

And honoured among foxes and pheasants by the gay house
Under the new made clouds and happy as the heart was long,
   In the sun born over and over,
     I ran my heedless ways,
   My wishes raced through the house-high hay
And nothing I cared, at my sky blue trades, that time allows
In all his tuneful turning so few and such morning songs
   Before the children green and golden
     Follow him out of grace,

Nothing I cared, in the lamb white days, that time would take me
Up to the swallow thronged loft by the shadow of my hand,
   In the moon that is always rising,
     Nor that riding to sleep
   I should hear him fly with the high fields
And wake to the farm forever fled from the childless land.
Oh as I was young and easy in the mercy of his means,
     Time held me green and dying
   Though I sang in my chains like the sea.

27 July ✶ Sea Fever ✶ John Masefield

John Masefield was a twentieth-century British poet and
novelist who served as Poet Laureate of the United Kingdom.
This poem describes the deep longing of its speaker to return
to the sea. Even though the imagery of the 'wheels' kicking
suggests that the ship in the poem is travelling during a
dangerous storm, the 'wild call' and the excitement of the
seafaring life is more exciting than the safety of life at home.

I must go down to the seas again, to the lonely sea and the sky,
And all I ask is a tall ship and a star to steer her by;
And the wheel's kick and the wind's song and the white sail's
    shaking,
And a grey mist on the sea's face, and a grey dawn breaking.

I must go down to the seas again, for the call of the running
    tide
Is a wild call and a clear call that may not be denied;
And all I ask is a windy day with the white clouds flying,
And the flung spray and the blown spume, and the sea-gulls
    crying.

I must go down to the seas again, to the vagrant gypsy life,
To the gull's way and the whale's way where the wind's like a
    whetted knife;
And all I ask is a merry yarn from a laughing fellow-rover,
And quiet sleep and a sweet dream when the long trick's over.

28 July ✳ MCMXIV ✳ Philip Larkin

'MCMXIV' is '1914' in Roman numerals, and in this poem Philip Larkin describes the devastation of the First World War, which began on 28 July 1914. The poem is a single sentence, spread over four verses.

Those long uneven lines
Standing as patiently
As if they were stretched outside
The Oval or Villa Park,
The crowns of hats, the sun
On moustached archaic faces
Grinning as if it were all
An August Bank Holiday lark;

And the shut shops, the bleached
Established names on the sunblinds,
The farthings and sovereigns,
And dark-clothed children at play
Called after kings and queens,
The tin advertisements
For cocoa and twist, and the pubs
Wide open all day;

And the countryside not caring:
The place-names all hazed over
With flowering grasses, and fields
Shadowing Domesday lines
Under wheat's restless silence;
The differently-dressed servants
With tiny rooms in huge houses,
The dust behind limousines;

Never such innocence,
Never before or since,
As changed itself to past
Without a word – the men
Leaving the gardens tidy,
The thousands of marriages,
Lasting a little while longer:
Never such innocence again.

29 July ✳ Seaweed ✳ D. H. Lawrence

In this short poem, D. H. Lawrence's use of alliterative '*sw*' sounds, as he describes the movement of the seaweed, creates a vivid picture of its movements in the water (as well as compressing the word 'seaweed' itself).

> Seaweed sways and sways and swirls
> as if swaying were its form of stillness;
> and it flushes against fierce rock
> it slips over it as shadows do, without hurting itself.

30 July ✳ The Inchcape Rock ✳ Robert Southey

Five years after the publication of this poem in 1802, work began on the construction of a lighthouse on Inchcape, which still stands today.

No stir in the air, no stir in the sea,
The Ship was still as she could be;
Her sails from heaven received no motion,
Her keel was steady in the ocean.

Without either sign or sound of their shock,
The waves flow'd over the Inchcape Rock;
So little they rose, so little they fell,
They did not move the Inchcape Bell.

The Abbot of Aberbrothok
Had placed that bell on the Inchcape Rock;
On a buoy in the storm it floated and swung,
And over the waves its warning rung.

When the Rock was hid by the surge's swell,
The Mariners heard the warning Bell;
And then they knew the perilous Rock,
And blest the Abbot of Aberbrothok

The Sun in the heaven was shining gay,
All things were joyful on that day;
The sea-birds scream'd as they wheel'd round,
And there was joyaunce in their sound.

The buoy of the Inchcape Bell was seen
A darker speck on the ocean green;
Sir Ralph the Rover walk'd his deck,
And fix'd his eye on the darker speck.

He felt the cheering power of spring,
It made him whistle, it made him sing;
His heart was mirthful to excess,
But the Rover's mirth was wickedness.

His eye was on the Inchcape Float;
Quoth he, 'My men, put out the boat,
And row me to the Inchcape Rock,
And I'll plague the Abbot of Aberbrothok.'

The boat is lower'd, the boatmen row,
And to the Inchcape Rock they go;
Sir Ralph bent over from the boat,
And he cut the Bell from the Inchcape Float.

Down sank the Bell with a gurgling sound,
The bubbles rose and burst around;
Quoth Sir Ralph, 'The next who comes to the Rock,
Won't bless the Abbot of Aberbrothok.'

Sir Ralph the Rover sail'd away,
He scour'd the seas for many a day;
And now grown rich with plunder'd store,
He steers his course for Scotland's shore.

So thick a haze o'erspreads the sky,
They cannot see the sun on high;
The wind hath blown a gale all day,
At evening it hath died away.

On the deck the Rover takes his stand,
So dark it is they see no land.
Quoth Sir Ralph, 'It will be lighter soon,
For there is the dawn of the rising Moon.'

'Canst hear,' said one, 'the breakers roar?
For methinks we should be near the shore.'
'Now, where we are I cannot tell,
But I wish we could hear the Inchcape Bell.'

They hear no sound, the swell is strong,
Though the wind hath fallen they drift along;
Till the vessel strikes with a shivering shock,
'Oh Christ! It is the Inchcape Rock!'

Sir Ralph the Rover tore his hair,
He curst himself in his despair;
The waves rush in on every side,
The ship is sinking beneath the tide.

But even in his dying fear,
One dreadful sound could the Rover hear;
A sound as if with the Inchcape Bell,
The Devil below was ringing his knell.

31 July ∗ A Smuggler's Song ∗ Rudyard Kipling

It is thought that Rudyard Kipling was inspired to write
this poem by hearing stories of smugglers during a stay in
Cornwall.

If you wake at midnight, and hear a horse's feet,
Don't go drawing back the blind, or looking in the street,
Them that ask no questions isn't told a lie.
Watch the wall my darling while the Gentlemen go by!
    Five and twenty ponies,
    Trotting through the dark –
    Brandy for the Parson,
    'Baccy for the Clerk;
    Laces for a lady; letters for a spy,
And watch the wall, my darling, while the Gentlemen go by!

Running round the woodlump if you chance to find
Little barrels, roped and tarred, all full of brandy-wine,
Don't you shout to come and look, nor use 'em for your play.
Put the brishwood back again – and they'll be gone next day!

If you see the stable-door setting open wide;
If you see a tired horse lying down inside;
If your mother mends a coat cut about and tore;
If the lining's wet and warm – don't you ask no more!

If you meet King George's men, dressed in blue and red,
You be careful what you say, and mindful what is said.
If they call you 'pretty maid', and chuck you 'neath the chin,
Don't you tell where no one is, nor yet where no one's been!

Knocks and footsteps round the house – whistles after dark –
You've no call for running out till the house-dogs bark.
Trusty's here, and *Pincher*'s here, and see how dumb they lie –
They don't fret to follow when the Gentlemen go by!

If you do as you've been told, likely there's a chance,
You'll be give a dainty doll, all the way from France,
With a cap of Valenciennes, and a velvet hood –
A present from the Gentlemen, along 'o being good!
　　Five and twenty ponies,
　　Trotting through the dark –
　　Brandy for the Parson,
　　'Baccy for the Clerk.
Them that asks no questions isn't told a lie –
Watch the wall, my darling, while the Gentlemen go by!

August

1 August ✳ Silver ✳ Walter de la Mare

Have you ever been for a walk at night and noticed how things
seem to look very different from how they do in the daytime?
In this poem, Walter de la Mare describes a different kind
of walk, as he imagines the moon herself walking across the
landscape, changing everything she sees by casting it in her
silvery light.

Slowly, silently, now the moon
Walks the night in her silver shoon;
This way, and that, she peers, and sees
Silver fruit upon silver trees;
One by one the casements catch
Her beams beneath the silvery thatch;
Couched in his kennel, like a log,
With paws of silver sleeps the dog;
From their shadowy cote the white breasts peep
Of doves in silver feathered sleep
A harvest mouse goes scampering by,
With silver claws, and silver eye;
And moveless fish in the water gleam,
By silver reeds in a silver stream.

2 August ✶ The Listeners ✶ Walter de la Mare

In this poem, Walter de la Mare tells the story of a lone
horseman's arrival at an empty house.

'Is there anybody there?' said the Traveller,
　Knocking on the moonlit door;
And his horse in the silence champed the grasses
　Of the forest's ferny floor:
And a bird flew up out of the turret,
　Above the Traveller's head:
And he smote upon the door again a second time;
　'Is there anybody there?' he said.
But no one descended to the Traveller;
　No head from the leaf-fringed sill
Leaned over and looked into his grey eyes,
　Where he stood perplexed and still.
But only a host of phantom listeners
　That dwelt in the lone house then
Stood listening in the quiet of the moonlight
　To that voice from the world of men:
Stood thronging the faint moonbeams on the dark stair,
　That goes down to the empty hall,
Hearkening in an air stirred and shaken
　By the lonely Traveller's call.
And he felt in his heart their strangeness,
　Their stillness answering his cry,
While his horse moved, cropping the dark turf,
　'Neath the starred and leafy sky;
For he suddenly smote on the door, even
　Louder, and lifted his head:—
'Tell them I came, and no one answered,
　That I kept my word,' he said.
Never the least stir made the listeners,

Though every word he spake
Fell echoing through the shadowiness of the still house
    From the one man left awake:
Ay, they heard his foot upon the stirrup,
    And the sound of iron on stone,
And how the silence surged softly backward,
    When the plunging hoofs were gone.

3 August ✳ Imagination ✳ James Baldwin

3 August 1492 was the day on which the Italian explorer Christopher Columbus sailed westwards from Spain into the Atlantic Ocean, intending to find a new trade route to Asia. Instead, he arrived in America, and his expedition was one of the first European voyages to make contact with this 'New World', although there were people living on the American continent long before Columbus arrived.

Imagination
creates the situation,
and, then, the situation
creates imagination.

It may, of course,
be the other way around:
Columbus was discovered
by what he found.

4 August ∗ If ∗ Rudyard Kipling

'If' is a famous inspirational poem, written from the perspective of a father who is offering advice to his son.

If you can keep your head when all about you
        Are losing theirs and blaming it on you;
If you can trust yourself when all men doubt you,
        But make allowance for their doubting too;
If you can wait and not be tired by waiting,
        Or being lied about, don't deal in lies,
Or being hated, don't give way to hating,
        And yet don't look too good, nor talk too wise:

If you can dream — and not make dreams your master;
        If you can think — and not make thoughts your aim;
If you can meet with Triumph and Disaster
        And treat those two impostors just the same;
If you can bear to hear the truth you've spoken
        Twisted by knaves to make a trap for fools,
Or watch the things you gave your life to, broken,
        And stoop and build 'em up with worn-out tools:

If you can make one heap of all your winnings
        And risk it on one turn of pitch-and-toss,
And lose, and start again at your beginnings
        And never breathe a word about your loss;
If you can force your heart and nerve and sinew
        To serve your turn long after they are gone,
And so hold on when there is nothing in you
        Except the Will which says to them: 'Hold on!'

If you can talk with crowds and keep your virtue,
     Or walk with Kings — nor lose the common touch,
If neither foes nor loving friends can hurt you,
     If all men count with you, but none too much;
If you can fill the unforgiving minute
     With sixty seconds' worth of distance run,
Yours is the Earth and everything that's in it,
     And — which is more — you'll be a Man, my son!

5 August ✷ If-ing ✷ Langston Hughes

Just like Kipling's 'If', this poem by Langston Hughes takes as its theme that simple two-letter word that can cover all things wished for, possible or imagined. While Kipling's poem lists a whole string of virtues — things that 'if' you can do them make you a wonderful person — Hughes's poem is all about the 'if' of having money.

If I had some small change
I'd buy me a mule,
Get on that mule and
Ride like a fool.

If I had some greenbacks
I'd buy me a Packard,
Fill it up with gas and
Drive that baby backward.

If I had a million
I'd get me a plane
And everybody in America'd
Think I was insane.

But I ain't got a million,

Fact is, ain't got a dime —

So just by if-ing

I have a good time!

6 August ✴ The Smile ✴ William Blake

How comforting do you find the idea of one true smile that can
end all misery if it can be smiled only once in a lifetime?

> There is a Smile of Love
> And there is a Smile of Deceit
> And there is a Smile of Smiles
> In which these two Smiles meet
>
> And there is a Frown of Hate
> And there is a Frown of disdain
> And there is a Frown of Frowns
> Which you strive to forget in vain
>
> For it sticks in the Hearts deep Core
> And it sticks in the deep Back bone
> And no Smile that ever was Smil'd
> But only one Smile alone
>
> That betwixt the Cradle & Grave
> It only once Smil'd can be
> But when it once is Smil'd
> There's an end to all Misery

7 August * A Poison Tree * William Blake

This poem uses a central image of a tree that echoes the Tree of Knowledge in the Biblical story. Blake seems to be suggesting that if you don't express your anger immediately, then it will grow and make you bitter.

I was angry with my friend;
I told my wrath, my wrath did end.
I was angry with my foe:
I told it not, my wrath did grow.

And I water'd it in fears,
Night & morning with my tears;
And I sunned it with smiles,
And with soft deceitful wiles.

And it grew both day and night.
Till it bore an apple bright;
And my foe beheld it shine,
And he knew that it was mine,

And into my garden stole,
When the night had veil'd the pole:
In the morning glad I see;
My foe outstretch'd beneath the tree.

8 August ✶ Drake's Drum ✶ Henry Newbolt

This poem refers to the death of Sir Francis Drake, who is
said to have commanded on his deathbed that his ship's drum
be taken back to his home in Devon. If it is beaten at times
of national crisis, so the story goes, he will rise again to save
England. 8 August 1588 is the date the English navy destroyed
the Spanish Armada.

Drake he's in his hammock an' a thousand miles away,
　(Capten, art tha sleepin' there below?)
Slung atween the round shot in Nombre Dios Bay,
　An' dreamin' arl the time o' Plymouth Hoe.
Yarnder lumes the Island, yarnder lie the ships,
　Wi' sailor lads a-dancing' heel-an'-toe,
An' the shore-lights flashin', an' the night-tide dashin',
　He sees et arl so plainly as he saw et long ago.

Drake he was a Devon man, an' ruled the Devon seas,
　(Capten, art tha' sleepin' there below?)
Rovin' tho' his death fell, he went wi' heart at ease,
　A' dreamin' arl the time o' Plymouth Hoe.
'Take my drum to England, hang et by the shore,
　Strike et when your powder's runnin' low;
If the Dons sight Devon, I'll quit the port o' Heaven,
　An' drum them up the Channel as we drumm'd them long ago.'

Drake he's in his hammock till the great Armadas come,
　(Capten, art tha sleepin' there below?)
Slung atween the round shot, listenin' for the drum,
　An' dreamin arl the time o' Plymouth Hoe.
Call him on the deep sea, call him up the Sound,
　Call him when ye sail to meet the foe;
Where the old trade's plyin' an' the old flag flyin'
　They shall find him ware an' wakin', as they found him long ago!

9 August * Cargoes * John Masefield

Britain has a long history of being a seafaring nation. This poem describes cargoes from all over the world.

Quinquireme of Nineveh from distant Ophir,
Rowing home to haven in sunny Palestine,
With a cargo of ivory,
And apes and peacocks,
Sandalwood, cedarwood, and sweet white wine.

Stately Spanish galleon coming from the Isthmus,
Dipping through the Tropics by the palm-green shores,
With a cargo of diamonds,
Emeralds, amythysts,
Topazes, and cinnamon, and gold moidores.

Dirty British coaster with a salt-caked smoke stack,
Butting through the Channel in the mad March days,
With a cargo of Tyne coal,
Road-rails, pig-lead,
Firewood, iron-ware, and cheap tin trays.

10 August * Hunter Trials * John Betjeman

A gymkhana is an equestrian event that consists of trials and timed games played while riding horses and ponies. And that's what John Betjeman is making fun of in this poem.

It's awf'lly bad luck on Diana,
    Her ponies have swallowed their bits;
She fished down their throats with a spanner
    And frightened them all into fits.

So now she's attempting to borrow.
    Do lend her some bits, Mummy, *do*;
I'll lend her my own for to-morrow,
    But to-day *I*'ll be wanting them too.

Just look at Prunella on Guzzle,
    The wizardest pony on earth;
Why doesn't she slacken his muzzle
    And tighten the breech in his girth?

I say, Mummy, there's Mrs. Geyser
    And doesn't she look pretty sick?
I bet it's because Mona Lisa
    Was hit on the hock with a brick.

Miss Blewitt says Monica threw it,
    But Monica says it was Joan,
And Joan's very thick with Miss Blewitt,
    So Monica's sulking alone.

And Margaret failed in her paces,
    Her withers got tied in a noose,
So her coronets caught in the traces
    And now all her fetlocks are loose.

Oh, it's me now. I'm terribly nervous.
  I wonder if Smudges will shy.
She's practically certain to swerve as
  Her Pelham is over one eye.

*

Oh wasn't it naughty of Smudges?
  Oh, Mummy, I'm sick with disgust.
She threw me in front of the Judges,
  And my silly old collarbone's bust.

11 August ✳ Triolet ✳ G. K. Chesterton

A triolet is a type of poetic form which originated in French medieval poetry. For the most part it is a poem of eight lines, and the first, fourth and seventh lines are identical. This poem is a joyful example of how a simple idea can create a comic picture, in this case that of a jellyfish falling down the stairs.

> I wish I were a jellyfish
> That cannot fall downstairs;
> Of all the things I wish to wish
> I wish I were a jellyfish
> That hasn't any cares
> And doesn't even have to wish
> 'I wish I were a jellyfish
> That cannot fall downstairs.'

12 August ✳ Blackberry-Picking ✳ Seamus Heaney

August in England is blackberry season – as Summer slowly turns into Autumn, the hedgerows become covered in berries. This poem by Seamus Heaney brilliantly evokes the rich sights and smells of late Summer, and the deliciousness of freshly picked blackberries: 'sweet / Like thickened wine'.

For Philip Hobsbaum

Late August, given heavy rain and sun
For a full week, the blackberries would ripen.
At first, just one, a glossy purple clot
Among others, red, green, hard as a knot.
You ate that first one and its flesh was sweet
Like thickened wine: summer's blood was in it
Leaving stains upon the tongue and lust for
Picking. Then red ones inked up and that hunger
Sent us out with milk cans, pea tins, jam pots
Where briars scratched and wet grass bleached our boots.
Round hayfields, cornfields and potato drills
We trekked and picked until the cans were full,
Until the tinkling bottom had been covered
With green ones, and on top big dark blobs burned
Like a plate of eyes. Our hands were peppered
With thorn pricks, our palms sticky as Bluebeard's.

We hoarded the fresh berries in the byre.
But when the bath was filled we found a fur,
A rat-grey fungus, glutting on our cache.
The juice was stinking too. Once off the bush
The fruit fermented, the sweet flesh would turn sour.
I always felt like crying. It wasn't fair
That all the lovely canfuls smelt of rot.
Each year I hoped they'd keep, knew they would not.

13 August ✶ After Blenheim ✶ Robert Southey

The Battle of Blenheim, one of the major battles of the War of the Spanish Succession, was fought on 13 August 1704.

It was a summer evening,
   Old Kaspar's work was done,
And he before his cottage door
   Was sitting in the sun;
And by him sported on the green
His little grandchild Wilhelmine.

She saw her brother Peterkin
   Roll something large and round,
Which he beside the rivulet
   In playing there had found;
He came to ask what he had found,
That was so large, and smooth, and round.

Old Kaspar took it from the boy,
   Who stood expectant by;
And then the old man shook his head,
   And, with a natural sigh,
''Tis some poor fellow's skull,' said he,
'Who fell in the great victory.

'I find them in the garden,
   For there's many here about;
And often when I go to plough
   The ploughshare turns them out.
For many thousand men,' said he,
'Were slain in that great victory.'

'Now tell us what 'twas all about,'
   Young Peterkin, he cries;
And little Wilhelmine looks up
   With wonder-waiting eyes;
'Now tell us all about the war,
And what they fought each other for.'

'It was the English,' Kaspar cried,
   'Who put the French to rout;
But what they fought each other for,
   I could not well make out;
But everybody said,' quoth he,
'That 'twas a famous victory.

'My father lived at Blenheim then,
   Yon little stream hard by;
They burnt his dwelling to the ground,
   And he was forced to fly;
So with his wife and child he fled,
Nor had he where to rest his head.

'With fire and sword the country round
   Was wasted far and wide,
And many a childing mother then
   And newborn baby died;
But things like that, you know, must be
At every famous victory.

'They say it was a shocking sight
   After the field was won;
For many thousand bodies here
   Lay rotting in the sun:
But things like that, you know, must be
After a famous victory.

'Great praise the Duke of Marlbro' won,
    And our good Prince Eugene.'
'Why, 'twas a very wicked thing!'
    Said little Wilhelmine.
'Nay. . . nay . . . my little girl,' quoth he,
'It was a famous victory.

'And everybody praised the Duke
    Who this great fight did win.'
'But what good came of it at last?'
    Quoth little Peterkin.
'Why that I cannot tell,' said he,
'But 'twas a famous victory.'

14 August ✳ End of the Day ✳ Anthony Watts

In this poem, Anthony Watts paints a vivid picture of the twilight scene he is describing using only a few words in each line.

> The old world turns
>   in its rusty socket;
> a ragged sky burns;
> the sea slops
>   in the moon's bucket;
> the sun's penny drops.

15 August ✳ *from* Macbeth ✳ William Shakespeare

This speech is a soliloquy, delivered by Macbeth straight
after he has received news of his wife's death. The historical
Scottish King Macbeth was killed on this day in 1057 by the
future King Malcolm III, though Shakespeare's play is far from
being a reliable 'history' of his reign.

> Tomorrow, and tomorrow, and tomorrow,
> Creeps in this petty pace from day to day,
> To the last syllable of recorded time;
> And all our yesterdays have lighted fools
> The way to dusty death. Out, out, brief candle!
> Life's but a walking shadow, a poor player,
> That struts and frets his hour upon the stage,
> And then is heard no more. It is a tale
> Told by an idiot, full of sound and fury,
> Signifying nothing.

16 August ✳ The Viking Terror ✳ Anon., translated by Kuno Meyer

Originally written in Old Irish, this poem was found in the margin of a manuscript which has been dated to around 850 AD — a time in which Irish coastal communities lived in constant fear of vicious Viking raiding parties. While we might think of bad weather as irritating, for the anonymous Irish poet who wrote these lines, turbulent seas were a blessing, guaranteeing safety from the Viking longboats which could not be sailed safely in a storm.

> Bitter is the wind tonight.
> It tosses the ocean's white hair:
> Tonight I fear not the fierce warriors of Norway
> Coursing on the Irish Sea.

17 August ✴ August ✴ John Updike

Like the poem that is included above as the entry for 28 June,
this poem is taken from the great American writer John
Updike's collection of children's poetry, *A Child's Calendar*.

> The sprinkler twirls.
> The summer wanes.
> The pavement wears
> Popsicle stains.
>
> The playground grass
> Is worn to dust.
> The weary swings
> Creak, creak with rust.
>
> The trees are bored
> With being green.
> Some people leave
> The local scene
>
> And go to seaside
> Bungalows
> And take off nearly
> All their clothes.

18 August ✳ The Forsaken Merman ✳
Matthew Arnold

In this poem, Matthew Arnold tells the sad story of a
merman – a creature who is human from the waist up, and a
fish from the waist down – and his human wife.

Come, dear children, let us away;
Down and away below!
Now my brothers call from the bay,
Now the great winds shoreward blow,
Now the salt tides seaward flow;
Now the wild white horses play,
Champ and chafe and toss in the spray.
Children dear, let us away!
This way, this way!

Call her once before you go—
Call once yet!
In a voice that she will know:
'Margaret! Margaret!'
Children's voices should be dear
(Call once more) to a mother's ear;

Children's voices, wild with pain—
Surely she will come again!
Call her once and come away;
This way, this way!
'Mother dear, we cannot stay!
The wild white horses foam and fret.'
Margaret! Margaret!

Come, dear children, come away down;
Call no more!
One last look at the white-wall'd town
And the little grey church on the windy shore,
Then come down!
She will not come though you call all day;
Come away, come away!

Children dear, was it yesterday
We heard the sweet bells over the bay?
In the caverns where we lay,
Through the surf and through the swell,
The far-off sound of a silver bell?
Sand-strewn caverns, cool and deep,
Where the winds are all asleep;
Where the spent lights quiver and gleam,
Where the salt weed sways in the stream,
Where the sea-beasts, ranged all round,
Feed in the ooze of their pasture-ground;
Where the sea-snakes coil and twine,
Dry their mail and bask in the brine;
Where great whales come sailing by,
Sail and sail, with unshut eye,
Round the world for ever and aye?
When did music come this way?
Children dear, was it yesterday?

Children dear, was it yesterday
(Call yet once) that she went away?
Once she sate with you and me,
On a red gold throne in the heart of the sea,
And the youngest sate on her knee.
She comb'd its bright hair, and she tended it well,
When down swung the sound of a far-off bell.
She sigh'd, she look'd up through the clear green sea;
She said: 'I must go, to my kinsfolk pray
In the little grey church on the shore to-day.

314

'Twill be Easter-time in the world—ah me!
And I lose my poor soul, Merman! here with thee.'
I said: 'Go up, dear heart, through the waves;
Say thy prayer, and come back to the kind sea-caves!'
She smiled, she went up through the surf in the bay.
Children dear, was it yesterday?

Children dear, were we long alone?
'The sea grows stormy, the little ones moan;
Long prayers,' I said, 'in the world they say;
Come!' I said; and we rose through the surf in the bay.
We went up the beach, by the sandy down
Where the sea-stocks bloom, to the white-wall'd town;
Through the narrow paved streets, where all was still,
To the little grey church on the windy hill.
From the church came a murmur of folk at their prayers,
But we stood without in the cold blowing airs.
We climb'd on the graves, on the stones worn with rains,
And we gazed up the aisle through the small leaded panes.
She sate by the pillar; we saw her clear:
'Margaret, hist! come quick, we are here!
Dear heart,' I said, 'we are long alone;
The sea grows stormy, the little ones moan.'
But, ah, she gave me never a look,
For her eyes were seal'd to the holy book!
Loud prays the priest; shut stands the door.
Come away, children, call no more!
Come away, come down, call no more!

Down, down, down!
Down to the depths of the sea!
She sits at her wheel in the humming town,
Singing most joyfully.
Hark what she sings: 'O joy, O joy,
For the humming street, and the child with its toy!
For the priest, and the bell, and the holy well;
For the wheel where I spun,

And the blessed light of the sun!'
And so she sings her fill,
Singing most joyfully,
Till the spindle drops from her hand,
And the whizzing wheel stands still.
She steals to the window, and looks at the sand,
And over the sand at the sea;
And her eyes are set in a stare;
And anon there breaks a sigh,
And anon there drops a tear,
From a sorrow-clouded eye,
And a heart sorrow-laden,
A long, long sigh;
For the cold strange eyes of a little Mermaiden
And the gleam of her golden hair.

Come away, away children
Come children, come down!
The hoarse wind blows coldly;
Lights shine in the town.
She will start from her slumber
When gusts shake the door;
She will hear the winds howling,
Will hear the waves roar.
We shall see, while above us
The waves roar and whirl,
A ceiling of amber,
A pavement of pearl.
Singing: 'Here came a mortal,
But faithless was she!
And alone dwell for ever
The kings of the sea.'

But, children, at midnight,
When soft the winds blow,
When clear falls the moonlight,
When spring-tides are low;

When sweet airs come seaward
From heaths starr'd with broom,
And high rocks throw mildly
On the blanch'd sands a gloom;
Up the still, glistening beaches,
Up the creeks we will hie,
Over banks of bright seaweed
The ebb-tide leaves dry.
We will gaze, from the sand-hills,
At the white, sleeping town;
At the church on the hill-side—
And then come back down.
Singing: 'There dwells a loved one,
But cruel is she!
She left lonely for ever
The kings of the sea.'

19 August ✷ The Forlorn Sea ✷ Stevie Smith

In this poem, Stevie Smith's narrator tells a strange, magical story about a princess who marries a fairy king, and moves to a fairy kingdom near a 'forlorn sea'.

Our Princess married
A fairy King,
It was a sensational
Wedding.

Now they live in a palace
Of porphyry,
Far, far away,
By the forlorn sea.

Sometimes people visit them,
Last week they invited me;
That is how I can tell you
They live by a forlorn sea.

(They said: Here's a magic carpet,
Come on this,
And when you arrive
We will give you a big kiss.)

I play in the palace garden,
I climb the sycamore tree,
Sometimes I swim
In the forlorn sea.

The King and the Princess are shadowy,
Yet beautiful,
They are waited on by white cats,
Who are dutiful.

It is like a dream
When they kiss and cuddle me,
But I like it, I like it,
I do not wish to break free.

So I eat all they give me
Because I have read
If you eat fairy food
You will never wake up in your own bed,

But will go on living,
As has happened to me,
Far, far away
By a forlorn sea.

20 August ✴ Thunder ✴ Elizabeth Bishop

This poem uses a fantasy world of gods and giants to explain
the causes of thunder.

And suddenly the giants tired of play. –
With huge, rough hands they flung the gods' gold balls
And silver harps and mirrors at the walls
Of Heaven, and trod, ashamed, where lay
The loveliness of flowers. Frightened Day
On white feet ran from out the temple halls,
The blundering dark was filled with great war-calls,
And Beauty, shamed, slunk silently away.

Be quiet, little wind among the leaves
That turn pale faces to the coming storm.
Be quiet, little foxes in your lairs,
And birds and mice be still – a giant grieves
For his forgotten might. Hark now the warm
And heavy stumbling down the leaden stairs!

21 August ∗ Bed in Summer ∗
Robert Louis Stevenson

Robert Louis Stevenson spent much of his childhood bed-bound due to illness, so he may well have had a particularly sharp memory of the misery of staying in bed while the world outside enjoys the longer hours of light in the Summer time.

In winter I get up at night
And dress by yellow candle-light.
In summer, quite the other way,
I have to go to bed by day.

I have to go to bed and see
The birds still hopping on the tree,
Or hear the grown-up people's feet
Still going past me in the street.

And does it not seem hard to you,
When all the sky is clear and blue,
And I should like so much to play,
To have to go to bed by day?

22 August ✳ Humpty Dumpty ✳ Anon.

On this day, 22 August 1485, Richard III was defeated by Henry Tudor at the Battle of Bosworth. There is a popular theory that Humpty Dumpty in this English nursery rhyme symbolizes Richard III, and his 'great fall' represents Richard falling from his horse.

> Humpty Dumpty sat on a wall,
> Humpty Dumpty had a great fall;
> All the king's horses and all the king's men
> Couldn't put Humpty together again.

23 August ✴ Little Red Riding Hood ✴ Roald Dahl

In this poem from his collection *Revolting Rhymes*, Roald Dahl takes the familiar story of Little Red Riding Hood and gives the ending an exciting, gruesome twist. Rather than relying upon the woodsman to come and save her and her grandmother, Dahl's stylish, dangerous Little Red Riding Hood is perfectly capable of taking care of herself . . .

As soon as Wolf began to feel
That he would like a decent meal,
He went and knocked on Grandma's door.
When Grandma opened it, she saw
The sharp white teeth, the horrid grin,
And Wolfie said, 'May I come in?'
Poor Grandmamma was terrified,
'He's going to eat me up!' she cried.

And she was absolutely right.
He ate her up in one big bite.
But Grandmamma was small and tough,
And Wolfie wailed, 'That's not enough!
I haven't yet begun to feel
That I have had a decent meal!'
He ran around the kitchen yelping,
'I've got to have a second helping!'
Then added with a frightful leer,
'I'm therefore going to wait right here
Till Little Miss Red Riding Hood
Comes home from walking in the wood.'
He quickly put on Grandma's clothes
(Of course he hadn't eaten those).
He dressed himself in coat and hat.
He put on shoes, and after that,
He even brushed and curled his hair,

Then sat himself in Grandma's chair.
In came the little girl in red.
She stopped. She stared. And then she said,

'What great big ears you have, Grandma.'
'All the better to hear you with,'
the Wolf replied.
'What great big eyes you have, Grandma.'
said Little Red Riding Hood.
'All the better to see you with,'
the Wolf replied.

He sat there watching her and smiled.
He thought, I'm going to eat this child.
Compared with her old Grandmamma,
She's going to taste like caviar.

Then Little Red Riding Hood said,
'But Grandma, what a lovely great big
furry coat you have on.'

'That's wrong!' cried Wolf.
'Have you forgot
To tell me what BIG TEETH I've got?
Ah well, no matter what you say,
I'm going to eat you anyway.'
The small girl smiles. One eyelid flickers.
She whips a pistol from her knickers.
She aims it at the creature's head,
And bang bang bang, she shoots him dead.
A few weeks later, in the wood,
I came across Miss Riding Hood.
But what a change! No cloak of red,
No silly hood upon her head.
She said, 'Hello, and do please note
My lovely furry wolfskin coat.'

24 August ✶ Goldilocks ✶ Carole Bromley

This poem is another rewriting of a traditional fairy tale, this time from Goldilocks's perspective.

I'd listened at the door; they were always there,
the daddy with the voice and the enormous chair,
the mummy with the pinny, stirring the vat;
banging his spoon, their spoilt wee brat.

The chance came soon; they were humouring
the kid, swinging him hand to hand,
There there, baby bear, let's leave our bowls,
walk in the forest till the porridge cools.

All the more for me; I walked in from the yard
climbed onto daddy's chair – far too hard.
You know the score – hard, soft, right,
hot, cold, fine; big, small, mine.

Point was I had the whole place to myself,
put telly on, took a bath, rearranged a shelf.
Then it was Who's been sitting in our chairs,
helping themselves? Beds are for bears

and this one's bust. Yeah, yeah, fair cop.
But they chased after me and didn't stop
till jumping out the window was the only way;
and there's me thinking they'd ask me to stay.

But I'll be back, you mark my words;
bears living in houses! It's just absurd;
bears eating porridge, bears wearing frocks –
next time they're out I'm changing the locks.

25 August ✷ Property for Sale ✷ Rachel Rooney

This poem is another re-imagining of a familiar story, and Rachel Rooney uses the understated form of a property advertisement to tell the story of the Three Little Pigs.

> Two houses up for sale.
> One stick, one straw.
> Both self-assembly,
> See pig next door.

26 August ✶ The Unknown Bird ✶ Edward Thomas

In this poem, Thomas describes meeting the mysterious bird
of the title. Just the memory of the bird's song can lift his
spirits.

Three lovely notes he whistled, too soft to be heard
If others sang; but others never sang
In the great beech-wood all that May and June.
No one saw him: I alone could hear him:
Though many listened. Was it but four years
Ago? or five? He never came again.

Oftenest when I heard him I was alone,
Nor could I ever make another hear.
La-la-la! he called, seeming far-off—
As if a cock crowed past the edge of the world,
As if the bird or I were in a dream.
Yet that he travelled through the trees and sometimes
Neared me, was plain, though somehow distant still
He sounded. All the proof is—I told men
What I had heard.

I never knew a voice,
Man, beast, or bird, better than this. I told
The naturalists; but neither had they heard
Anything like the notes that did so haunt me,
I had them clear by heart and have them still.
Four years, or five, have made no difference. Then
As now that La-la-la! was bodiless sweet:
Sad more than joyful it was, if I must say
That it was one or other, but if sad
'Twas sad only with joy too, too far off
For me to taste it. But I cannot tell

If truly never anything but fair
The days were when he sang, as now they seem.
This surely I know, that I who listened then,
Happy sometimes, sometimes suffering
A heavy body and a heavy heart,
Now straightway, if I think of it, become
Light as that bird wandering beyond my shore.

27 August ✳ How to Cut a Pomegranate ✳
Imtiaz Dharker

In this poem the pomegranate is more than just a fruit. Its
exotic taste transforms it into a symbol of a distant home, with
each seed containing a wealth of flavours, sounds and sights.

'Never,' said my father,
'Never cut a pomegranate
through the heart. It will weep blood.
Treat it delicately, with respect.

'Just slit the upper skin across four quarters.
This is a magic fruit,
so when you split it open, be prepared
for the jewels of the world to tumble out,
more precious than garnets,
more lustrous than rubies,
lit as if from inside.
Each jewel contains a living seed.
Separate one crystal.
Hold it up to catch the light.
Inside is a whole universe.
No common jewel can give you this.'

Afterwards, I tried to make necklaces
of pomegranate seeds.
The juice spurted out, bright crimson,
and stained my fingers, then my mouth.
I didn't mind. The juice tasted of gardens
I had never seen, voluptuous
with myrtle, lemon, jasmine,
and alive with parrots' wings.

The pomegranate reminded me
that somewhere I had another home.

329

28 August * Dawn * Paul Laurence Dunbar

This short stanza by the American poet Paul Laurence Dunbar takes the moment of sunrise as its subject.

> An angel, robed in spotless white,
> Bent down and kissed the sleeping Night.
> Night woke to blush; the sprite was gone.
> Men saw the blush and called it Dawn.

29 August ✳ Prayer (I) ✳ George Herbert

Prayer can be difficult to describe. Here, the seventeenth-century poet George Herbert explains what praying means to him.

Prayer the Church's banquet, angels' age,
>God's breath in man returning to his birth,
>The soul in paraphrase, heart in pilgrimage,
The Christian plummet sounding heav'n and earth;
Engine against th' Almighty, sinners' tow'r,
>Reversed thunder, Christ-side-piercing spear,
>The six-days' world transposing in an hour,
A kind of tune, which all things hear and fear;
Softness, and peace, and joy, and love, and bliss,
>Exalted manna, gladness of the best,
>Heaven in ordinary, man well drest,
The milky way, the bird of Paradise,
>Church-bells beyond the stars heard, the soul's blood,
>The land of spices; something understood.

This poem by C. S. Lewis, perhaps better known as the author of the *Chronicles of Narnia* books, was written in 1948, and tells a story based on Noah's Ark. In Lewis's reimagining, Noah's sons, Shem, Ham and Japhet, are too lazy to let in the unicorn, meaning the world will be deprived of these creatures.

The sky was low, the sounding rain was falling dense and dark,
And Noah's sons were standing at the window of the Ark.

The beasts were in, but Japhet said, 'I see one creature more
Belated and unmated there come knocking at the door.'

'Well, let him knock,' said Ham, 'Or let him drown or learn to
   swim.
We're overcrowded as it is; we've got no room for him.'

'And yet it knocks, how terribly it knocks,' said Shem, 'Its feet
Are hard as horn – but oh the air that comes from it is sweet.'

'Now hush,' said Ham, 'You'll waken Dad, and once he comes
   to see
What's at the door, it's sure to mean more work for you and me.'

Noah's voice came roaring from the darkness down below,
'Some animal is knocking. Take it in before we go.'

Ham shouted back, and savagely he nudged the other two,
'That's only Japhet knocking down a brad-nail in his shoe.'

Said Noah, 'Boys, I hear a noise that's like a horse's hoof.'
Said Ham, 'Why, that's the dreadful rain that drums upon the
   roof.'

Noah tumbled up on deck and out he put his head;
His face went grey, his knees were loosed, he tore his beard
   and said,

'Look, look! It would not wait. It turns away. It takes its flight.
Fine work you've made of it, my sons, between you all tonight!

'Even if I could outrun it now, it would not turn again –
Not now. Our great discourtesy has earned its high disdain.

'Oh noble and unmated beast, my sons were all unkind;
In such a night what stable and what manger will you find?

'Oh golden hoofs, oh cataracts of mane, oh nostrils wide
With indignation! Oh the neck wave-arched, the lovely pride!

'Oh long shall be the furrows ploughed across the hearts of men
Before it comes to stable and to manger once again.

'And dark and crooked all the ways in which our race shall walk,
And shrivelled all their manhood like a flower with broken stalk,

'And all the world, oh Ham, may curse the hour when you
   were born;
Because of you the Ark must sail without the Unicorn.'

31 August ✳ The Destruction of Sennacherib ✳ George Gordon, Lord Byron

'The Destruction of Sennacherib' is a retelling of a tale told in the second part of the Book of Kings in the Bible.

The Assyrian came down like the wolf on the fold,
And his cohorts were gleaming in purple and gold;
And the sheen of their spears was like stars on the sea,
When the blue wave rolls nightly on deep Galilee.

Like the leaves of the forest when Summer is green,
That host with their banners at sunset were seen:
Like the leaves of the forest when Autumn hath blown,
That host on the morrow lay wither'd and strown.

For the Angel of Death spread his wings on the blast,
And breathed in the face of the foe as he passed;
And the eyes of the sleepers waxed deadly and chill,
And their hearts but once heaved, and for ever grew still!

And there lay the steed with his nostril all wide,
But through it there rolled not the breath of his pride;
And the foam of his gasping lay white on the turf,
And cold as the spray of the rock-beating surf.

And there lay the rider distorted and pale,
With the dew on his brow, and the rust on his mail:
And the tents were all silent, the banners alone,
The lances unlifted, the trumpet unblown.

And the widows of Ashur are loud in their wail,
And the idols are broke in the temple of Baal;
And the might of the Gentile, unsmote by the sword,
Hath melted like snow in the glance of the Lord!

September

1 September * Aeroplanes * Herbert Read

On 1 September 1939, Germany invaded Poland. The Allied Powers had vowed to help Poland if it was attacked, and so, two days later, Britain, France and members of the Commonwealth declared war on Germany, marking the beginning of World War Two. The war would last for nearly six years, and would cause over 60 million casualties.

A dragonfly
in a flecked grey sky.

Its silvered planes
break the wide and still
harmony of space.

Around it shells
flash
their fumes
burgeoning to blooms
smoke-liles that float
along the sky.

Among them darts
a dragonfly.

2 September ✴ Slough ✴ John Betjeman

In between the First and Second World Wars, the British town of Slough in Berkshire was used as a dumping ground for war surplus materials, before becoming a site of manufacturing and home to over 850 new factories. John Betjeman wrote this poem in 1937, lamenting the onset of industrialization.

Come, friendly bombs, and fall on Slough
It isn't fit for humans now,
There isn't grass to graze a cow
    Swarm over, Death!

Come, bombs, and blow to smithereens
Those air-conditioned, bright canteens,
Tinned fruit, tinned meat, tinned milk, tinned beans,
    Tinned minds, tinned breath.

Mess up the mess they call a town—
A house for ninety-seven down
And once a week a half-a-crown
    For twenty years.

And get that man with double chin
Who'll always cheat and always win,
Who washes his repulsive skin
    In women's tears,

And smash his desk of polished oak
And smash his hands so used to stroke
And stop his boring dirty joke
    And make him yell.

But spare the bald young clerks who add
The profits of the stinking cad;
It's not their fault that they are mad,
    They've tasted Hell.

It's not their fault they do not know
The birdsong from the radio,
It's not their fault they often go
    To Maidenhead

And talk of sport and makes of cars
In various bogus-Tudor bars
And daren't look up and see the stars
    But belch instead.

In labour-saving homes, with care
Their wives frizz out peroxide hair
And dry it in synthetic air
    And paint their nails.

Come, friendly bombs, and fall on Slough
To get it ready for the plough.
The cabbages are coming now;
    The earth exhales.

3 September ✳ Composed Upon Westminster Bridge, September 3, 1802 ✳ William Wordsworth

This poem describes London and the River Thames, viewed from Westminster Bridge in the early morning. Wordsworth was travelling to Calais with his sister Dorothy at the time, and in her journal, Dorothy wrote this of the sight: 'Yet the sun shone so brightly with such a pure light that there was even something like the purity of one of nature's own grand Spectacles.'

Earth has not anything to show more fair:
Dull would he be of soul who could pass by
A sight so touching in its majesty:
This City now doth, like a garment, wear
The beauty of the morning; silent, bare,
Ships, towers, domes, theatres, and temples lie
Open unto the fields, and to the sky;
All bright and glittering in the smokeless air.
Never did sun more beautifully steep
In his first splendour, valley, rock, or hill;
Ne'er saw I, never felt, a calm so deep!
The river glideth at his own sweet will:
Dear God! the very houses seem asleep;
And all that mighty heart is lying still!

4 September ✶ The Solitary Reaper ✶
William Wordsworth

In this poem, Wordsworth's speaker describes the experience
of seeing a girl singing in a field as she reaps, cutting and
binding the grain. Wordsworth speculates about what kind of
song the girl could be singing.

Behold her, single in the field,
Yon solitary Highland Lass!
Reaping and singing by herself;
Stop here, or gently pass!
Alone she cuts and binds the grain,
And sings a melancholy strain;
O listen! for the Vale profound
Is overflowing with the sound.

No Nightingale did ever chaunt
More welcome notes to weary bands
Of travellers in some shady haunt,
Among Arabian sands:
A voice so thrilling ne'er was heard
In spring-time from the Cuckoo-bird,
Breaking the silence of the seas
Among the farthest Hebrides.

Will no one tell me what she sings?
Perhaps the plaintive numbers flow
For old, unhappy, far-off things,
And battles long ago:
Or is it some more humble lay,
Familiar matter of today?
Some natural sorrow, loss, or pain,
That has been, and may be again?

Whate'er the theme, the Maiden sang
As if her song could have no ending;
I saw her singing at her work,
And o'er the sickle bending;—
I listened, motionless and still;
And, as I mounted up the hill,
The music in my heart I bore,
Long after it was heard no more.

5 September ✳ Ring a Ring o' Roses ✳ Anon.

This song is a nursery rhyme which was first printed in England in 1881. There are many versions of this rhyme, including some that originate in Germany, Switzerland and the Netherlands. Some people believe that the rhyme dates from the Great Plague in 1665, or earlier breakouts of the Black Death, and that the lyrics describe the symptoms of the disease. From 2–6 September 1666 the Great Fire of London raged through the city, destroying many of the buildings and – perhaps– the plague along with it.

> Ring a ring o' roses,
> A pocket full of posies,
> A-tishoo! A-tishoo!
> We all fall down.

6 September ✶ Homework! Oh, Homework! ✶
Jack Prelutsky

Although there are some exciting things about the beginning
of term, this poem takes as its subject something that many
students dread: homework!

Homework! Oh, Homework!
I hate you! You stink!
I wish I could wash you away in the sink, if only a bomb
would explode you to bits.
Homework! Oh, homework!
You're giving me fits.

I'd rather take baths
with a man-eating shark, or wrestle a lion
alone in the dark,
eat spinach and liver,
pet ten porcupines,
than tackle the homework my teacher assigns.

Homework! Oh, homework! You're last on my list,
I simply can't see
why you even exist,

if you just disappeared
it would tickle me pink. Homework! Oh, homework!
    I hate you! You stink!

7 September ✶ Talk Us Through It, Charlotte ✶ Allan Ahlberg

Allan Ahlberg has written over twenty books for children over the course of his career, many of which were illustrated by his wife, Janet. You might know some of them, such as *The Jolly Postman* and *Each Peach Pear Plum*. The heroine of this poem outplays all of the boys on the field.

Well I shouldn't've been playin' really
Only there to watch me brother
My friend fancies his friend, y'know.
Anyway they was a man short.

Stay out on the wing, they said
Give 'em something to think about.
So I did that for about an hour;
Never passed to me or anything.

The ball kind of rebounded to me.
I thought, I'll have a little run with it.
I mean, they wasn't passin' to me
Was they? So off I went.

I ran past the first boy
He sort of fell over.
It was a bit slippery on that grass
I will say that for him.

Two more of 'em come at me
Only they sort of tackled each other
Collided – arh. I kept going.
There was this great big fat boy.

One way or another I kicked it
Through his legs and run round him.
That took a time. Me brother
Was shouting, Pass it to me, like.

Well like I said, I'd been there an hour.
They never give *me* a pass
Never even spoke to me
Or anything. So I kept going.

Beat this other boy somehow
Then there was just the goalie.
Out he came, spreadin' himself
As they say. I was really worried.

I thought he was going to hug me.
So I dipped me shoulder like they do
And the goalie moved one way, y'know
And I slammed it in the net.

Turned out afterwards it was the winner.
The manager said I was very good.
He wants me down at trainin' on Tuesday.
My friend says she's comin' as well.

'Arithmetic' is the name for the part of Maths that deals with addition, subtraction, multiplication and division. Can you work any of these sums out?

Arithmetic is where numbers fly like pigeons in and out of your
  head.
Arithmetic tells you how many you lose or win if you know how
  many you had before you lost or won.
Arithmetic is seven eleven all good children go to heaven — or
  five six bundle of sticks.
Arithmetic is numbers you squeeze from your head to your
  hand to your pencil to your paper till you get the answer.
Arithmetic is where the answer is right and everything is nice
  and you can look out of the window and see the blue sky —
  or the answer is wrong and you have to start all over and try
  again and see how it comes out this time.
If you take a number and double it and double it again and then
  double it a few more times, the number gets bigger and bigger
  and goes higher and higher and only arithmetic can tell you
  what the number is when you decide to quit doubling.
Arithmetic is where you have to multiply — and you carry the
  multiplication table in your head and hope you won't lose it.
If you have two animal crackers, one good and one bad, and you
  eat one and a striped zebra with streaks all over him eats the
  other, how many animal crackers will you have if somebody
  offers you five six seven and you say No no no and you say
  Nay nay nay and you say Nix nix nix?
If you ask your mother for one fried egg for breakfast and she
  gives you two fried eggs and you eat both of them, who is
  better in arithmetic, you or your mother?

9 September ✴ The Hurt Boy and the Birds ✴ John Agard

This poem takes bullying as its subject. Unable to talk to humans, the boy in this poem finds strength and inspiration through talking to birds.

The hurt boy talked to the birds
and fed them the crumbs of his heart.

It was not easy to find the words
for secrets he hid under his skin.
The hurt boy spoke of a bully's fist
that made his face a bruised moon –
his spectacles stamped to ruin.

It was not easy to find the words
for things that nightly hissed
as if his pillow was a hideaway for creepy-crawlies –
the note sent to the girl he fancied
held high in mockery.

But the hurt boy talked to the birds
and their feathers gave him welcome –

Their wings taught him new ways to become.

10 September ✳ The Sorting Hat Song ✳
J. K. Rowling

Ever since *Harry Potter and the Philosopher's Stone* was
published in 1997, J. K Rowling's series about the young
students at the Hogwarts School of Witchcraft and Wizardry
have been hugely popular. The Sorting Hat is a magical talking
hat that decides which of the four Hogwarts houses –
Gryffindor, Ravenclaw, Hufflepuff and Slytherin – new
students are assigned to. The Sorting Hat sings a song during
the opening banquet at the beginning of the school year, and
this is the song that appears in the first book.

Oh you may not think I'm pretty,
But don't judge on what you see,
I'll eat myself if you can find
A smarter hat than me.
You can keep your bowlers black,
Your top hats sleek and tall,
For I'm the Hogwarts Sorting Hat
And I can cap them all.
There's nothing hidden in your head
The Sorting Hat can't see,
So try me on and I will tell you
Where you ought to be.
You might belong in Gryffindor,
Where dwell the brave at heart,
Their daring, nerve, and chivalry
Set Gryffindors apart;
You might belong in Hufflepuff,
Where they are just and loyal,
Those patient Hufflepuffs are true
And unafraid of toil;

Or yet in wise old Ravenclaw,
if you've a ready mind,
Where those of wit and learning,
Will always find their kind;
Or perhaps in Slytherin
You'll make your real friends,
Those cunning folks use any means
To achieve their ends.
So put me on! Don't be afraid!
And don't get in a flap!
You're in safe hands (though I have none)
For I'm a Thinking Cap!

11 September ✳ The Convergence of the Twain ✳ Simon Armitage

This poem by Simon Armitage was written as a memorial to the events of 11 September 2001, when four passenger aircraft were hijacked and crashed, with two of the planes hitting the twin towers of the World Trade Center in New York. In this poem, Armitage adopts the same style as Thomas Hardy's poem of the same title, which you can find as the entry for 15 April, which also commemorated a disaster: the sinking of the *Titanic* in 1912.

I

Here is an architecture of air.
Where dust has cleared,
nothing stands but free sky, unlimited and sheer.

II

Smoke's dark bruise
has paled, soothed
by wind, dabbed at and eased by rain, exposing the wound.

III

Over the spoil of junk,
rescuers prod and pick,
shout into tangled holes. What answers back is aftershock.

IV

All land lines are down.
Reports of mobile phones
are false. One half-excoriated Apple Mac still quotes the Dow
  Jones.

Shop windows are papered
with faces of the disappeared.
As if they might walk from the ruins – chosen, spared.

VI

With hindsight now we track
the vapour-trail of each flight-path
arcing through blue morning, like a curved thought.

VII

And in retrospect plot
the weird prospect
of a passenger plane beading an office-block.

VIII

But long before that dawn,
with those towers drawing
in worth and name to their full height, an opposite was forming,

IX

a force
still years and miles off,
yet moving headlong forwards, locked on a collision course.

X

Then time and space
contracted, so whatever distance
held those worlds apart thinned to an instant.

XI

During which, cameras framed
moments of grace
before the furious contact wherein earth and heaven fused.

12 September ✶ On the Other Side of the Door ✶ Jeff Moss

The American writer Jeff Moss was perhaps best known for his award-winning work on the children's television programme *Sesame Street*. He was also the writer of several collections of children's poetry.

On the other side of the door
I can be a different me,
As smart and as brave and as funny or strong
As a person could want to be.
There's nothing too hard for me to do,
There's no place I can't explore
Because everything can happen
On the other side of the door.

On the other side of the door
I don't have to go alone.
If you come, too, we can sail tall ships
And fly where the wind has flown.
And wherever we go, it is almost sure
We'll find what we're looking for
Because everything can happen
On the other side of the door.

13 September ✷ Now I Lay Me Down to Sleep ✷
Anon.

This prayer-poem dates from the eighteenth century, when Christian children were taught to pray at bedtime for their safety and the safety of the ones they loved.

> Now I lay me down to sleep,
> I pray the Lord my soul to keep,
> If I should die before I wake
> I pray the Lord my soul to take.

14 September ✶ Psalm 23

'The Lord is my Shepherd' is among the most recognized of the poems contained in the Book of Psalms. Psalm 23 takes as its subject the relationship between God and man, comparing it to the relationship between a shepherd and his sheep. Psalms such as this one would have been treasured by the Puritan pilgrims who set sail for America around this date in September 1620: their journey across the Atlantic in search of a new life was a leap of faith, and the comfort of a deep trust in a loving God would have been indispensable.

The Lord is my shepherd; I shall not want.
He maketh me to lie down in green pastures: he leadeth me
    beside the still waters.
He restoreth my soul: he leadeth me in the paths of
    righteousness for his name's sake.
Yea, though I walk through the valley of the shadow of death,
    I will fear no evil: for thou art with me; thy rod and thy staff
    they comfort me.
Thou preparest a table before me in the presence of mine
    enemies: thou anointest my head with oil; my cup runneth
    over.
Surely goodness and mercy shall follow me all the days of my
    life: and I will dwell in the house of the Lord for ever.

15 September ✷ The Lord's Prayer

The Lord's Prayer is a prayer given by Jesus to his disciples during the Sermon on the Mount.

> Our Father, which art in heaven,
> Hallowed be thy Name.
> Thy Kingdom come.
> Thy will be done in earth,
> As it is in heaven.
> Give us this day our daily bread.
> And forgive us our trespasses,
> As we forgive them that trespass against us.
> And lead us not into temptation,
> But deliver us from evil.
> For thine is the kingdom,
> The power, and the glory,
> For ever and ever.
> Amen.

16 September ✳ The Iroquois Prayer

This prayer of thanks is a tradition passed on by the Iroquois, a confederacy of Native American tribes who lived in upstate New York and the area surrounding the Great Lakes before the advent of the modern United States. There are still Iroquois communities living in Canada and America.

We return thanks to our mother, the earth, which sustains us.
We return thanks to the rivers and streams, which supply us
    with water.
We return thanks to all herbs, which furnish medicines for the
    cure of our diseases.
We return thanks to the corn, and to her sisters, the beans and
    squash, which give us life. We return thanks to the bushes
    and trees, which provide us with fruit.
We return thanks to the wind which, moving the air, has
    banished diseases.
We return thanks to the moon and the stars, which have given
    us their light when the sun was gone.
We return thanks to our grandfather He-no, who has given to
    us his rain.
We return thanks to the sun, that he has looked upon the earth
    with a beneficent eye. Lastly, we return thanks to the Great
    Spirit, in whom is embodied all goodness, and who directs
    all things for the good of his children.

17 September ✶ The Easterner's Prayer

This anonymous poem purports to be an English version of a Muslim prayer. It is not, however, a translation; references to the fact that the speaker is not actually an 'Easterner' both open and close the poem.

I pray the prayer the Easterners do —
May the peace of Allah abide with you!
Wherever you stay, wherever you go,
May the beautiful palms of Allah grow,
Through days of labour and nights of rest,
The love of good Allah make you blest,
So I touch my heart as Easterners do —
May the peace of Allah abide with you!
Salaam Alaikum
(Peace be unto you).

18 September ✳ The Mool Mantar

Sikhism first developed in South Asia during the fifteenth century, and today there are over 25 million Sikhs living throughout the world. The Mool Mantar is the first line of the sacred book of the Sikhs, the Guru Granth Sahib; it outlines the basic beliefs of Sikhism regarding the nature of God as omnipresent and eternal.

Ik Onkar
There is only one God
Sat Nam
Eternal truth is His name
Karta Purakh
He is the creator
Nir Bhau
He is without fear
Nir Vair
He is without hate
Akal Murat
Immortal, without form
Ajuni
Beyond birth and death
Saibhang
He is the enlightener
Gur Prasaad
He can be reached through the mercy
    and grace of the true Guru

19 September ✶ Now May Every Living Thing

With over 370 million followers worldwide, Buddhism is one of the world's major religions, and is centred on the teachings of Buddha, Siddhartha Gautama, who embarked on a quest for enlightenment around the sixth century BC. He is thought to have written the simple blessing printed here. While there are many different forms of Buddhism, and specific teachings vary accordingly, there are some important tenets which are shared between them all: a belief in pacifism and the importance of living a non-violent life; the notion that nothing is permanent or fixed, and that change is always possible; and an emphasis on the importance of meditation and self-development in order to reach a state of enlightenment, known as nirvana.

Now may every living thing, young or old,
weak or strong, living near or far, known or
unknown, living or departed or yet unborn,
may every living thing be full of bliss.

20 September ✶ Tichborne's Elegy ✶
Chidiock Tichborne

Chidiock Tichborne was executed on 20 September 1586 for his involvement in a plot to murder Queen Elizabeth I and replace her with the Catholic Mary Queen of Scots. On the eve of his execution, Tichborne wrote a letter to his wife Agnes in which he included this elegy.

My prime of youth is but a frost of cares;
My feast of joy is but a dish of pain,
My crop of corn is but a field of tares,
And all my good is but vain hope of gain:
The day is past, and yet I saw no sun,
And now I live, and now my life is done.

My tale was heard, and yet it was not told,
My fruit is fallen, and yet my leaves are green,
My youth is spent, and yet I am not old,
I saw the world, and yet I was not seen:
My thread is cut, and yet it is not spun,
And now I live, and now my life is done.

I sought my death, and found it in my womb,
I looked for life, and saw it was a shade,
I trod the earth, and knew it was my tomb,
And now I die, and now I was but made;
The glass is full, and now the glass is run,
And now I live, and now my life is done.

21 September ✳ Pied Beauty ✳
Gerard Manley Hopkins

In this poem, Gerard Manley Hopkins uses 'dappled things'
to mean those that are not traditionally considered beautiful,
defending diversity and variety.

Glory be to God for dappled things –
  For skies of couple-colour as a brinded cow;
    For rose-moles all in stipple upon trout that swim;
Fresh-firecoal chestnut-falls; finches' wings;
  Landscape plotted and pieced – fold, fallow, and plough;
    And áll trádes, their gear and tackle and trim.

All things counter, original, spare, strange;
  Whatever is fickle, freckled (who knows how?)
    With swift, slow; sweet, sour; adazzle, dim;
He fathers-forth whose beauty is past change:
                Praise him.

22 September ✳ *from* Meditation XVII ✳
John Donne

On 22 September 1735, Robert Walpole, who is considered
the first Prime Minister of Great Britain, took up residence in
10 Downing Street — a town house in central London which,
to this day, is the official home of the British Prime Minister.
Edward Heath, who was the British Prime Minster from 1970–
1974, quoted these famous (prose) lines by John Donne and
added, 'Today no island is an island. That applies as much to
the price of bread as it does to political influence.'

No man is an island entire of itself; every man is a piece of
the continent, a part of the main; if a clod be washed away
by the sea, Europe is the less, as well as if a promontory
were, as well as any manner of thy friends or of thine
own were; any man's death diminishes me, because I am
involved in mankind. And therefore never send to know for
whom the bell tolls; it tolls for thee.

23 September ✳ When I Heard the Learn'd Astronomer ✳ Walt Whitman

On this day in 1846, the German astronomer Johann Gottfried Galle discovered the planet Neptune. An 'astronomer' is a scientist who studies stars, planets and space. Walt Whitman wrote this poem in 1865, so the astronomer in this poem might have mentioned Neptune in his lecture.

When I heard the learn'd astronomer,
When the proofs, the figures, were ranged in columns
     before me,
When I was shown the charts and diagrams, to add, divide,
     and measure them,
When I sitting heard the astronomer where he lectured
     with much applause in the lecture-room,
How soon unaccountable I became tired and sick,
Till rising and gliding out I wander'd off by myself,
In the mystical moist night-air, and from time to time,
Look'd up in perfect silence at the stars.

24 September ✳ A Psalm of Life ✳
Henry Wadsworth Longfellow

On this day in 1940, King George VI instituted the George Cross – a silver cross-shaped medal that could be awarded for acts of heroism outside the battlefield. This inspirational poem by the American writer Henry Wadsworth Longfellow encourages its audience to be positive and heroic in life, in 'the world's broad field of battle'.

What the Heart of the Young Man
Said to the Psalmist.

Tell me not, in mournful numbers,
 'Life is but an empty dream!'
For the soul is dead that slumbers,
 And things are not what they seem.

Life is real! Life is earnest!
 And the grave is not its goal;
'Dust thou art, to dust returnest,'
 Was not spoken of the soul.

Not enjoyment, and not sorrow,
 Is our destined end or way;
But to act, that each to-morrow
 Find us farther than to-day.

Art is long, and Time is fleeting,
 And our hearts, though stout and brave,
Still, like muffled drums, are beating
 Funeral marches to the grave.

In the world's broad field of battle,
    In the bivouac of Life,
Be not like dumb, driven cattle!
    Be a hero in the strife!

Trust no Future, howe'er pleasant!
    Let the dead Past bury its dead!
Act,— act in the living Present!
    Heart within, and God o'erhead!

Lives of great men all remind us
    We can make our lives sublime,
And, departing, leave behind us
    Footprints on the sands of time;

Footprints, that perhaps another,
    Sailing o'er life's solemn main,
A forlorn and shipwrecked brother,
    Seeing, shall take heart again.

Let us, then, be up and doing,
    With a heart for any fate;
Still achieving, still pursuing,
    Learn to labour and to wait.

25 September ✻ The Tyger ✻ William Blake

'The Tyger' is taken from William Blake's 1794 collection *Songs of Experience*, and is one of his most memorable poems. Blake's tiger is certainly terrifying, stalking 'the forests of the night' with its burning eyes.

Tyger, Tyger, burning bright,
In the forests of the night;
What immortal hand or eye
Could frame thy fearful symmetry?

In what distant deeps or skies.
Burnt the fire of thine eyes?
On what wings dare he aspire?
What the hand, dare seize the fire?

And what shoulder, & what art,
Could twist the sinews of thy heart?
And when thy heart began to beat,
What dread hand? & what dread feet?

What the hammer? what the chain?
In what furnace was thy brain?
What the anvil? what dread grasp,
Dare its deadly terrors clasp?

When the stars threw down their spears
And water'd heaven with their tears:
Did he smile his work to see?
Did he who made the Lamb make thee?

Tyger, Tyger, burning bright,
In the forests of the night:
What immortal hand or eye
Dare frame thy fearful symmetry?

26 September ✶ Astrophysics Lesson ✶ Ade Hall

Have you ever looked up at the night sky and wondered how it all works? How is the moon held in place, and why does it sometimes disappear? Why does the sun set, and how far away are those distantly twinkling stars? In this poem a school teacher uses fruit to try to demonstrate the positions of stars and planets.

I took an orange and a plum
To demonstrate the Earth and Sun;
held in place by gravity –
Our little planet, you and me.

I grabbed some grapes for all the stars
And cast them out so wide and far;
Distant suns and foreign moons
In all four corners of the room.

The wonders of the galaxy
Spread out before class 2BT.
'Where did they come from?' someone cried;
'From the fruit bowl' I replied.

27 September ✶ My Boy Jack ✶ Rudyard Kipling

John Kipling, who was known as Jack, was the only son of
the poet Rudyard Kipling. When the First World War broke
out in 1914, his father used his influence to get Jack a military
commission, despite his poor eyesight. Jack went missing
in the Battle of Loos on the 27 September 1915, six weeks
after his eighteenth birthday. His body was not found in the
aftermath of the battle, and it was not until 1992 that his grave
was identified in St Mary's Cemetery, Haisnes.

'Have you news of my boy Jack?'
    Not this tide.
'When d'you think that he'll come back?'
    Not with this wind blowing, and this tide.

'Has any one else had word of him?'
    Not this tide.
For what is sunk will hardly swim,
    Not with this wind blowing, and this tide.

'Oh, dear, what comfort can I find?'
    None this tide,
    Nor any tide,
Except he did not shame his kind—
    Not even with that wind blowing, and that tide.

Then hold your head up all the more,
    This tide,
    And every tide;
Because he was the son you bore,
    And gave to that wind blowing and that tide!

28 September ✶ Full Moon and Little Frieda ✶
Ted Hughes

Ted Hughes wrote this poem in the Summer of 1962, when he
was living in Devon. It describes an incident that happened in
the garden of his house, Court Green, with his young daughter
Frieda.

A cool small evening shrunk to a dog bark and the
    clank of a bucket –

And you listening.
A spider's web, tense for the dew's touch.
A pail lifted, still and brimming – mirror
To tempt a first star to a tremor.

Cows are going home in the lane there, looping the
    hedges with their warm wreaths of breath –
A dark river of blood, many boulders,
Balancing unspilled milk.

'Moon!' you cry suddenly, 'Moon! Moon!'

The moon has stepped back like an artist gazing
    amazed at a work

That points at him amazed.

29 September ✳ The Song of Mr Toad ✳ Kenneth Grahame

Kenneth Grahame is best known for writing *The Wind in the Willows*, a much-loved children's classic documenting the adventures of four characterful animals: Rat, Mole, Badger and the subject of this poem, the charismatic but bonkers Mr Toad.

The world has held great Heroes,
As history-books have showed;
But never a name to go down to fame
Compared with that of Toad!

The clever men at Oxford
Know all that there is to be knowed.
But they none of them knew one half as much
As intelligent Mr Toad!

The animals sat in the Ark and cried,
Their tears in torrents flowed.
Who was it said, 'There's land ahead'?
Encouraging Mr Toad!

The Army all saluted
As they marched along the road.
Was it the King? Or Kitchener?
No. It was Mr Toad!

The Queen and her Ladies-in-waiting
Sat at the window and sewed.
She cried, 'Look! who's that handsome man?'
They answered, 'Mr Toad.'

30 September ✳ Thirty Days Hath September ✳
Michael Rosen

This rhyming couplet makes fun of the famous rhyme for remembering how many days there are in each month. The speaker of this poem only manages one month out of twelve – luckily his ability to find rhymes is much stronger than his memory!

> Thirty days hath September,
> All the rest I can't remember.

October

1 October ∗ The Pheasant ∗ Sylvia Plath

In this poem, the American poet Sylvia Plath is addressing
her husband, Ted Hughes. Hughes was a keen game-shooter,
having grown up in the Yorkshire countryside, and Plath is
asking him not to kill the pheasant of the poem's title.

You said you would kill it this morning.
Do not kill it. It startles me still,
The jut of that odd, dark head, pacing

Through the uncut grass on the elm's hill.
It is something to own a pheasant,
Or just to be visited at all.

I am not mystical: it isn't
As if I thought it had a spirit.
It is simply in its element.

That gives it a kingliness, a right.
The print of its big foot last winter,
The trail-track, on the snow in our court

The wonder of it, in that pallor,
Through crosshatch of sparrow and starling.
Is it its rareness, then? It is rare.

But a dozen would be worth having,
A hundred, on that hill – green and red,
Crossing and recrossing: a fine thing!

It is such a good shape, so vivid.
It's a little cornucopia.
It unclaps, brown as a leaf, and loud,

Settles in the elm, and is easy.
It was sunning in the narcissi.
I trespass stupidly. Let be, let be.

2 October ✴ Fall, Leaves, Fall ✴ Emily Brontë

Emily Brontë was a poet and novelist who lived in the West Riding of Yorkshire, England, for most of her life. She is best known for her novel, *Wuthering Heights*, which was published in 1847.

Fall, leaves, fall; die, flowers, away;
Lengthen night and shorten day;
Every leaf speaks bliss to me
Fluttering from the autumn tree.
I shall smile when wreaths of snow
Blossom where the rose should grow;
I shall sing when night's decay
Ushers in a drearier day.

3 October ✶ Pencil and Paint ✶ Eleanor Farjeon

In the two verses of this poem, Eleanor Farjeon uses drawing and painting to compare the visual differences between Autumn and Winter.

> Winter has a pencil
> For pictures clear and neat,
> She traces the black tree-tops
> Upon a snowy sheet.
>
> But autumn has a palette
> And a painting-brush instead,
> And daubs the leaves for pleasure
> With yellow, brown, and red.

4 October ✶ St Francis and the Birds ✶
Seamus Heaney

St Francis of Assisi was the founder of the Franciscan order of
the Catholic Church, and he is remembered and celebrated for
his special relationship with animals, which is what Seamus
Heaney is drawing on in this poem. He is also known for his
generosity to the poor and his willingness to help lepers. He
died on 4 October 1226, and he was canonized as a saint
in 1228.

When Francis preached love to the birds
They listened, fluttered, throttled up
Into the blue like a flock of words
Released for fun from his holy lips.
Then wheeled back, whirred about his head,
Pirouetted on brothers' capes.
Danced on the wing, for sheer joy played
And sang, like images took flight.
Which was the best poem Francis made,
His argument true, his tone light.

5 October ∗ Abou Ben Adhem ∗ Leigh Hunt

Abou Ben Adhem was a Muslim mystic – also known as a
Sufi – who lived in Persia, and was venerated as a saint
after his death, which happened around AD 777. He is often
compared to St Francis of Assisi, because he gave up a
luxurious life in favour of one devoted to prayer and helping
his fellow man.

Abou Ben Adhem (may his tribe increase!)
Awoke one night from a deep dream of peace,
And saw, within the moonlight in his room,
Making it rich, and like a lily in bloom,
An angel writing in a book of gold:—
Exceeding peace had made Ben Adhem bold,
And to the presence in the room he said,
'What writest thou?'—The vision raised its head,
And with a look made of all sweet accord,
Answered, 'The names of those who love the Lord.'
'And is mine one?' said Abou. 'Nay, not so,'
Replied the angel. Abou spoke more low,
But cheerly still; and said, 'I pray thee, then,
Write me as one that loves his fellow men.'

The angel wrote, and vanished. The next night
It came again with a great wakening light,
And showed the names whom love of God had blest,
And lo! Ben Adhem's name led all the rest.

6 October ✳ Messages ✳ Matt Goodfellow

National Poetry Day in the UK usually falls on the first
Thursday in October. This poem was especially written for
National Poetry Day 2016's theme: 'messages'.

look closely and you'll find them
everywhere

in fields of patterned grasses
drafted by the hare

embroidered by the bluebells
through a wood

in scattered trails of blossom
stamped into the mud

scorched by heather-fire
across the moors

in looping snail-trails
scrawled on forest floors

scored across the sky
by screaming swifts

in rolling, twisting peaks
of drifting mountain mist

scribbled by an ocean
on the sand

look closely: you will see
and understand

7 October ✳ Birthday ✳ Rachel Rooney

Autumn is a time when the wind starts blowing strongly, pulling leaves off trees and turning umbrellas inside out. In this poem Rachel Rooney personifies the wind, transforming it into a character having a tantrum on their birthday.

Wind was angry,
slammed the door.
Smash went the glass
on the kitchen floor.

Out in the garden
Wind shook trees,
kicked up a fuss
and a pile of leaves.

Wind was howling,
started to shout.
Who blew the candles
on my birthday cake out?

8 October ✳ Lord Ullin's Daughter ✳
Thomas Campbell

This ballad by Thomas Campbell, set in the Scottish highlands, tells the tale of a dangerous journey through a storm. While the autumnal wind in the previous poem knocks over glasses and slams doors, in 'Lord Ullin's Daughter' the storm impacts the lives of those who travel in it in a far more tragic way.

A Chieftain, to the Highlands bound,
　　Cries, 'Boatman, do not tarry;
And I'll give thee a silver pound
　　To row us o'er the ferry.'

'Now who be ye would cross Lochgyle,
　　This dark and stormy water?'
'Oh! I'm the chief of Ulva's isle,
　　And this Lord Ullin's daughter.

'And fast before her father's men
　　Three days we've fled together,
For should he find us in the glen,
　　My blood would stain the heather.

'His horsemen hard behind us ride;
　　Should they our steps discover,
Then who will cheer my bonny bride
　　When they have slain her lover?'

Outspoke the hardy Highland wight:
　　'I'll go, my chief – I'm ready:
It is not for your silver bright,
　　But for your winsome lady.

'And by my word, the bonny bird
    In danger shall not tarry:
So, though the waves are raging white,
    I'll row you o'er the ferry.'

By this the storm grew loud apace,
    The water-wraith was shrieking;
And in the scowl of heaven each face
    Grew dark as they were speaking.

But still, as wilder blew the wind,
    And as the night grew drearer,
Adown the glen rode armed men –
    Their trampling sounded nearer.

'Oh! Haste thee, haste!' the lady cries,
    'Though tempests round us gather;
I'll meet the raging of the skies,
    But not an angry father.'

The boat has left a stormy land,
    A stormy sea before her –
When oh! Too strong for human hand,
    The tempest gathered o'er her.

And still they rowed amidst the roar
    Of waters fast prevailing;
Lord Ullin reach'd that fatal shore –
    His wrath was chang'd to wailing.

For sore dismay'd, through storm and shade,
    His child he did discover;
One lovely hand she stretch'd for aid,
    And one was round her lover.

'Come back! Come back!' he cried in grief,
    'Across this stormy water;
And I'll forgive your Highland chief,
    My daughter! – oh, my daughter!'

'Twas vain: the loud waves lash'd the shore,
    Return or aid preventing;
The waters wild went o'er his child,
    And he was left lamenting.

9 October ✷ She Dwelt Among the Untrodden Ways ✷ William Wordsworth

This short lyric is one of Wordsworth's series of five poems that focused upon unrequited love for the eponymous Lucy, who may or may not have actually existed.

She dwelt among the untrodden ways
    Beside the springs of Dove,
A Maid whom there were none to praise
    And very few to love:

A violet by a mossy stone
    Half hidden from the eye!
– Fair as a star, when only one
    Is shining in the sky.

She lived unknown, and few could know
    When Lucy ceased to be;
But she is in her grave, and, oh,
    The difference to me!

10 October ✳ Xbox, Xbox – A Love Poem ✳
Kenn Nesbitt

Ada Lovelace was a talented British mathematician, and daughter of poet Lord Byron. She is widely considered to be the first computer programmer due to her significant work in the 1830s on her friend Babbage's Analytical Engine. Ada Lovelace Day, the annual commemoration of her and her achievements, falls in October, and also celebrates the ongoing achievements of women in Science, Technology, Mathematics and Engineering.

Xbox, Xbox,
you're the one for me.
I also love my 3DS
and my Nintendo Wii.

GameCube, GameBoy,
Apple iPod Touch.
I never thought that I would ever
be in love this much.

Pac-Man, Sonic,
Mario, and Link.
Your names are etched inside my mind
in everlasting ink.

Run, jump, flip, hang,
double-jump, and climb.
That's all I want to do
with every second of my time.

This is true love.
Yes, it's plain to see.
Xbox, Xbox,
will you marry me?

11 October ✶ Kubla Khan ✶
Samuel Taylor Coleridge

Written in October 1797 but not published until 1816, Samuel
Taylor Coleridge claimed that 'Kubla Khan' was inspired by
a dream. In a preface to his 1816 collection, he describes how
he woke from his dream with a 'distinct recollection' and
'eagerly wrote down the lines that are here preserved', before
he was interrupted by 'a person on business from Porlock'. On
returning to his writing an hour later, however, he found that
his trance had been broken.

In Xanadu did Kubla Khan
A stately pleasure-dome decree:
Where Alph, the sacred river, ran
Through caverns measureless to man
  Down to a sunless sea.
So twice five miles of fertile ground
With walls and towers were girdled round;
And there were gardens bright with sinuous rills,
Where blossomed many an incense-bearing tree;
And here were forests ancient as the hills,
Enfolding sunny spots of greenery.

But oh! that deep romantic chasm which slanted
Down the green hill athwart a cedarn cover!
A savage place! as holy and enchanted
As e'er beneath a waning moon was haunted
By woman wailing for her demon-lover!
And from this chasm, with ceaseless turmoil seething,
As if this earth in fast thick pants were breathing,
A mighty fountain momently was forced:
Amid whose swift half-intermitted burst
Huge fragments vaulted like rebounding hail,

Or chaffy grain beneath the thresher's flail:
And 'mid these dancing rocks at once and ever
It flung up momently the sacred river.
Five miles meandering with a mazy motion
Through wood and dale the sacred river ran,
Then reached the caverns measureless to man,
And sank in tumult to a lifeless ocean;
And 'mid this tumult Kubla heard from far
Ancestral voices prophesying war!
  The shadow of the dome of pleasure
  Floated midway on the waves;
  Where was heard the mingled measure
  From the fountain and the caves.
It was a miracle of rare device,
A sunny pleasure-dome with caves of ice!

  A damsel with a dulcimer
  In a vision once I saw:
  It was an Abyssinian maid
  And on her dulcimer she played,
  Singing of Mount Abora.
  Could I revive within me
  Her symphony and song,
  To such a deep delight 'twould win me,
That with music loud and long,
I would build that dome in air,
That sunny dome! those caves of ice!
And all who heard should see them there,
And all should cry, Beware! Beware!
His flashing eyes, his floating hair!
Weave a circle round him thrice,
And close your eyes with holy dread
For he on honey-dew hath fed,
And drunk the milk of Paradise.

12 October ✶ Ozymandias ✶ Percy Bysshe Shelley

Similarly to Coleridge's 'Kubla Khan', Percy Bysshe Shelley's sonnet 'Ozymandias' takes as its subject a fantastical place in a distant land. The poem is the result of a sonnet competition between Shelley and his friend Horace Smith. They both wrote on the same topic: a huge ruined statue in Egypt.

I met a traveller from an antique land,
Who said: 'Two vast and trunkless legs of stone
Stand in the desert . . . Near them, on the sand,
Half sunk, a shattered visage lies, whose frown,
And wrinkled lip, and sneer of cold command,
Tell that its sculptor well those passions read
Which yet survive, stamped on these lifeless things,
The hand that mocked them, and the heart that fed;
And on the pedestal, these words appear:
'My name is Ozymandias, king of kings;
Look on my works, ye Mighty, and despair!'
Nothing beside remains. Round the decay
Of that colossal wreck, boundless and bare
The lone and level sands stretch far away.

13 October ✶ To Autumn ✶ John Keats

In 1819 John Keats wrote a celebrated series of odes, now regarded as some of the finest poetry in the English language, the last of which is 'To Autumn'. The 'ode' is a poetic form in which a particular subject in discussed and celebrated – alongside his ode to Autumn, Keats took as his subjects the goddess Psyche, a nightingale, a Grecian urn, and the emotion melancholy.

Season of mists and mellow fruitfulness,
　Close bosom-friend of the maturing sun;
Conspiring with him how to load and bless
　With fruit the vines that round the thatch-eves run;
To bend with apples the moss'd cottage-trees,
　And fill all fruit with ripeness to the core;
　　To swell the gourd, and plump the hazel shells
With a sweet kernel; to set budding more,
And still more, later flowers for the bees,
Until they think warm days will never cease,
　　For summer has o'er-brimm'd their clammy cells.

Who hath not seen thee oft amid thy store?
　Sometimes whoever seeks abroad may find
Thee sitting careless on a granary floor,
　Thy hair soft-lifted by the winnowing wind;
Or on a half-reap'd furrow sound asleep,
　Drows'd with the fume of poppies, while thy hook
　　Spares the next swath and all its twined flowers:
And sometimes like a gleaner thou dost keep
　Steady thy laden head across a brook;
　Or by a cyder-press, with patient look,
　　Thou watchest the last oozings hours by hours.

Where are the songs of Spring? Ay, where are they?
  Think not of them, thou hast thy music too,—
While barred clouds bloom the soft-dying day,
  And touch the stubble-plains with rosy hue;
Then in a wailful choir the small gnats mourn
  Among the river sallows, borne aloft
    Or sinking as the light wind lives or dies;
And full-grown lambs loud bleat from hilly bourn;
  Hedge-crickets sing; and now with treble soft
  The red-breast whistles from a garden-croft;
    And gathering swallows twitter in the skies.

14 October ✶ The Battle of Hastings ✶
Marriott Edgar

The Battle of Hastings was a day-long battle that occurred
on 14 October 1066 between the Anglo-Saxon English and
the Norman army, who were invading. The Normans were
victorious, and William, the Duke of Normandy – also known
as William the Conqueror – was crowned King William I of
England ten weeks later. This poem, however, does not take
this pivotal moment in history *too* seriously.

> I'll tell of the Battle of Hastings,
> As happened in days long gone by,
> When Duke William became King of England,
> And 'Arold got shot in the eye.
>
> It were this way – one day in October
> The Duke, who were always a toff,
> Having no battles on at the moment,
> Had given his lads a day off.
>
> They'd all taken boats to go fishing,
> When some chap in t' Conqueror's ear
> Said 'Let's go and put breeze up the Saxons;'
> Said Bill – 'By gum, that's an idea.'
>
> Then turning around to his soldiers,
> He lifted his big Norman voice,
> Shouting – 'Hands up who's coming to England.'
> That was swank cos they hadn't no choice.
>
> They started away about tea-time –
> The sea was so calm and so still,
> And at quarter to ten the next morning
> They arrived at a place called Bexhill.

King 'Arold came up as they landed –
His face full of venom and 'ate –
He said 'If you've come for Regatta
You've got here just six weeks too late.'

At this William rose, cool but 'aughty,
And said 'Give us none of your cheek;
You'd best have your throne re-upholstered,
I'll be wanting to use it next week.'

When 'Arold heard this 'ere defiance,
With rage he turned purple and blue,
And shouted some rude words in Saxon,
To which William answered – 'And you.'

'Twere a beautiful day for a battle;
The Normans set off with a will,
And when both sides was duly assembled,
They tossed for the top of the hill.

King 'Arold he won the advantage,
On the hill-top he took up his stand,
With his knaves and his cads all around him,
On his 'orse with his 'awk in his 'and.

The Normans had nowt in their favour,
Their chance of a victory seemed small,
For the slope of the field were against them,
And the wind in their faces an' all.

The kick-off were sharp at two-thirty,
And soon as the whistle had went
Both sides started banging each other
Till, the swineherds could hear them in Kent.

The Saxons had best line of forwards,
Well armed both with buckler and sword –
But the Normans had best combination,
And when half-time came neither had scored.

So the Duke called his cohorts together
And said – 'Let's pretend that we're beat,
Once we get Saxons down on the level
We'll cut off their means of retreat.'

So they ran – and the Saxons ran after,
Just exactly as William had planned,
Leaving 'Arold alone on the hill-top
On his 'orse with his 'awk in his 'and.

When the Conqueror saw what had happened,
A bow and an arrow he drew;
He went right up to 'Arold and shot him.
He were off-side, but what could they do?

The Normans turned round in a fury,
And gave back both parry and thrust,
Till the fight were all over bar shouting,
And you couldn't see Saxons for dust.

And after the battle were over
They found 'Arold so stately and grand,
Sitting there with an eye-full of arrow
On his 'orse with his 'awk in his 'and.

15 October ✷ When I Was One-and-Twenty ✷
A. E. Housman

This poem was published in A. E. Housman's *A Shropshire Lad* and, like many of the poems in that collection, it is narrated by a speaker looking back on his youth. Here he regrets not listening to some wise advice.

When I was one-and-twenty
    I heard a wise man say,
'Give crowns and pounds and guineas
    But not your heart away;
Give pearls away and rubies
    But keep your fancy free.'
But I was one-and-twenty,
    No use to talk to me.

When I was one-and-twenty
    I heard him say again,
'The heart out of the bosom
    Was never given in vain;
'Tis paid with sighs a plenty
    And sold for endless rue.'
And I am two-and-twenty,
    And oh, 'tis true, 'tis true.

16 October ✶ l (a ✶ E. E. Cummings

In this poem a simple Autumnal image is transformed into a visual riddle. We cannot just read this poem – we have to decipher it. Cummings breaks up each word of his poem, placing fragments of words on separate lines. With the longest line being the last ('iness'), reading this poem is like watching a leaf drift down from a tree before settling on the ground.

> l (a
>
> le
> af
> fa
> ll
>
> s)
> one
> l
>
> iness

17 October ✷ Spiderweb ✷ Kay Ryan

Kay Ryan is an award-winning American poet who often writes short poems, avoiding the first-person 'I'. At first, this poem appears to be a detailed description of the spider's work as it weaves its web, encouraging the reader to inhabit the spider's mind, rather than the human's. The final two sentences of the poem, however, move the focus of the poem outwards, drawing out a similarity between life of all kinds – humans, animals, and even arachnoid!

From other
angles the
fibers look
fragile, but
not from the
spider's, always
hauling coarse
ropes, hitching
lines to the
best posts
possible. It's
heavy work
everyplace,
fighting sag,
winching up
give. It
isn't ever
delicate
to live.

18 October * Someone * Walter de la Mare

This poem by Walter de la Mare has a similar theme to 'The Listeners' (*see* 2 August). This time, the narrator of the poem is roused from his sleep by a knock at the door but, when he goes to answer, he realizes that there is nobody there. The descriptions of the natural world outside the door, however, suggests that the narrator is not really alone, as the nocturnal world is full of creatures.

Someone came knocking
At my wee, small door;
Someone came knocking;
I'm sure, sure, sure;
I listened, I opened,
I looked to left and right,
But nought there was a stirring
In the still dark night;
Only the busy beetle
Tap-tapping in the wall,
Only from the forest
The screech-owl's call,
Only the cricket whistling
While the dewdrops fall,
So I know not who came knocking,
At all, at all, at all.

19 October ✳ A Prayer for Travellers ✳ Anon.

Gaelic is a Celtic language spoken in Ireland, and this is a traditional Irish Gaelic prayer. Celtic literature often uses natural imagery to illustrate God interacting with his people, as can be seen in this poem. 'May the road rise up to meet you' wishes travellers good luck for their upcoming journeys.

> May the road rise up to meet you.
> May the wind be always at your back.
> May the sun shine warm upon your face;
> The rains fall soft upon your fields.
> And until we meet again,
> May God hold you in the palm of His hand.

20 October ✳ The Guest House ✳ Rumi, translated by Reynold A. Nicholson

In this poem it almost sounds as if the thirteenth-century Persian poet Rumi is telling his readers to embrace dark thoughts, shame and malice. But what he is really saying is to 'invite them in'; don't ignore your feelings. They may be of some higher significance.

> This being human is a guest house,
> Every morning a new arrival.
>
> A joy, a depression, a meanness,
> some momentary awareness comes
> as an unexpected visitor.
>
> Welcome and entertain them all!
> Even if they are a crowd of sorrows,
> who violently sweep your house
> empty of its furniture,
> still treat each guest honourably.
> He may be clearing you out for some new delight.
>
> The dark thought, the shame, the malice,
> meet them at the door laughing,
> and invite them in.
>
> Be grateful for whoever comes,
> because each has been sent
> as a guide from beyond.

21 October ✳ *from* The Battle of Trafalgar ✳ William King

The Battle of Trafalgar was a naval battle fought between British forces and the combined navies of Spain and France on 21 October 1805. Before the battle, the commander of the British Navy, Admiral Horatio Nelson, sent a terse communication to his forces: 'England expects that every man will do his duty'. Though Nelson was killed during the battle, the outcome was a resounding victory for the British, who destroyed the French and Spanish forces without losing a ship.

The last great signal Nelson did unfold,
Albion, record! in characters of gold!
'England expects that ev'ry man this day,
Will do his duty and his worth display.'
Warm'd at the words, brave Nelson's gallant crew
Mow'd down whole hosts! and heaps of heroes slew;
Like grateful sons – obeyed their gallant chief
Whilst the lost hero filled their souls with grief.

22 October ✳ Inscription on the Monument of a Newfoundland Dog ✳ George Gordon, Lord Byron

Dogs are often said to be 'man's best friend'. Lord Byron wrote this poem as an epitaph to his Newfoundland, Boatswain, and it can be found inscribed on the dog's tomb at Newstead Abbey, Byron's estate. Even though Boatswain died of rabies, which is highly infectious, reports from the time record that Byron nursed him personally until his death.

When some proud son of man returns to earth,
Unknown to glory but upheld by birth,
The sculptor's art exhausts the pomp of woe,
And storied urns record who rests below:
When all is done, upon the tomb is seen
Not what he was, but what he should have been.
But the poor dog, in life the firmest friend,
The first to welcome, foremost to defend,
Whose honest heart is still his master's own,
Who labours, fights, lives, breathes for him alone,
Unhonour'd falls, unnotic'd all his worth,
Denied in heaven the soul he held on earth,
While man, vain insect! hopes to be forgiven,
And claims himself a sole exclusive heaven.
Oh man! thou feeble tenant of an hour,
Debas'd by slavery, or corrupt by power,
Who knows thee well, must quit thee with disgust,
Degraded mass of animated dust!
Thy love is lust, thy friendship all a cheat,
Thy smiles hypocrisy, thy words deceit!
By nature vile, ennobled but by name,
Each kindred brute might bid thee blush for shame.
Ye! who behold perchance this simple urn,
Pass on – it honours none you wish to mourn.
To mark a friend's remains these stones arise;
I never knew but one – and here he lies.

23 October * El Alamein * John Jarmain

During World War Two, on 23 October 1942, the Battle of
El Alamein began in North Africa. The British commander
Montgomery led the Eighth Army to victory over German
Field Marshal Rommel's Afrika Korps, and it proved to be a
turning point in the war in Africa. An army officer and a war
poet, John Jarmain wrote this poem a year after fighting at El
Alamein. Tragically he was killed by shrapnel in Normandy in
June 1944, when he was just thirty-three.

There are flowers now, they say, at Alamein;
Yes, flowers in the minefields now.
So those that come to view that vacant scene,
Where death remains and agony has been
Will find the lilies grow –
Flowers, and nothing that we know.

So they rang the bells for us and Alamein,
Bells which we could not hear:
And to those that heard the bells, what could it mean,
That name of loss and pride, El Alamein?
– Not the murk and harm of war,
But their hope, their own warm prayer.

It will become a staid historic name,
That crazy sea of sand!
Like Troy or Agincourt its single fame
Will be the garland for our brow, our claim,
On us a fleck of glory to the end:
And there our dead will keep their holy ground.

But this is not the place that we recall,
The crowded desert crossed with foaming tracks,
The one blotched building, lacking half a wall,
The grey-faced men, sand powdered over all;
The tanks, the guns, the trucks,
The black, dark-smoking wrecks.

So be it: none but us has known that land:
El Alamein will still be only ours
And those ten days of chaos in the sand.
Others will come who cannot understand,
Will halt beside the rusty minefield wires
And find there – flowers.

24 October ✳ *from* Henry V ✳ William Shakespeare

This is Shakespeare's version of a rousing speech delivered by King Henry V of England before the battle of Agincourt in 1415. In Shakespeare's play, it is a response to one of Henry's noblemen, the Earl of Westmoreland, who worries that the English army are heavily outnumbered by the French. St Crispin's Day actually falls on 25 October, but it appears here a day early as the Battle of Balaclava was also fought on that day.

This day is called the feast of Crispian:
He that outlives this day, and comes safe home,
Will stand a tip-toe when the day is named,
And rouse him at the name of Crispian.
He that shall live this day, and see old age,
Will yearly on the vigil feast his neighbours,
And say, 'To-morrow is Saint Crispian.'
Then will he strip his sleeve and show his scars,
And say, 'These wounds I had on Crispin's day.'
Old men forget; yet all shall be forgot,
But he'll remember with advantages
What feats he did that day. Then shall our names,
Familiar in his mouth as household words –
Harry the King, Bedford and Exeter,
Warwick and Talbot, Salisbury and Gloucester –
Be in their flowing cups freshly remember'd.
This story shall the good man teach his son;
And Crispin Crispian shall ne'er go by,
From this day to the ending of the world,
But we in it shall be remembered;
We few, we happy few, we band of brothers;
For he today that sheds his blood with me
Shall be my brother; be he ne'er so vile,

This day shall gentle his condition;
And gentlemen in England now a-bed
Shall think themselves accursed they were not here,
And hold their manhoods cheap whiles any speaks
That fought with us upon Saint Crispin's day.

25 October ✶ The Charge of the Light Brigade ✶ Alfred, Lord Tennyson

Alfred, Lord Tennyson, wrote 'The Charge of the Light Brigade' after reading a newspaper account of the disastrous British cavalry charge against Russian forces at the Battle of Balaclava, which was fought on 25 October 1854. The ill-fated charge was the result of a miscommunication in the chain of command, and many of the 600 soldiers died.

Half a league, half a league,
  Half a league onward,
All in the valley of Death
  Rode the six hundred.
'Forward, the Light Brigade!
Charge for the guns!' he said.
Into the valley of Death
  Rode the six hundred.

'Forward, the Light Brigade!'
Was there a man dismayed?
Not though the soldier knew
  Someone had blundered.
Theirs not to make reply,
Theirs not to reason why,
Theirs but to do and die.
Into the valley of Death
  Rode the six hundred.

Cannon to right of them,
Cannon to left of them,
Cannon in front of them
  Volleyed and thundered;
Stormed at with shot and shell,

Boldly they rode and well,
Into the jaws of Death,
Into the mouth of Hell
  Rode the six hundred.

Flashed all their sabres bare,
Flashed as they turned in air
Sabring the gunners there,
Charging an army, while
  All the world wondered.
Plunged in the battery-smoke
Right through the line they broke;
Cossack and Russian
Reeled from the sabre-stroke
  Shattered and sundered.
Then they rode back, but not
  Not the six hundred.

Cannon to right of them,
Cannon to left of them,
Cannon behind them
  Volleyed and thundered;
Stormed at with shot and shell,
While horse and hero fell.
They that had fought so well
Came through the jaws of Death,
Back from the mouth of Hell,
All that was left of them,
  Left of six hundred.

When can their glory fade?
O the wild charge they made!
  All the world wondered.
Honour the charge they made!
Honour the Light Brigade,
  Noble six hundred!

26 October ✶ *from* Auguries of Innocence ✶
William Blake

Though 'Auguries of Innocence' is thought to have been written in the first few years of the nineteenth century, the poem was not published until 1866 – long after William Blake had died. These four lines are characteristically enigmatic of Blake: each line contains a paradox, with a tiny grain of sand holding a world in it, and eternity lasting just sixty minutes.

> To see a World in a Grain of Sand
> And a Heaven in a Wild Flower
> Hold Infinity in the palm of your hand
> And Eternity in an hour

27 October ✶ Anglo-Saxon riddle ✶ Anon.

The Anglo-Saxons, a people who inhabited Great Britain from the fifth century and who dominated the country until the Norman Conquest of 1066, loved telling each other riddles. They had a rich literary tradition, and perhaps the most well-known work from the Anglo-Saxon period is the epic poem *Beowulf*, written in Old English, the ancient ancestor of the language we speak today. This riddle transforms a thing that we don't usually think of as a person into a 'wonderful warrior' with a fickle personality – and the solution to this puzzle is something both beautiful and extremely dangerous!

A wonderful warrior exists on earth.
Two dumb creatures make him grow bright between them.
Enemies use him against one another.
His strength is fierce but a woman can tame him.
He will meekly serve both men and women
If they know the trick of looking after him
And feeding him properly.
He makes people happy.
He makes their lives better.
But if they let him grow proud
This ungrateful friend soon turns against them.

28 October ✳ The New Colossus ✳ Emma Lazarus

On 28 October 1886 an official ceremony of dedication marked the opening of the Statue of Liberty – a gift from the people of France to America. One of the most instantly recognizable symbols of America, the statue depicts the robed Roman goddess Libertas, the embodiment of liberty. The American poet Emma Lazarus wrote her sonnet 'The New Colossus' in 1883. The poem was engraved on a bronze plaque and mounted on the pedestal of the statue in 1903.

Not like the brazen giant of Greek fame,
With conquering limbs astride from land to land;
Here at our sea-washed, sunset gates shall stand
A mighty woman with a torch, whose flame
Is the imprisoned lightning, and her name
Mother of Exiles. From her beacon-hand
Glows world-wide welcome; her mild eyes command
The air-bridged harbor that twin cities frame.
'Keep, ancient lands, your storied pomp!' cries she
With silent lips. 'Give me your tired, your poor,
Your huddled masses yearning to breathe free,
The wretched refuse of your teeming shore.
Send these, the homeless, tempest-tost to me,
I lift my lamp beside the golden door!'

29 October ✳ Leaves ✳ Ted Hughes

In this poem, Ted Hughes puts an original twist on the
traditional pastoral theme of the changing of the seasons,
as he documents the process of Summer turning into
Autumn, and then Winter, through the journey of the leaves.
Throughout the piece, every aspect of the natural world is
personified, from the trees to the whistling wind.

Who's killed the leaves?
Me, says the apple, I've killed them all.
Fat as a bomb or a cannonball
I've killed the leaves.

Who sees them drop?
Me, says the pear, they will leave me all bare
So all the people can point and stare.
I see them drop.

Who'll catch their blood?
Me, me, me, says the marrow, the marrow.
I'll get so rotund that they'll need a wheelbarrow.
I'll catch their blood.

Who'll make their shroud?
Me, says the swallow, there's just time enough
Before I must pack all my spools and be off.
I'll make their shroud.

Who'll dig their grave?
Me, says the river, with the power of the clouds
A brown deep grave I'll dig under my floods.
I'll dig their grave.

Who'll be their parson?
Me, says the Crow, for it is well known
I study the bible right down to the bone.
I'll be their parson.

Who'll be chief mourner?
Me, says the wind, I will cry through the grass
The people will pale and go cold when I pass.
I'll be chief mourner.

Who'll carry the coffin?
Me, says the sunset, the whole world will weep
To see me lower it into the deep.
I'll carry the coffin.

Who'll sing a psalm?
Me, says the tractor, with my gear-grinding glottle
I'll plough up the stubble and sing through my throttle.
I'll sing the psalm.

Who'll toll the bell?
Me, says the robin, my song in October
Will tell the still gardens the leaves are over.
I'll toll the bell.

30 October ✳ A Boxing We Will Go ✳ Anon.

On 30 October 1974, Muhammad Ali, whom many call the greatest sportsman of all time, fought the fight of his life and knocked out the then heavyweight boxing champion of the world, George Foreman. The event's name was the Rumble in the Jungle, and it took place in Zaire (now the Democratic Republic of the Congo). This nineteenth-century poem talks about the importance of boxing in Great Britain and names the three star boxers of the time. All of them would stand up to Boney, better known as Napoleon Bonaparte.

Throw pistols, poniards, swords aside,
And all such deadly tools;
Let boxing be the Briton's pride,
The science of their schools.
Since boxing is a manly game,
And Briton's recreation;
By boxing we will raise our fame,
'Bove any other nation
Mendoza, Bully, Molineux
Each nature's weapon wield;
Who each at Boney would stand true,
And never to him yield.

31 October ✷ Down Vith Children! ✷ Roald Dahl

We now celebrate Halloween by dressing up as ghosts, ghouls, vampires or villains, and trick-or-treating in search of piles of sweets, but 31 October – also known as All Hallows' Eve – is an ancient feast associated with the remembrance of the dead in the Christian liturgical calendar. The tradition of dressing up for Halloween dates back to at least the sixteenth century. While we dress up on Halloween to look terrifying, the evil witches of Roald Dahl's poem, taken from his book *The Witches*, have to dress up to look like humans – underneath their daily disguises they are truly gruesome!

Down vith children! Do them in!
Boil their bones and fry their skin!
Bish them, sqvish them, bash them, mash them!
Brrreak them, shake them, slash them, smash them!
Offer chocs vith magic powder!
Say, 'Eat up!' then say it louder.
Crrram them full of sticky eats,
Send them home still guzzling sveets.
And in the morning little fools
Go marching off to separate schools.
A girl feels sick and goes all pale.
She yells, 'Hey look! I've grrrown a tail!'
A boy who's standing next to her
Screams, 'Help! I think I'm grrrowing fur!'
Another shouts, 'Vee look like frrreaks!
There's viskers growing on our cheeks!'
A boy who vos extremely tall
Cries out, 'Vot's wrong? I'm grrrowing small!'
Four tiny legs begin to sprrrout
From everybody rrround about.
And all at vunce, all in a trrrice,
There are no children! Only MICE!

In every school is mice galore
All rrrunning rrround the school-rrroom floor!
And all the poor demented teachers
Is yelling, 'Hey, who are these crrreatures?'
They stand upon the desks and shout,
'Get out, you filthy mice! Get out!
Vill someone fetch some mouse-trrraps, please!
And don't forrrget to bring the cheese!'
Now mouse-trrraps come and every trrrap
Goes snippy-snip and snappy-snap.
The mouse-trrraps have a powerful spring,
The springs go crack and snap and ping!
Is lovely noise for us to hear!
Is music to a vitch's ear!
Dead mice is every place arrround,
Piled two feet deep upon the grrround,
Vith teachers searching left and rrright,
But not a single child in sight!
The teachers cry, 'Vot's going on?
Oh vhere have all the children gone?
Is half-past nine and as a rrrule
They're never late as this for school!'
Poor teachers don't know vot to do.
Some sit and rrread, and just a few
Amuse themselves throughout the day
By sveeping all the mice avay.
AND ALL US VITCHES SHOUT 'HOORAY!'

November

1 November ✶ No! ✶ Thomas Hood

Thomas Hood was a nineteenth-century English author, poet and humorist. This poem is an example of a kind of extended pun, as Hood's list of phrases beginning with 'no' is revealed by the final line to be a list of all the negative characteristics of the month of November.

No sun—no moon!
   No morn—no noon—
No dawn—no dust—no proper time of day.
No warmth, no cheerfulness, no healthful ease,
  No comfortable feel in any member—
No shade, no shine, no butterflies, no bees,
   No fruits, no flowers, no leaves, no birds,
     November!

2 **November** ✴ *from* Macbeth ✴
William Shakespeare

This passage is taken from Act 4, Scene 1 of Shakespeare's
Macbeth, one of his darkest and most famous tragedies.
The mysterious witches who have prophesied Macbeth's
ascent to the throne of Scotland chant this haunting rhyme
while brewing a potion. Their spells and prophecies cause
Macbeth more harm than good, for at the end of the play
both the villainous Macbeth and his power-hungry wife suffer
grisly fates. This passage is a particularly good one to learn
off by heart – it's filled with memorable rhymes and catchy
alliteration.

> Double, double, toil and trouble;
> Fire burn, and cauldron bubble.
>
> Fillet of a fenny snake,
> In the cauldron boil and bake;
> Eye of newt and toe of frog,
> Wool of bat and tongue of dog,
> Adder's fork and blind-worm's sting,
> Lizard's leg and owlet's wing,
> For a charm of powerful trouble,
> Like a hell-broth boil and bubble.
>
> Double, double, toil and trouble;
> Fire burn, and cauldron bubble.
>
> Scale of dragon, tooth of wolf,
> Witches' mummy, maw and gulf
> Of the ravin'd salt-sea shark,
> Root of hemlock digg'd i' the dark,
> Scale of dragon, tooth of wolf,

Witches' mummy, maw and gulf
Of the ravin'd salt-sea shark,
Root of hemlock digg'd i' the dark,
Add thereto a tiger's chaudron,
For the ingredients of our cauldron.

Double, double, toil and trouble;
Fire burn and cauldron bubble.

3 November ✶ The Girl with Many Eyes ✶ Tim Burton

The American Tim Burton is best known for his film-directing work that includes *The Nightmare Before Christmas* and film adaptations of Roald Dahl's *Charlie and the Chocolate Factory* and Lewis Carroll's *Alice in Wonderland*. He is also a writer and an artist, and much of his work reflects his quirky and fantastical imagination.

> One day in the park,
> I had quite a surprise.
> I met a girl,
> who had many eyes.
>
> She was really quite pretty
> (and also quite shocking)
> and I noticed she had a mouth,
> so we ended up talking.
>
> We talked about flowers,
> and her poetry classes,
> and the problems she'd have
> if she ever wore glasses.
>
> It's great to know a girl
> who has so many eyes,
> but you get really wet
> when she breaks down and cries.

4 November ✶ Dulce et Decorum Est ✶ Wilfred Owen

Wilfred Owen, a poet and soldier who served in the First World War, composed 'Dulce et Decorum Est' while recovering from shell-shock in 1917. The title is taken from a passage of Horace, the Roman poet, who wrote that 'dulce et decorum est pro patria mori': 'it is sweet and fitting to die for one's country.' While Horace meant to praise the bravery of the Roman army, in Owen's poem the phrase takes on a bitter irony. Owen's descriptions of war are not lofty and idealized but brutally graphic. He attacks the military propaganda of the time which encouraged 'children ardent for some desperate glory' to serve in the war, setting the supposed sweetness of glory in battle in contrast with the horrendous reality. Owen was killed in action on 4 November 1918, a week before the signing of the Armistice and the end of the war. He was twenty-five years old.

Bent double, like old beggars under sacks,
Knock-kneed, coughing like hags, we cursed through sludge,
Till on the haunting flares we turned our backs
And towards our distant rest began to trudge.
Men marched asleep. Many had lost their boots
But limped on, blood-shod. All went lame; all blind;
Drunk with fatigue; deaf even to the hoots
Of gas-shells dropping softly behind.

Gas! GAS! Quick, boys!—An ecstasy of fumbling
Fitting the clumsy helmets just in time;
But someone still was yelling out and stumbling
And flound'ring like a man in fire or lime . . .
Dim through the misty panes and thick green light,
As under a green sea, I saw him drowning.
In all my dreams before my helpless sight,
He plunges at me, guttering, choking, drowning.

If in some smothering dreams, you too could pace
Behind the wagon that we flung him in,
And watch the white eyes writhing in his face,
His hanging face, like a devil's sick of sin;
If you could hear, at every jolt, the blood
Come gargling from the froth-corrupted lungs,
Obscene as cancer, bitter as the cud
Of vile, incurable sores on innocent tongues, –
My friend, you would not tell with such high zest
To children ardent for some desperate glory,
The old Lie: Dulce et decorum est
Pro patria mori.

5 November ✷ Remember, Remember ✷ Anon.

In 1605 a group of Catholics plotted to blow up the House of Lords during the State Opening of Parliament. The explosion would have reduced Parliament to a pile of rubble and killed the Protestant King James I. An anonymous letter revealing the plot led to a search of the House of Lords on the night of 4 November – and the discovery of Guy Fawkes guarding 36 barrels of gunpowder! Guy Fawkes and the Gunpowder Plot are now remembered every year on 5 November in the form of extravagant firework displays, and huge bonfires with a straw dummy of Guy traditionally thrown on the top.

Remember, remember the fifth of November
Gunpowder, treason and plot.
I see no reason why gunpowder treason
Should ever be forgot.

Guy Fawkes, Guy, 'twas his intent
To blow up king and parliament.
Three score barrels were laid below
To prove old England's overthrow.

By God's mercy he was catch'd
With a darkened lantern and burning match.
So holler, boys, holler, boys, let the bells ring.
Holler, boys, holler, boys, God save the king!

And what shall we do with him?
Burn him!

6 November ✶ *from* Amours de Voyage ✶
Arthur Hugh Clough

Wilfred Owen was not the first poet to interrogate Horace's phrase 'Dulce et decorum est pro patria mori'. This extract is taken from Arthur Hugh Clough's mid-nineteenth-century poem 'Amours de Voyage', set during the Siege of Rome in 1849. Here, too, Horace's patriotic phrase is shown to be an idealistic, unrealistic vision of war.

Dulce it is, and decorum, no doubt, for the country to fall, — to
Offer one's blood an oblation to Freedom, and die for the Cause;
   yet
Still, individual culture is also something, and no man
Finds quite distinct the assurance that he of all others is called
   on,
Or would be justified even, in taking away from the world that
Precious creature, himself. Nature sent him here to abide here;
Else why send him at all? Nature wants him still, it is likely;
On the whole, we are meant to look after ourselves; it is certain
Each has to eat for himself, digest for himself, and in general
Care for his own dear life, and see to his own preservation;
Nature's intentions, in most things uncertain, in this are decisive;
Which, on the whole, I conjecture the Romans will follow, and I
   shall.
So we cling to our rocks like limpets; Ocean may bluster,
Over and under and round us; we open our shells to imbibe our
Nourishment, close them again, and are safe, fulfilling the
   purpose
Nature intended, — a wise one, of course, and a noble, we doubt
   not.
Sweet it may be and decorous, perhaps, for the country to die;
   but,
On the whole, we conclude the Romans won't do it, and I sha'n't.

7 November ✱ *from* As You Like It ✱
William Shakespeare

This song is sung at the end of the second act of Shakespeare's comedy *As You Like It*, when the runaway gentleman, Orlando, and his old faithful servant, Adam, arrive at the court of an exiled Duke who is living as an outlaw in the Forest of Arden. Despite the song's many references to human ingratitude and feigned friendship, the travellers receive a hearty welcome at the feast.

> Blow, blow, thou winter wind,
>   Thou art not so unkind
>   As man's ingratitude;
>   Thy tooth is not so keen,
> Because thou art not seen,
>   Although thy breath be rude.
> Heigh-ho! sing, heigh-ho! unto the green holly:
> Most friendship is feigning, most loving mere folly:
>   Then, heigh-ho, the holly!
>   This life is most jolly.
>
> Freeze, freeze, thou bitter sky,
> That dost not bite so nigh
>   As benefits forgot:
> Though thou the waters warp,
>   Thy sting is not so sharp
>   As friend remembered not.
> Heigh-ho! sing, heigh-ho! unto the green holly . . .
> Most friendship is feigning, most loving mere folly:
>   Then, heigh-ho, the holly!
>   This life is most jolly.

8 November ✳ Solitude ✳ A. A. Milne

Do you have a place you can go when you feel like being on your own? Sometimes we all feel like we need a bit of time to ourselves. 'Solitude' means the state of being alone, and this poem by A. A. Milne describes a place where the speaker can find solitude, and peace and quiet.

> I have a house where I go
>   When there's too many people,
> I have a house where I go
>   Where no one can be;
> I have a house where I go,
> Where nobody ever says 'No'
> Where no one says anything – so
>   There is no one but me.

9 November ✳ Divali ✳ David Harmer

Divali is India's largest festival, and a national holiday in India, Nepal, Sri Lanka and Singapore. It falls in the Hindu month of Kartik, which is usually sometime in October or November. 'Divali' means 'rows of lighted lamps', and it is a festival of light and joy: people often celebrate by decorating their houses or shops with colourful lights and lamps. The festival worships Lord Ganesh for welfare and prosperity, and the goddess Lakshmi for wealth and wisdom.

Winter stalks us
like a leopard in the mountains
scenting prey.

It grows dark,
bare trees stick black bars
across the moon's silver eye.

I will light my lamp for you
Lakshmi,
drive away the darkness.

Welcome you into my home
Lakshmi,
beckon you from every window

With light that blazes
out like flames
across the somber sky.

Certain houses
crouch in shadow, do not hear
your gentle voice.

Will not feel
your gentle heartbeat
bring prosperity and fortune.

Darkness hunts them
like a leopard in the mountains
stalking prey.

10 November * *from* The Song of Hiawatha *
Henry Wadsworth Longfellow

The Song of Hiawatha is an epic poem by Henry Wadsworth
Longfellow that was published in America in 1855. The hero
of the poem is the Native American Hiawatha, the son of the
beautiful Wenonah and the West Wind. The poem was loosely
based on Native American legends, although Longfellow was
not very faithful to them, and it is largely set on the shore
of Lake Superior, which is called Gitchigume by the Ojibwe
Native Americans.

By the shores of Gitche Gumee,
By the shining Big-Sea-Water,
Stood the wigwam of Nokomis,
Daughter of the Moon, Nokomis.
Dark behind it rose the forest,
Rose the black and gloomy pine-trees,
Rose the firs with cones upon them;
Bright before it beat the water,
Beat the clear and sunny water,
Beat the shining Big-Sea-Water.
    There the wrinkled old Nokomis
Nursed the little Hiawatha,
Rocked him in his linden cradle.
Bedded soft in moss and rushes,
Safely bound with reindeer sinews;
Stilled his fretful wail by saying,
'Hush! the Naked Bear will hear thee!'
Lulled him into slumber, singing,
'Ewa-yea! my little owlet!
Who is this, that lights the wigwam?
With his great eyes lights the wigwam?
Ewa-yea! my little owlet!'

Many things Nokomis taught him
Of the stars that shine in heaven;
Showed him Ishkoodah, the comet,
Ishkoodah, with fiery tresses;
Showed the Death-Dance of the spirits,
Warriors with their plumes and war-clubs,
Flaring far away to northward
In the frosty nights of Winter;
Showed the vorad whit road in heaven,
Pathway of the ghosts, the shadows,
Running straight across the heaven,
Crowded with the ghosts, the shadows.

11 November ✷ The Soldier ✷ Rupert Brooke

On 11 November 1918, the fighting ceased on the Western Front, marking the end of World War One. At the eleventh hour of the eleventh day of the eleventh month, people all round the world hold a two-minute silence to mark their respect for the dead. 11 November is known as Armistice or Remembrance Day. Rupert Brooke was a poet and a soldier who enlisted to fight in the First World War. This poem was written in 1914, just as the war was about to begin, and is one of the most well-known poems from the war: it is notable for its lack of gruesome imagery, and a seemingly idealistic vision of how noble it is to die for your country.

If I should die, think only this of me:
    That there's some corner of a foreign field
That is for ever England. There shall be
    In that rich earth a richer dust concealed;
A dust whom England bore, shaped, made aware,
    Gave, once, her flowers to love, her ways to roam;
A body of England's, breathing English air,
    Washed by the rivers, blest by suns of home.

And think, this heart, all evil shed away,
    A pulse in the eternal mind, no less
        Gives somewhere back the thoughts by England given;
Her sights and sounds; dreams happy as her day;
    And laughter, learnt of friends; and gentleness,
        In hearts at peace, under an English heaven.

12 November ✳ 'No One Cares Less than I' ✳ Edward Thomas

In this poem Edward Thomas can be seen to parody the opening lines of Brooke's 'The Soldier'. In response to Brooke's notion that, should he die in 'some corner of a foreign field', that place shall be 'for ever England', Thomas responds that he doesn't care whether he is 'destined to lie / Under a foreign clod'. Here the poet warns the reader of the dangers of patriotism and the glorification of war. Thomas died on 9 April 1917 in Pas-de-Calais, France. He was thirty-nine years old.

'No one cares less than I,
Nobody knows but God,
Whether I am destined to lie
Under a foreign clod,'
Were the words I made to the bugle call in the morning.

But laughing, storming, scorning,
Only the bugles know
What the bugles say in the morning,
And they do not care, when they blow
The call that I heard and made words to early this morning.

13 November ✶ Does it Matter? ✶ Siegfried Sassoon

Siegfried Sassoon joined the British Army shortly before the outbreak of the First World War in 1914. By 1917, many of his friends and comrades had been killed, including his brother, and despite being awarded the Military Cross for several acts of bravery, he was bitterly disillusioned with the war. Many of Sassoon's poems contain a powerful anti-war message, and 'Does it Matter?' is no exception. The bitter sarcasm of the title is carried through the rest of the poem, as he describes men whose lives and bodies have been ruined by war.

Does it matter? – losing your legs?
For people will always be kind,
And you need not show that you mind
When others come in after hunting
To gobble their muffins and eggs.

Does it matter? – losing your sight?
There's such splendid work for the blind;
And people will always be kind,
As you sit on the terrace remembering
And turning your face to the light.

Do they matter from those dreams – the pit?
You can drink and forget and be glad,
And people won't say that you're mad;
For they'll know that you've fought for your country,
And no one will worry a bit.

14 November ✶ Anthem for Doomed Youth ✶ Wilfred Owen

This First World War poem takes the surprising form of a sonnet – a form usually associated with love poetry. Among the deadliest of conflicts in human history, World War One saw the deaths of over 17 million people. Owen's poetry marks an attempt to deal with this immense loss of human life – and also an acknowledgement that such loss is beyond comprehension.

What passing-bells for these who die as cattle?
   – Only the monstrous anger of the guns.
   Only the stuttering rifles' rapid rattle
Can patter out their hasty orisons.
No mockeries now for them; no prayers nor bells;
   Nor any voice of mourning save the choirs, –
The shrill, demented choirs of wailing shells;
   And bugles calling for them from sad shires.

What candles may be held to speed them all?
   Not in the hands of boys, but in their eyes
Shall shine the holy glimmers of goodbyes.
   The pallor of girls' brows shall be their pall;
Their flowers the tenderness of patient minds,
And each slow dusk a drawing-down of blinds.

15 November ✴ Fiere Good Nicht ✴ Jackie Kay (after Gussie Lord Davis)

This poem is taken from the award-winning Scottish poet Jackie Kay's 2011 collection, *Fiere*, and it's a perfect poem to read just before going to bed. In the Scots dialect, 'fiere' means 'mate' or 'companion' – and this is just one of the many Scots terms used in the poem.

When you've had your last one for the road,
a Linkwood, a Talisker, a Macallan,
and you've finished your short story
and played one more time Nacht und Traume
with Roland Hayes singing sweetly;
and pictured yourself on the road,
the one that stretches to infinity,
and said good night to your dead,
and fathomed the links in the long day –
then it's time to say Goodnight fiere,
and lay your highland head on your feather pillow,
far away – in England, Canada, New Zealand –
and coorie in, coorie in, coorie in.
The good dreams are drifting quietly doon,
like a figmaleerie, my fiere, my dearie,
and you'll sleep as soond as a peerie,
and you, are turning slowly towards the licht:
Goodnight fiere, fiere, Good Nicht.

16 November ✳ The Wind and the Moon ✳
George MacDonald

On mid-November nights, the wind can blow bitterly and
moonlight can make the frost-covered earth shimmer and
sparkle. This fantastic poem by George MacDonald imagines
both the wind and the moon as people, supplying them with
personalities and feelings. The poem has a strange visual
shape, juxtaposing very short and rather long lines in a
way which imitates the gusts of wind, blowing fiercely for a
moment before subsiding. With its quick-fire rhymes and
humorous twist, this is a great poem to read aloud.

Said the Wind to the Moon, 'I will blow you out;
You stare
In the air
Like a ghost in a chair,
Always looking what I am about –
I hate to be watched; I'll blow you out.'

The Wind blew hard, and out went the Moon.
So deep
On a heap
Of clouds to sleep,
Down lay the Wind, and slumbered soon,
Muttering low, 'I've done for that Moon.'

He turned in his bed; she was there again!
On high
In the sky,
With her one ghost eye,
The Moon shone white and alive and plain.
Said the Wind, 'I will blow you out again.'

The Wind blew hard, and the Moon grew slim.
'With my sledge
And my wedge,
I have knocked off her edge!
If only I blow right fierce and grim,
The creature will soon be slimmer than slim.'

He blew and he blew, and she thinned to a thread.
'One puff
More's enough
To blow her to snuff!
One good puff more where the last was bred,
And glimmer, glimmer, glum will go the thread.'

He blew a great blast, and the thread was gone.
In the air
Nowhere
Was a moonbeam bare;
Far off and harmless the shy stars shone –
Sure and certain the Moon was gone!

The Wind he took to his revels once more;
On down
In town,
Like a merry-mad clown.
He leaped and hallooed with whistle and roar –
'What's that?' The glimmering thread once more!

He flew in a rage – he danced and blew;
But in vain
Was the pain
Of his bursting brain;
For still the broader the Moon-scrap grew,
The broader he swelled his big cheeks and blew.

Slowly she grew – till she filled the night,
And shone
On her throne
In the sky alone,
A matchless, wonderful silvery light,
Radiant and lovely, the queen of the night.

Said the Wind: 'What a marvel of power am I!
With my breath,
In good faith
I blew her to death!
First blew her away right out of the sky –
Then blew her in; what strength have I!'

But the Moon she knew nothing about the affair;
For high
In the sky,
With her one white eye,
Motionless, miles above the air,
She had never heard the great Wind blare.

17 November ✶ The Duke of Fire and the Duchess of Ice ✶ Carol Ann Duffy

We all know the phrase 'Opposites attract', but can you imagine how difficult life would be if spending time with your opposite meant turning into a puddle? Like the previous poem, this piece by the Poet Laureate Carol Ann Duffy is about an unlikely couple – a duke made of fire and a duchess of ice.

Passionate love for the Duke of Fire
the Duchess of Ice felt.
One kiss was her heart's desire,
but with one kiss she would melt.

She dreamed of him in his red pantaloons,
in his orange satin blouse,
in his crimson cravat,
in his tangerine hat,
in his vermilion dancing shoes.

One kiss, one kiss,
lips of flame on frost,
one kiss, pure bliss,
and never count the cost.

She woke. She went to the bathroom.
She took a freezing shower –
her body as pale as a stalagmite,
winter's frailest flower.

The Duke of Fire stood there,
radiant, ablaze with love,
and the Duchess of Ice cared nothing
for anything in the world.

She spoke his name,
her voice was snow,
kissed him, kissed him again,
and in his warm, passionate arms
turned to water, tears, rain.

18 November ✳ Overheard on a Saltmarsh ✳ Harold Munro

This imagined conversation is an especially good poem for two people to read aloud, with one person taking the role of the jealous goblin, and the other acting out the part of the beautiful nymph.

Nymph, nymph, what are your beads?

Green glass, goblin. Why do you stare at them?

Give them me.

        No.

Give them me. Give them me.

                No.

Then I will howl all night in the reeds,
lie in the mud and howl for them.

Goblin, why do you love them so?

They are better than stars or water,
Better than voices of winds that sing,
Better than any man's fair daughter,
Your green glass beads on a silver ring.

Hush, I stole them out of the moon.

Give me your beads, I want them.

                No.

I will howl in a deep lagoon
For your green glass beads, I love them so.
Give them me. Give them.

                No.

19 November ✶ The Gettysburg Address ✶ Abraham Lincoln

On 19 November 1863, President Abraham Lincoln delivered the Gettysburg Address at the Consecration ceremony of the National Cemetery at Gettysburg, on the site of one of the climactic battles of the American Civil War. The speech is acclaimed for its beauty and brevity, as well as its masterful use of various rhetorical devices.

Four score and seven years ago our fathers brought forth on this continent, a new nation, conceived in Liberty, and dedicated to the proposition that all men are created equal.

Now we are engaged in a great civil war, testing whether that nation, or any nation so conceived and so dedicated, can long endure. We are met on a great battlefield of that war. We have come to dedicate a portion of that field, as a final resting place for those who here gave their lives that that nation might live. It is altogether fitting and proper that we should do this.

But, in a larger sense, we can not dedicate – we can not consecrate – we can not hallow – this ground. The brave men, living and dead, who struggled here, have consecrated it, far above our poor power to add or detract. The world will little note, nor long remember what we say here, but it can never forget what they did here. It is for us the living, rather, to be dedicated here to the unfinished work which they who fought here have thus far so nobly advanced. It is rather for us to be here, dedicated to the great task remaining before us – that from these honored dead we take increased devotion to that cause for which they gave the last full measure of devotion – that we here highly resolve that these dead shall not have died in vain – that this nation, under God, shall have a new birth of freedom – and that government of the people, by the people, for the people, shall not perish from the earth.

20 November ✳ The Moon was but a Chin of Gold ✳ Emily Dickinson

In this poem, Emily Dickinson marvels at the changes that happen to the moon every month: the narrator of the poem seems surprised that the moon can evolve so quickly from a thin 'chin of gold' to a full, 'perfect face' just over the course of 'a Night or two'.

The Moon was but a Chin of Gold
A Night or two ago—
And now she turns Her perfect Face
Upon the World below—

Her Forehead is of Amplest Blonde—
Her Cheek—a Beryl hewn—
Her Eye unto the Summer Dew
The likest I have known—

Her Lips of Amber never part—
But what must be the smile
Upon Her Friend she could confer
Were such Her Silver Will—

And what a privilege to be
But the remotest Star—
For Certainty She take Her Way
Beside Your Palace Door—

Her Bonnet is the Firmament—
The Universe—Her Shoe—
The Stars—the Trinkets at Her Belt—
Her Dimities—of Blue—

21 November ✳ A Word is Dead ✳
Emily Dickinson

Emily Dickinson wrote many brief poems, but this is one of
her shortest pieces. Although some people believe that words
'die' once they are spoken, Dickinson is suggesting that they
begin to take on a whole new life once they have been said.

A word is dead
When it is said,
Some say.
I say it just
Begins to live
That day.

22 **November** ✶ The Runaway ✶ Robert Frost

A 'Morgan' is a small and sturdy type of horse bred in New England. The colt in this poem has never seen snow before. He runs around his pasture panicking: he doesn't understand the cold, wet prickles all over his coat, and white dots swirling around, obscuring his vision.

Once when the snow of the year was beginning to fall,
We stopped by a mountain pasture to say, 'Whose colt?'
A little Morgan had one forefoot on the wall,
The other curled at his breast. He dipped his head
And snorted to us. And then we saw him bolt.
We heard the miniature thunder where he fled,
And we saw him, or thought we saw him, dim and gray,
Like a shadow across instead of behind the flakes.
The little fellow's afraid of the falling snow.
He never saw it before. It isn't play
With the little fellow at all. He's running away.
He wouldn't believe when his mother told him, 'Sakes,
It's only weather.' He thought she didn't know!
So this is something he has to bear alone
And now he comes again with a clatter of stone,
He mounts the wall again with whited eyes
Dilated nostrils, and tail held straight up straight.
He shudders his coat as if to throw off flies.
'Whoever it is that leaves him out so late,
When all other creatures have gone to stall and bin,
Ought to be told to come and take him in.'

23 November ✳ Nothing Gold Can Stay ✳
Robert Frost

Here the colours of nature fade as Winter approaches, and nothing can stop the passing of time.

> Nature's first green is gold,
> Her hardest hue to hold.
> Her early leaf's a flower;
> But only so an hour.
> Then leaf subsides to leaf.
> So Eden sank to grief,
> So dawn goes down to day.
> Nothing gold can stay.

24 November ✳ Winter Poem ✳ Nikki Giovanni

Nikki Giovanni is one of the most celebrated living African-American poets, and is particularly well known for her powerful political poetry. This little poem, however, takes as its subject Winter weather. The poet brings the wintry setting of the poem to life, giving snowflakes the ability to feel happy. While the poem acknowledges that the beautiful snow cannot last forever, the final image is of new life springing up after the freezing Winter weather has departed.

once a snowflake fell
on my brow and i loved
it so much and i kissed
it and it was happy and called its cousins
and brothers and a web
of snow engulfed me then
i reached to love them all
and i squeezed them and they became
a spring rain and i stood perfectly
still and was a flower

25 November ✳ The New-England Boy's Song about Thanksgiving Day ✳ Lydia Maria Child

Thanksgiving is a holiday that remembers and gives thanks for the kindness that the first pilgrims to America were shown by the Native Americans from the Wampanoag tribe. In 1863, Abraham Lincoln set aside the last Thursday in November as an official national day of Thanksgiving. Nowadays, the holiday is usually celebrated by families and friends enjoying a meal together, often with turkey as the main dish. This poem, by Lydia Maria Child, draws on childhood memories of visits to her grandfather's house.

> Over the river, and through the wood,
>   To Grandfather's house we go;
>   The horse knows the way,
>   To carry the sleigh,
>   Through the white and drifted snow.

> Over the river, and through the wood,
>   To Grandfather's house away!
>   We would not stop
>   For doll or top,
>   For 'tis Thanksgiving day.

> Over the river, and through the wood,
>   Oh, how the wind does blow!
>   It stings the toes,
>   And bites the nose,
>   As over the ground we go.

Over the river, and through the wood,
  With a clear blue winter sky,
    The dogs do bark,
    And children hark,
  As we go jingling by.

Over the river, and through the wood,
  To have a first-rate play –
    Hear the bells ring
    Ting-a-ling-ding,
  Hurra for Thanksgiving day!

Over the river, and through the wood –
  No matter for winds that blow;
    Or if we get
    The sleigh upset,
  Into a bank of snow.

Over the river, and through the wood,
  To see little John and Ann;
    We will kiss them all,
    And play snow-ball,
  And stay as long as we can.

Over the river, and through the wood,
  Trot fast, my dapple grey!
    Spring over the ground,
    Like a hunting hound,
  For 'tis Thanksgiving day!

Over the river, and through the wood,
  And straight through the barn-yard gate;
    We seem to go
    Extremely slow,
  It is so hard to wait.

Over the river, and through the wood,
 Old Jowler hears our bells;
  He shakes his pow,
  With a loud bow-wow,
 And thus the news he tells.

Over the river, and through the wood –
 When Grandmother sees us come,
  She will say, Oh dear,
  The children are here,
 Bring a pie for every one.

Over the river, and through the wood –
 Now Grandmother's cap I spy!
  Hurra for the fun!
  Is the pudding done?
 Hurra for the pumpkin pie!

26 November ✳ Not Waving but Drowning ✳ Stevie Smith

This poem by Stevie Smith was published in 1957. In an interview about the poem, Smith said that it was about how many people pretend out of bravery that they are 'very jolly and ordinary sort of chaps', when, actually, they find life to be a real struggle – they're not waving, but drowning.

Nobody heard him, the dead man,
But still he lay moaning:
I was much further out than you thought
And not waving but drowning.

Poor chap, he always loved larking
And now he's dead
It must have been too cold for him his heart gave way,
They said.

Oh, no no no, it was too cold always
(Still the dead one lay moaning)
I was much too far out all my life
And not waving but drowning.

27 November * Do Not Go Gentle into that Good Night * Dylan Thomas

Although 'Do not go gentle' is commonly thought to have been written about Thomas's dying father, it was actually composed in 1947, five years before his father died. The poet here rails against death and tells us to put up a fight.

Do not go gentle into that good night,
Old age should burn and rave at close of day;
Rage, rage against the dying of the light.

Though wise men at their end know dark is right,
Because their words had forked no lightning they
Do not go gentle into that good night.

Good men, the last wave by, crying how bright
Their frail deeds might have danced in a green bay,
Rage, rage against the dying of the light.

Wild men who caught and sang the sun in flight,
And learn, too late, they grieved it on its way,
Do not go gentle into that good night.

Grave men, near death, who see with blinding sight
Blind eyes could blaze like meteors and be gay,
Rage, rage against the dying of the light.

And you, my father, there on the sad height,
Curse, bless, me now with your fierce tears, I pray.
Do not go gentle into that good night.
Rage, rage against the dying of the light.

28 November ✶ *from* The Highwayman ✶
Alfred Noyes

First published in 1906, 'The Highwayman' is an evocative narrative poem relating the tragic tale of a highwayman and his lover Bess.

The wind was a torrent of darkness among the gusty trees.
The moon was a ghostly galleon tossed upon cloudy seas.
The road was a ribbon of moonlight over the purple moor,
And the highwayman came riding—
    Riding—riding—
The highwayman came riding, up to the old inn-door.

He'd a French cocked-hat on his forehead, a bunch of lace at
    his chin,
A coat of the claret velvet, and breeches of brown doe-skin.
They fitted with never a wrinkle. His boots were up to the
    thigh.
And he rode with a jewelled twinkle,
    His pistol butts a-twinkle,
His rapier hilt a-twinkle, under the jewelled sky.

Over the cobbles he clattered and clashed in the dark inn-yard.
He tapped with his whip on the shutters, but all was locked
    and barred.
He whistled a tune to the window, and who should be waiting
    there
But the landlord's black-eyed daughter,
    Bess, the landlord's daughter,
Plaiting a dark red love-knot into her long black hair.

And dark in the dark old inn-yard a stable-wicket creaked
Where Tim the ostler listened. His face was white and peaked.
His eyes were hollows of madness, his hair like mouldy hay,
But he loved the landlord's daughter,
     The landlord's red-lipped daughter.
Dumb as a dog he listened, and he heard the robber say—

'One kiss, my bonny sweetheart, I'm after a prize to-night,
But I shall be back with the yellow gold before the morning
   light;
Yet, if they press me sharply, and harry me through the day,
Then look for me by moonlight,
     Watch for me by moonlight,
I'll come to thee by moonlight, though hell should bar the
   way.'

He rose upright in the stirrups. He scarce could reach her
   hand,
But she loosened her hair in the casement. His face burnt like
   a brand
As the black cascade of perfume came tumbling over his
   breast;
And he kissed its waves in the moonlight
     (O, sweet black waves in the moonlight!),
Then he tugged at his rein in the moonlight, and galloped
   away to the west.

29 November ✳ When You Are Old ✳ W. B. Yeats

Yeats wrote this poem for Maud Gonne, a frequent muse of his, and he emphasizes his belief that, although many have loved her for her youth and beauty, he will be constant in his admiration even when she is 'old and grey'.

When you are old and grey and full of sleep,
And nodding by the fire, take down this book,
And slowly read, and dream of the soft look
Your eyes had once, and of their shadows deep;

How many loved your moments of glad grace,
And loved your beauty with love false or true,
But one man loved the pilgrim soul in you,
And loved the sorrows of your changing face;

And bending down beside the glowing bars,
Murmur, a little sadly, how Love fled
And paced upon the mountains overhead
And hid his face amid a crowd of stars.

30 November ✷ Funeral Blues ✷ W. H. Auden

'Funeral Blues' was read out in its entirety in the romantic comedy *Four Weddings and a Funeral*, and has become one of Auden's best-known poems. 'Funeral Blues' details the grief of the speaker for their lover, moving from imagery of the couple's shared domestic life – clocks and telephones – to demanding that the whole nation join in the mourning, even the traffic policemen and the 'public doves'.

Stop all the clocks, cut off the telephone,
Prevent the dog from barking with a juicy bone,
Silence the pianos and with muffled drum
Bring out the coffin, let the mourners come.

Let aeroplanes circle moaning overhead
Scribbling on the sky the message, He is dead.
Put crepe bows round the white necks of the public doves,
Let the traffic policemen wear black cotton gloves.

He was my North, my South, my East and West,
My working week and my Sunday rest,
My noon, my midnight, my talk, my song;
I thought that love would last for ever: I was wrong.

The stars are not wanted now: put out every one;
Pack up the moon and dismantle the sun;
Pour away the ocean and sweep up the wood.
For nothing now can ever come to any good.

457

December

1 December ✶ Rosa Parks ✶ Jan Dean

Rosa Parks was a heroine of the American Civil Rights movement who defied the racially 'segregated' seating on her local bus.

she sorts the drawer
knives at the left
forks at the right
spoons in the middle
like neat silver petals
curved inside each other

the queue sorts itself
snaking through the bus
whites at the front
blacks at the back

but people are not knives
not forks
not spoons
their bones are full of stardust
their hearts full of songs
and the sorting on the bus
is just plain wrong

so Rosa says no
and Rosa won't go
to the place for her race

she'll face up to all the fuss
but she's said goodbye
to the back of the bus

2 December ✳ Still I Rise ✳ Maya Angelou

'Still I Rise' is a powerful poem in which the speaker declares an intention to transcend the bitter realities of black experience in America. The verses gradually break down and are replaced by a repeated statement of defiance: 'I rise.' Angelou said it was her favourite of her own poems.

> You may write me down in history
> With your bitter, twisted lies,
> You may trod me in the very dirt
> But still, like dust, I'll rise.
>
> Does my sassiness upset you?
> Why are you beset with gloom?
> 'Cause I walk like I've got oil wells
> Pumping in my living room.
>
> Just like moons and like suns,
> With the certainty of tides,
> Just like hopes springing high,
> Still I'll rise.
>
> Did you want to see me broken?
> Bowed head and lowered eyes?
> Shoulders falling down like teardrops,
> Weakened by my soulful cries?
>
> Does my haughtiness offend you?
> Don't you take it awful hard
> 'Cause I laugh like I've got gold mines
> Diggin' in my own backyard.

You may shoot me with your words,
You may cut me with your eyes,
You may kill me with your hatefulness,
But still, like air, I'll rise.

Does my sexiness upset you?
Does it come as a surprise
That I dance like I've got diamonds
At the meeting of my thighs?

Out of the huts of history's shame
I rise
Up from a past that's rooted in pain
I rise
I'm a black ocean, leaping and wide,
Welling and swelling I bear in the tide.

Leaving behind nights of terror and fear
I rise
Into a daybreak that's wondrously clear
I rise
Bringing the gifts that my ancestors gave,
I am the dream and the hope of the slave.
I rise
I rise
I rise.

3 December * Napoleon * Walter de la Mare

In the Winter of 1812, Napoleon's army was advancing into Russia. This ill-advised campaign during the bitterly cold Russian Winter eventually led to the destruction of the French army. This short poem is framed as a speech from Napoleon to his troops during this campaign, but it might as well be a soliloquy. For Napoleon, the Russian landscape only reflects his inner emptiness and isolation.

'What is the world, O soldiers?
   It is I:
I, this incessant snow,
   This northern sky;
Soldiers, this solitude
   Through which we go
     Is I.'

4 December ✶ The Ends of the Earth ✶
George the Poet

George Mpanga, better known by his stage name George the Poet, is a British spoken-word artist, whose poetry focuses on political and social issues. This poem talks about the importance and value of children in society. Spoken-word poetry is intended to be read aloud – try performing this one aloud and see how many internal rhymes and clever bits of wordplay suddenly come to life!

A child is not a portion of an adult.
It's not a partial being.
A child is an absolute person,
An entire life.

The fact that the child is developing
Doesn't mean it's incomplete.
This just makes it especially important for the
Child to drink and eat, and get a decent wink of sleep,
Many children are given less than children deserve;
Such is the world they entered at birth.
But all it takes is one friend . . . one friend
Who's willing to go to the end of the earth.

For children in the hardest circumstances,
A friend who gives in to no resistance.
Whether down the road or around the globe.
One who's prepared to go the distance,
One who's not scared to show persistence.
No task is too tall, no ask is too small
To send through . . . to attend to.
You could be a friend, too.
Go to the ends of the Earth, for children.

5 December * Snow and Snow * Ted Hughes

In this poem Ted Hughes uses personification to describe
the snow. Here, he imagines different types of snowfall to be
different kinds of people, even picturing their clothing.

Snow is sometimes a she, a soft one.
Her kiss on your cheek, her finger on your sleeve
In early December, on a warm evening,
And you turn to meet her, saying 'It's snowing!'
But it is not. And nobody's there.
Empty and calm is the air.

Sometimes the snow is a he, a sly one.
Weakly he signs the dry stone with a damp spot.
Waifish he floats and touches the pond and is not.
Treacherous-beggarly he falters, and taps at the window.
A little longer he clings to the grass-blade tip
Getting his grip.

Then how she leans, how furry foxwrap she nestles
The sky with her warm, and the earth with her softness.
How her lit crowding fairylands sink through the space-silence
To build her palace, till it twinkles in starlight –
Too frail for a foot
Or a crumb of soot.

Then how his muffled armies move in all night
And we wake and every road is blockaded
Every hill taken and every farm occupied
And the white glare of his tents is on the ceiling.
And all that dull blue day and on into the gloaming
We have to watch more coming.

464

Then everything in the rubbish-heaped world
Is a bridesmaid at her miracle.
Dunghills and crumbly dark old barns are bowed in the chapel
of her sparkle.
The gruesome boggy cellars of the wood
Are a wedding of lace
Now taking place.

6 December ✶ The Thought-Fox ✶ Ted Hughes

This poem from 1957 is based upon a dream that Ted Hughes had when he was a student. Hughes wasn't enjoying his English degree, and he dreamed that a fox came to him as a representative of the poets he was studying, telling him to stop. He then changed degree courses to Anthropology, the study of human societies through time.

I imagine this midnight moment's forest:
Something else is alive
Beside the clock's loneliness
And this blank page where my fingers move.

Through the window I see no star:
Something more near
though deeper within darkness
Is entering the loneliness:

Cold, delicately as the dark snow
A fox's nose touches twig, leaf;
Two eyes serve a movement, that now
And again now, and now, and now

Sets neat prints into the snow
Between trees, and warily a lame
Shadow lags by stump and in hollow
Of a body that is bold to come

Across clearings, an eye,
A widening deepening greenness,
Brilliantly, concentratedly,
Coming about its own business

Till, with a sudden sharp hot stink of fox,
It enters the dark hole of the head.
The window is starless still; the clock ticks,
The page is printed.

7 December ✳ The Darkling Thrush ✳ Thomas Hardy

One of Hardy's most acclaimed poems, 'The Darkling Thrush' was originally titled 'The Century's End, 1900'. Like many of Hardy's poems, this one is filled with rich natural imagery.

I leant upon a coppice gate
    When Frost was spectre-grey,
And Winter's dregs made desolate
    The weakening eye of day.
The tangled bine-stems scored the sky
    Like strings of broken lyres,
And all mankind that haunted nigh
    Had sought their household fires.

The land's sharp features seemed to be
    The Century's corpse outleant,
His crypt the cloudy canopy,
    The wind his death-lament.
The ancient pulse of germ and birth
    Was shrunken hard and dry,
And every spirit upon earth
    Seemed fervourless as I.

At once a voice arose among
    The bleak twigs overhead
In a full-hearted evensong
    Of joy illimited;
An aged thrush, frail, gaunt, and small,
    In blast-beruffled plume,
Had chosen thus to fling his soul
    Upon the growing gloom.

So little cause for carollings
    Of such ecstatic sound
Was written on terrestrial things
    Afar or nigh around,
That I could think there trembled through
    His happy good-night air
Some blessed Hope, whereof he knew
    And I was unaware.

8 December ✳ Birds at Winter Nightfall ✳
Thomas Hardy

Here, Thomas Hardy uses repetition to create a feeling of excitement and joy. Although the birds themselves are never described, we know that they have been there because the berries – one of their favourite snacks – have all disappeared.

> Around the house the flakes fly faster,
> And all the berries now are gone
> From holly and cotoneaster
> Around the house. The flakes fly! – faster
> Shutting indoors that crumb-outcaster
> We used to see upon the lawn
> Around the house. The flakes fly faster,
> And all the berries now are gone!

9 December ✷ Town Owl ✷ Laurie Lee

Laurie Lee was an English writer who grew up in the Slad
Valley in Gloucestershire, and his poems are admired for
capturing both the wartime uncertainty of the 1940s and the
beauty and peace of the English countryside. In this poem,
Lee describes an experience he had with an owl, something he
described later as a 'miracle visitation'.

On eves of cold, when slow coal fires,
rooted in basements, burn and branch,
brushing with smoke the city air;

When quartered moons pale in the sky,
and neons glow along the dark
like deadly nightshade on a briar;

Above the muffled traffic then
I hear the owl, and at his note
I shudder in my private chair.

For like an auger he has come
to roost among our crumbling walls,
his blooded talons sheathed in fur.

Some secret lure of time it seems
has called him from his country wastes
to hunt a newer wasteland here.

And where the candelabra swung
bright with the dancers' thousand eyes,
now his black, hooded pupils stare,

And where the silk-shoed lovers ran
with dust of diamonds in their hair,
he opens now his silent wing,

And, like a stroke of doom, drops down,
and swoops across the empty hall,
and plucks a quick mouse off the stair . . .

10 December ✷ Light the Festive Candles ✷
Aileen Lucia Fisher

In this poem, Aileen Lucia Fisher uses each of the stanzas to symbolize the lighting of the nine candles that make up the menorah, a special-nine branch candle holder that is an important part of the Hanukkah celebrations. Hanukkah is a Jewish festival that starts on the 25th day of the Hebrew month of Kislah (usually between late November and late December in the Gregorian calendar) and it lasts for eight days. The festival celebrates the victory of the Maccabees – the Jewish patriots – over the Seleucid army, which was far larger. It also celebrates a miracle that occurred, where a single day's supply of olive oil allowed the menorah in the Temple in Jerusalem to remain alight for eight days.

(For Hanukkah)

Light the first of eight tonight –
the farthest candle to the right.

Light the first and second, too,
when tomorrow's day is through.

Then light three, and then light four –
every dusk one candle more

Till all eight burn bright and high,
honoring a day gone by

When the Temple was restored,
rescued from the Syrian lord,

And an eight-day feast proclaimed –
The Festival of Lights – well named

To celebrate the joyous day
when we regained the right to pray
to our one God in our own way.

11 December ✳ Remembering Snow ✳ Brian Patten

Isn't it strange how a snowfall seems to change everything?
In this poem, Brian Patten's narrator describes a snowy night
that transforms the 'grubby little street' that he knows so well,
seeming to create the whole world anew.

I did not sleep last night.
The falling snow was beautiful and white.
I dressed, sneaked down the stairs
And opened wide the door.
I had not seen such snow before.
Our grubby little street had gone;
The world was brand-new, and everywhere
There was a pureness in the air.
I felt such peace. Watching every flake
I felt more and more awake.
I thought I'd learned all there was to know
About the trillion million different kinds
Of swirling frosty falling flakes of snow.
But that was not so.
I had not known how vividly it lit
The world with such a peaceful glow.
Upstairs my mother slept.
I could not drag myself away from that sight
To call her down and have her share
That mute miracle of snow.
It seemed to fall for me alone.
How beautiful our grubby little street had grown!

12 December ✶ Snow in the Suburbs ✶
Thomas Hardy

In this poem, Thomas Hardy is describing a snowy scene in
the suburbs. Although the poem's human speaker is enjoying
the snow, it isn't quite as much fun for the animals stuck
outside in it, as the comical image of the sparrow stuck under
a snowfall the same size as itself and the black cat seeking
shelter show.

Every branch big with it,
Bent every twig with it;
Every fork like a white web-foot;
Every street and pavement mute:
Some flakes have lost their way, and grope back upward when
Meeting those meandering down they turn and descend again.
The palings are glued together like a wall,
And there is no waft of wind with the fleecy fall.

A sparrow enters the tree,
Whereon immediately
A snow-lump thrice his own slight size
Descends on him and showers his head and eye
And overturns him,
And near inurns him,
And lights on a nether twig, when its brush
Starts off a volley of other lodging lumps with a rush.

The steps are a blanched slope,
Up which, with feeble hope,
A black cat comes, wide-eyed and thin;
And we take him in.

13 December ✴ *from* The Prelude ✴ William Wordsworth

In this passage, an extract from his autobiographical work *The Prelude*, Wordsworth remembers a happy evening skating at sunset in Winter during his childhood in the Lake District. He recalls the joy and excitement of skating with his companions, capturing the energy and excitement as he compares the skaters to chasing hounds, but he is set a little apart from the group as he skates off alone. While skating solo, he is able to appreciate the sublime, awe-inspiring wonder of the mountains and the lakes that surround him, a familiar theme in his poetry.

> And in the frosty season, when the sun
> Was set, and visible for many a mile
> The cottage windows blazed through twilight gloom,
> I heeded not their summons: happy time
> It was indeed for all of us – for me
> It was a time of rapture! Clear and loud
> The village clock tolled six, – I wheeled about,
> Proud and exulting like an untired horse
> That cares not for his home. All shod with steel,
> We hissed along the polished ice in games
> Confederate, imitative of the chase
> And woodland pleasures, – the resounding horn,
> The pack loud chiming, and the hunted hare.
> So through the darkness and the cold we flew,
> And not a voice was idle; with the din
> Smitten, the precipices rang aloud;
> The leafless trees and every icy crag
> Tinkled like iron; while far distant hills
> Into the tumult sent an alien sound
> Of melancholy not unnoticed, while the stars

Eastward were sparkling clear, and in the west
The orange sky of evening died away.
Not seldom from the uproar I retired
Into a silent bay, or sportively
Glanced sideway, leaving the tumultuous throng,
To cut across the reflex of a star
That fled, and, flying still before me, gleamed
Upon the glassy plain; and oftentimes,
When we had given our bodies to the wind,
And all the shadowy banks on either side
Came sweeping through the darkness, spinning still
The rapid line of motion, then at once
Have I, reclining back upon my heels,
Stopped short; yet still the solitary cliffs
Wheeled by me – even as if the earth had rolled
With visible motion her diurnal round!
Behind me did they stretch in solemn train,
Feebler and feebler, and I stood and watched
Till all was tranquil as a dreamless sleep.

14 December ✳ What Are Heavy? ✳ Christina Rossetti

Christina Rossetti was a poet who, as well as writing longer works, also published a book of nursery rhymes, *Sing-Song*. Although this poem has a jaunty feel, due to its short length and its 'sing-song' structure, it creates a thoughtful atmosphere. Rossetti was a devoted Christian, and the call-and-response style of the poem is similar to the way some prayers are phrased in Christian church services, called 'catechisms'.

> What are heavy? Sea-sand and sorrow:
> What are brief? To-day and to-morrow:
> What are frail? Spring blossoms and youth:
> What are deep? The ocean and truth.

15 December ∗ Slip into Sleep ∗ Mandy Coe

Do you ever roll around in bed, unable to get to sleep in spite of every effort at lying still and counting sheep? This meditative poem by Mandy Coe, with its soothing use of repetition and single rhyme of 'sleep' and 'deep', is a brilliant one to remember when you climb into bed.

> Slip your toes into sleep
> Slip your heels into sleep
> Slip your knees into sleep
> Slip your hips into sleep
> Breathe soft, breathe deep
> Slip into sleep
>
> Slip your middle into sleep
> Slip your chest into sleep
> Slip your shoulders into sleep
> Slip your arms into sleep
> Breathe soft, breathe deep
> Slip into sleep
>
> Slip your elbows into sleep
> Slip your wrists into sleep
> Slip your fingers into sleep
> Breathe soft, breathe deep
> Slip into sleep
>
> Slip your neck into sleep
> Slip your chin into sleep
> Slip your lips into sleep
> Breathe soft, breathe deep
> Slip into sleep

Slip your nose into sleep
Slip your eyes into sleep
Slip your hair into sleep
Breathe soft, breathe deep
Slip into sleep

16 December ✳ In the Last Quarter ✳ Dave Calder

Haunted by a huge bright moon and featuring a strange
magical event, this poem by Dave Calder is another that is
perfect for night-time.

She sat at the table under the small light.
Outside the window the moon rose huge and yellow, slow,
   swollen, weighing down the night.

She turned the pages of a book, pages that
were dry and stiff; and the book's spine creaked each time she
   moved her hand to hold them flat.

From somewhere a wind began to stir the room – cups
   chinked softly on their hooks, in a vase the dusty flowers
   brushed together; soon

the shelves, the pots and plates, began to tremble
with the edgy aching sound of something about to break and
   under the swaying lamp she could no longer tell

one word from another. She put her head down,
one ear pressed on the book as if to listen, and watched leaves
   twist across the floor, drift into mounds

around her feet and up against the wall;
leaves swirling and falling till the room was lost in them and
   their rustling whisper like the scurrying of small

animals or the parched voices of the dead. And then her
   eyelids fluttered, shut; and the wind also dropped, sudden,
   and in the room everything fell silent.

The lamp hung above her, its shadow didn't change. Her chair
    stopped creaking, and the leaves
lay deep enough to drown in; like tiny hands or flames

the leaves lay from wall to wall, high
as her waist, as the window. Not a sigh. Beyond the glass the
    moon swept, bright and staring, into a frozen sky.

17 December ✷ High Flight ✷
John Gillespie Magee, Jr.

On this day in 1903, the first ever aeroplane ride took place near Kitty Hawk, North Carolina. This was thanks to two mechanically minded brothers called Orville and Wilbur Wright. 'High Flight' is a sonnet celebrating the joys of being airborne, written in 1941 by another American, John Gillespie Magee, Jr. A pilot in the Royal Canadian Air Force, Magee was only nineteen when he wrote 'High Flight' on the back of an envelope and sent it to his parents.

Oh! I have slipped the surly bonds of Earth
And danced the skies on laughter-silvered wings;
Sunward I've climbed, and joined the tumbling mirth
Of sun-split clouds, and done a hundred things
You have not dreamed of: wheeled and soared and swung
High in the sunlit silence. Hov'ring there,
I've chased the shouting wind along, and flung
My eager craft through footless halls of air . . .
Up, up the long, delirious, burning blue
I've topped the wind-swept heights with easy grace
Where never lark nor even eagle flew
And, while with silent lifting mind I've trod
The high untrespassed sanctity of space,
Put out my hand, and touched the face of God.

18 December ✶ A Week to Christmas ✶
John Cotton

In this poem by John Cotton, the seven rhyming stanzas each
represents a day of the week leading up to Christmas.

Sunday with six whole days to go,
How we'll endure it I don't know!

Monday the goodies are in the making,
Spice smells of pudding and mince pies a-baking.

Tuesday, Dad's home late and quiet as a mouse
He smuggles packages into the house.

Wednesday's the day for decorating the tree.
Will the lights work again? We'll have to see!

Thursday's for last minute shopping and hurry,
We've never seen Mum in quite such a flurry!

Friday is Christmas Eve when we'll lie awake
Trying to sleep before the day break.

And that special quiet of Christmas morn
When out there somewhere Christ was born.

19 December * Christmas * John Betjeman

John Betjeman was a practising Anglican, and the religious side of his character comes through in some of his poems, particularly those that are inspired by Christmas. This poem both celebrates the secular traditions of the Christmas season, such as the wrapped gifts and decorations, as a time that brings people together, and expresses doubts about the true meaning of the Christian festival, illustrated by the repetition of the rhetorical question 'Is it true?'. The poem is ultimately a hopeful one, however, as Betjeman reveals his faith in the Nativity story, and optimism about the way Christmas can bring people together.

The bells of waiting Advent ring,
    The Tortoise stove is lit again
And lamp-oil light across the night
    Has caught the streaks of winter rain
In many a stained-glass window sheen
From Crimson Lake to Hooker's Green.

The holly in the windy hedge
    And round the Manor House the yew
Will soon be stripped to deck the ledge,
    The altar, font and arch and pew,
So that the villagers can say
'The church looks nice' on Christmas Day.

Provincial public houses blaze,
    And Corporation tramcars clang,
On lighted tenements I gaze
    Where paper decorations hang,
And bunting in the red Town Hall
Says 'Merry Christmas to you all'.

And London shops on Christmas Eve
  Are strung with silver bells and flowers
As hurrying clerks the City leave
  To pigeon-haunted classic towers,
And marbled clouds go scudding by
The many-steepled London sky.

And girls in slacks remember Dad,
  And oafish louts remember Mum,
And sleepless children's hearts are glad.
  And Christmas-morning bells say 'Come!'
Even to shining ones who dwell
Safe in the Dorchester Hotel.

And is it true? And is it true?
  This most tremendous tale of all,
Seen in a stained-glass window's hue,
  A Baby in an ox's stall ?
The Maker of the stars and sea
Become a Child on earth for me?

And is it true ? For if it is,
  No loving fingers tying strings
Around those tissued fripperies,
  The sweet and silly Christmas things,
Bath salts and inexpensive scent
And hideous tie so kindly meant,

No love that in a family dwells,
  No carolling in frosty air,
Nor all the steeple-shaking bells
  Can with this single Truth compare –
That God was Man in Palestine
And lives to-day in Bread and Wine.

20 December ✳ Talking Turkeys ✳
Benjamin Zephaniah

Benjamin Zephaniah is a British Jamaican poet, lyricist and writer who often incorporates Jamaican dialect into his work. This poem, and the book of the same name, enjoyed huge success upon their release in 1994.

> Be nice to yu turkeys dis christmas
> Cos' turkeys just wanna hav fun
> Turkeys are cool, turkeys are wicked
> An every turkey has a Mum.
> Be nice to yu turkeys dis christmas,
> Don't eat it, keep it alive,
> It could be yu mate, an not on yu plate
> Say, Yo! Turkey I'm on your side.
>
> I got lots of friends who are turkeys
> An all of dem fear christmas time,
> Dey wanna enjoy it, dey say humans destroyed it
> An humans are out of dere mind,
> Yeah, I got lots of friends who are turkeys
> Dey all hav a right to a life,
> Not to be caged up an genetically made up
> By any farmer an his wife.
>
> Turkeys just wanna play reggae
> Turkeys just wanna hip-hop
> Can yu imagine a nice young turkey saying,
> 'I cannot wait for de chop',
> Turkeys like getting presents, dey wanna watch
>   christmas TV,
> Turkeys hav brains an turkeys feel pain
> In many ways like yu an me.

I once knew a turkey called
Turkey
He said 'Benji explain to me please,
Who put de turkey in christmas
An what happens to christmas trees?',
I said 'I am not too sure turkey
But it's nothing to do wid Christ Mass
Humans get greedy an waste more dan need be
An business men mek loadsa cash'.

Be nice to yu turkey dis christmas
Invite dem indoors fe sum greens
Let dem eat cake an let dem partake
In a plate of organic grown beans,
Be nice to yu turkey dis christmas
An spare dem de cut of de knife,
Join Turkeys United an dey'll be delighted
An yu will mek new friends 'FOR LIFE'.

21 December ✳ Amazing Peace ✳ Maya Angelou

This Christmas poem imagines a lasting peace between
the adherents of all major religions, 'Baptist and Buddhist,
Methodist and Muslim'. The poet finds a remarkable power in
the softly spoken word 'peace', which can triumph over war and
violence. Angelou, who was recognized throughout her life as a
political figure and civil rights activist, concludes the poem by
addressing the word 'peace' to her brothers and sisters in the
human race, before finally speaking the word to her own soul.

Thunder rumbles in the mountain passes
And lightning rattles the eaves of our houses.
Flood waters await us in our avenues.

Snow falls upon snow, falls upon snow to avalanche
Over unprotected villages.
The sky slips low and grey and threatening.

We question ourselves.
What have we done to so affront nature?
We worry God.
Are you there? Are you there really?
Does the covenant you made with us still hold?

Into this climate of fear and apprehension, Christmas enters,
Streaming lights of joy, ringing bells of hope
And singing carols of forgiveness high up in the bright air.
The world is encouraged to come away from rancor,
Come the way of friendship.

It is the Glad Season.
Thunder ebbs to silence and lightning sleeps quietly in the
    corner.

Flood waters recede into memory.
Snow becomes a yielding cushion to aid us
As we make our way to higher ground.

Hope is born again in the faces of children
It rides on the shoulders of our aged as they walk into their
     sunsets.
Hope spreads around the earth. Brightening all things,
Even hate which crouches breeding in dark corridors.

In our joy, we think we hear a whisper.
At first it is too soft. Then only half heard.
We listen carefully as it gathers strength.
We hear a sweetness.
The word is Peace.
It is loud now. It is louder.
Louder than the explosion of bombs.

We tremble at the sound. We are thrilled by its presence.
It is what we have hungered for.
Not just the absence of war. But, true Peace.
A harmony of spirit, a comfort of courtesies.
Security for our beloveds and their beloveds.

We clap hands and welcome the Peace of Christmas.
We beckon this good season to wait a while with us.
We, Baptist and Buddhist, Methodist and Muslim, say come.
     Peace.
Come and fill us and our world with your majesty.
We, the Jew and the Jainist, the Catholic and the Confucian,
Implore you, to stay a while with us.
So we may learn by your shimmering light
How to look beyond complexion and see community.

It is Christmas time, a halting of hate time.

On this platform of peace, we can create a language
To translate ourselves to ourselves and to each other.

At this Holy Instant, we celebrate the Birth of Jesus Christ
Into the great religions of the world.
We jubilate the precious advent of trust.
We shout with glorious tongues at the coming of hope.
All the earth's tribes loosen their voices
To celebrate the promise of Peace.

We, Angels and Mortals, Believers and Non-Believers,
Look heavenward and speak the word aloud.
Peace. We look at our world and speak the word aloud.
Peace. We look at each other, then into ourselves
And we say without shyness or apology or hesitation.

Peace, My Brother.
Peace, My Sister.
Peace, My Soul.

22 December ✳ Mary's Burden ✳ Eleanor Farjeon

Christmas Day is traditionally the celebration of the birth of the
baby Jesus, which came at the end of a long and difficult journey
for Mary and her husband Joseph. In this poem, Eleanor Farjeon
imagines Mary being relieved of the 'burden' of her pregnancy,
only to be burdened in a different way, with worries about all that
her son will have to bear, as the saviour of mankind.

My Baby, my Burden,
Tomorrow the morn
I shall go lighter
And you will be born.

I shall go lighter,
But heavier too
For seeing the burden
That falls upon you.

The burden of love,
The burden of pain,
I'll see you bear both
Among men once again.

Tomorrow you'll bear it
Your burden alone,
Tonight you've no burden
That is not my own

My Baby, my Burden,
Tomorrow the morn
I shall go lighter
And you will be born.

492

23 December ✳ Help Wanted ✳ Timothy Tocher

This poem by Timothy Tocher takes its inspiration from 'A Visit from St Nicholas', which you can find over the page. Tocher's poem is a comic reinterpretation of the familiar image of Father Christmas and his faithful reindeer, imagining a poster advertising for new reindeer to take over from Dasher, Dancer, Rudolf and the rest.

Santa needs new reindeer.
The first bunch has grown old.
Dasher has arthritis;
Comet hates the cold.
Prancer's sick of staring
at Dancer's big behind.
Cupid married Blitzen
and Donder lost his mind.
Dancer's mad at Vixen
for stepping on his toes.
Vixen's being thrown out –
she laughed at Rudolph's nose.
If you are a reindeer
we hope you will apply.
There is just one tricky part:
You must know how to fly.

24 December ✶ A Visit from St Nicholas ✶ Clement Clarke Moore

'A Visit from St Nicholas' is possibly the one poem which has most influence on modern depictions of St Nicholas, or Santa Claus, across the English-speaking world. It is said that Moore wrote the poem for his family on Christmas Eve, 1822, and never intended for it to be published.

'Twas the night before Christmas, when all through the house
Not a creature was stirring, not even a mouse;
The stockings were hung by the chimney with care,
In hopes that St Nicholas soon would be there;
The children were nestled all snug in their beds;
While visions of sugar-plums danced in their heads;
And mamma in her 'kerchief, and I in my cap,
Had just settled our brains for a long winter's nap –
When out on the lawn there arose such a clatter,
I sprang from my bed to see what was the matter.
Away to the window I flew like a flash,
Tore open the shutters and threw up the sash.
The moon on the breast of the new-fallen snow,
Gave a lustre of midday to objects below;
When what to my wondering eyes did appear,
But a miniature sleigh and eight tiny reindeer,
With a little old driver so lively and quick,
I knew in a moment it must be St Nick.
More rapid than eagles his coursers they came,
And he whistled, and shouted, and called them by name:
'Now, *Dasher*! now, *Dancer*! now, *Prancer* and *Vixen*!
On, *Comet*! on, *Cupid*! on, *Doner* and *Blitzen*!
To the top of the porch! to the top of the wall!
Now dash away! dash away! dash away all!'
As leaves that before the wild hurricane fly,

When they meet with an obstacle, mount to the sky;
So up to the house-top the coursers they flew
With the sleigh full of toys, and St Nicholas too –
And then, in a twinkling, I heard on the roof
The prancing and pawing of each little hoof.
As I drew in my head, and was turning around,
Down the chimney St Nicholas came with a bound.
He was dressed all in fur, from his head to his foot,
And his clothes were all tarnished with ashes and soot;
A bundle of toys he had flung on his back,
And he looked like a pedlar just opening his pack.
His eyes – how they twinkled! his dimples, how merry!
His cheeks were like roses, his nose like a cherry!
His droll little mouth was drawn up like a bow,
And the beard on his chin was as white as the snow;
The stump of a pipe he held tight in his teeth,
And the smoke, it encircled his head like a wreath;
He had a broad face and a little round belly
That shook, when he laughed, like a bowl full of jelly.
He was chubby and plump, a right jolly old elf,
And I laughed when I saw him, in spite of myself;
A wink of his eye and a twist of his head
Soon gave me to know I had nothing to dread;
He spoke not a word, but went straight to his work,
And filled all the stockings; then turned with a jerk,
And laying his finger aside of his nose,
And giving a nod, up the chimney he rose;
He sprang to his sleigh, to his team gave a whistle,
And away they all flew like the down of a thistle.
But I heard him exclaim, ere he drove out of sight:
'Happy Christmas to all, and to all a good night!'

25 December ✳ The Twelve Days of Christmas ✳
Anon.

This popular carol was originally published without music, as a poem, in the eighteenth century. 'The Twelve Days of Christmas' run from Christmas Day to the eve of Epiphany on 5 January.

On the first day of Christmas,
my true love sent to me
A partridge in a pear tree.

On the second day of Christmas,
my true love sent to me
Two turtle doves,
And a partridge in a pear tree.

On the third day of Christmas,
my true love sent to me
Three French hens,
Two turtle doves,
And a partridge in a pear tree.

On the fourth day of Christmas,
my true love sent to me
Four calling birds,
Three French hens,
Two turtle doves,
And a partridge in a pear tree.

On the fifth day of Christmas,
my true love sent to me
Five golden rings,
Four calling birds,

Three French hens,
Two turtle doves,
And a partridge in a pear tree.

On the sixth day of Christmas,
my true love sent to me
Six geese a-laying,
Five golden rings,
Four calling birds,
Three French hens,
Two turtle doves,
And a partridge in a pear tree.

On the seventh day of Christmas,
my true love sent to me
Seven swans a-swimming,
Six geese a-laying,
Five golden rings,
Four calling birds,
Three French hens,
Two turtle doves,
And a partridge in a pear tree.

On the eighth day of Christmas,
my true love sent to me
Eight maids a-milking,
Seven swans a-swimming,
Six geese a-laying,
Five golden rings,
Four calling birds,
Three French hens,
Two turtle doves,
And a partridge in a pear tree.

On the ninth day of Christmas,
my true love sent to me
Nine ladies dancing,
Eight maids a-milking,
Seven swans a-swimming,
Six geese a-laying,
Five golden rings,
Four calling birds,
Three French hens,
Two turtle doves,
And a partridge in a pear tree.

On the tenth day of Christmas,
my true love sent to me
Ten lords a-leaping,
Nine ladies dancing,
Eight maids a-milking,
Seven swans a-swimming,
Six geese a-laying,
Five golden rings,
Four calling birds,
Three French hens,
Two turtle doves,
And a partridge in a pear tree.

On the eleventh day of Christmas,
my true love sent to me
Eleven pipers piping,
Ten lords a-leaping,
Nine ladies dancing,
Eight maids a-milking,
Seven swans a-swimming,
Six geese a-laying,
Five golden rings,
Four calling birds,
Three French hens,

Two turtle doves,
And a partridge in a pear tree.

On the twelfth day of Christmas,
my true love sent to me
Twelve drummers drumming,
Eleven pipers piping,
Ten lords a-leaping,
Nine ladies dancing,
Eight maids a-milking,
Seven swans a-swimming,
Six geese a-laying,
Five golden rings,
Four calling birds,
Three French hens,
Two turtle doves,
And a partridge in a pear tree!

26 December ✳ King John's Christmas ✳
A. A. Milne

This is a light-hearted idea of how one of the more
controversial monarchs of medieval England might have spent
Christmas.

> King John was not a good man –
>   He had his little ways.
> And sometimes no one spoke to him
>   For days and days and days.
> And men who came across him,
>   When walking in the town,
> Gave him a supercilious stare,
> Or passed with noses in the air –
> And bad King John stood dumbly there,
>   Blushing beneath his crown.
>
> King John was not a good man,
>   And no good friends had he.
> He stayed in every afternoon . . .
>   But no one came to tea.
> And, round about December,
>   The cards upon his shelf
> Which wished him lots of Christmas cheer,
> And fortune in the coming year,
> Were never from his near and dear,
>   But only from himself.

King John was not a good man,
    Yet had his hopes and fears.
They'd given him no present now
    For years and years and years.
But every year at Christmas,
    While minstrels stood about,
Collecting tribute from the young
For all the songs they might have sung,
He stole away upstairs and hung
    A hopeful stocking out.

King John was not a good man,
    He lived his live aloof;
Alone he thought a message out
    While climbing up the roof.
He wrote it down and propped it
    Against the chimney stack:
'TO ALL AND SUNDRY – NEAR AND FAR –
F. Christmas in particular.'
And signed it not 'Johannes R.'
    But very humbly, 'Jack'.

'I want some crackers,
    And I want some candy;
I think a box of chocolates
    Would come in handy;
I don't mind oranges,
    I do like nuts!
And I SHOULD like a pocket-knife
That really cuts.
And, oh! Father Christmas, if you love me at all,
    Bring me a big, red, india-rubber ball!'

King John was not a good man –
   He wrote this message out,
And gat him to this room again,
   Descending by the spout.
And all that night he lay there,
   A prey to hopes and fears.
   'I think that's him a-coming now!'
   (Anxiety bedewed his brow.)
   'He'll bring one present, anyhow –
   The first I've had for years.'

'Forget about the crackers,
   And forget the candy;
I'm sure a box of chocolates
   Would never come in handy;
I don't like oranges,
   I don't want nuts,
And I HAVE got a pocket-knife
   That almost cuts.
But, oh! Father Christmas, if you love me at all,
Bring me a big, red, india-rubber ball!'

King John was not a good man –
   Next morning when the sun
Rose up to tell a waiting world
   That Christmas had begun,
And people seized their stockings,
   And opened them with glee,
And crackers, toys and games appeared,
And lips with sticky sweets were smeared,
King John said grimly: 'As I feared,
   Nothing again for me!'

'I did want crackers,
    And I did want candy;
I know a box of chocolates
    Would come in handy;
I do love oranges,
    I did want nuts!
I haven't got a pocket-knife -
    Not one that cuts.
And, oh! if Father Christmas, had loved me at all,
He would have brought a big, red, india-rubber ball!'

King John stood by the window,
    And frowned to see below
The happy bands of boys and girls
    All playing in the snow.
A while he stood there watching,
    And envying them all . . .
When through the window big and red
There hurtled by his royal head,
And bounced and fell upon the bed,
    An india-rubber ball!

AND, OH, FATHER CHRISTMAS,
    MY BLESSINGS ON YOU FALL
        FOR BRINGING HIM
        A BIG, RED,
        INDIA-RUBBER
        BALL!

27 December ∗ At Nine of the Night ∗
Charles Causley

In this poem, Charles Causley takes a familiar, snowy
Christmas scene and turns it on its head, leaving the reader
full of questions. Who is the stranger wrapped in a red
cloak? Is it the stable-boy, or is it someone altogether more
mysterious?

At nine of the night I opened my door
That stands midway between moor and moor,
And all around me, silver-bright,
I saw that the world had turned to white.

Thick was the snow on field and hedge
And vanished was the river-sedge,
Where winter skilfully had wound
A shining scarf without a sound.

And as I stood and gazed my fill
A stable-boy came down the hill.
With every step I saw him take
Flew at his heel a puff of flake.

His brow was whiter than the hoar,
A beard of freshest snow he wore,
And round about him, snowflake starred,
A red horse-blanket from the yard.

In a red cloak I saw him go,
His back was bent, his step was slow,
And as he laboured through the cold
He seemed a hundred winters old.

I stood and watched the snowy head,
The whiskers white, the cloak of red.
'A Merry Christmas!' I heard him cry.
'The same to you, old friend,' said I.

28 December ✷ In the Bleak Midwinter ✷ Christina Rossetti

In the early 1870s, Christina Rossetti wrote this poem in response to an advert in the magazine *Scribner's Monthly* that was looking for a Christmas poem. Rossetti describes the birth of the baby Jesus, before stating that it doesn't matter if you can't afford to give anything expensive or impressive: it's enough just to give your heart. The poem has been set to music many times, and remains a popular Christmas carol.

> In the bleak midwinter
>   Frosty wind made moan,
> Earth stood hard as iron,
>   Water like a stone;
> Snow had fallen, snow on snow,
>   Snow on snow,
> In the bleak midwinter
>   Long ago.
>
> Our God, Heaven cannot hold Him,
>   Nor earth sustain;
> Heaven and earth shall flee away
>   When He comes to reign.
> In the bleak midwinter
>   A stable place sufficed
> The Lord God Almighty,
>   Jesus Christ.

Enough for Him, whom cherubim
   Worship night and day,
A breastful of milk,
   And a mangerful of hay;
Enough for Him, whom angels
   Fall down before,
The ox and ass and camel
   Which adore.

Angels and archangels
   May have gathered there,
Cherubim and seraphim
   Thronged the air;
But His mother only,
   In her maiden bliss,
Worshipped the beloved
   With a kiss.

What can I give Him,
   Poor as I am?
If I were a shepherd,
   I would bring a lamb;
If I were a Wise Man,
   I would do my part;
Yet what I can I give Him:
   Give my heart.

29 December ★ Innocents' Song ★
Charles Causley

28 and 29 December are known, by the Catholic Church and the Greek Orthodox Church respectively, as the Day of the Innocents. This marks the Biblical story in which King Herod, having been warned that a child had been born who was the future king, ordered the slaughter of all the male children in Bethlehem. This poem by Charles Causley creates a frightening picture of these events, with the intricate descriptions of the 'smiling stranger' creating a sinister atmosphere, before he is revealed in the final verse to be Herod himself.

Who's that knocking on the window,
Who's that standing at the door,
What are all those presents
Laying on the kitchen floor?

Who is the smiling stranger
With hair as white as gin,
What is he doing with the children
And who could have let him in?

Why has he rubies on his fingers,
A cold, cold crown on his head,
Why, when he caws his carol,
Does the salty snow run red?

Why does he ferry my fireside
As a spider on a thread,
His fingers made of fuses
And his tongue of gingerbread?

Why does the world before him
Melt in a million suns,
Why do his yellow, yearning eyes
Burn like saffron buns?

Watch where he comes walking
Out of the Christmas flame,
Dancing, double-talking:

Herod is his name.

30 December ✳ Crossing the Bar ✳
Alfred, Lord Tennyson

In this beautiful poem the speaker describes himself setting
sail in the evening – an image which is a metaphor for passing
from life into death. The term 'bar' here means a bank of
sand or pebbles across a harbour – an obstacle that must be
traversed in order to sail into the ocean. The poem is filled
with imagery connected to endings, such as the evening
star and bell, twilight and farewells. Shortly before he died,
Tennyson asked that 'Crossing the Bar' be placed at the end of
every anthology of his poetical works.

Sunset and evening star,
    And one clear call for me!
And may there be no moaning of the bar,
    When I put out to sea,

But such a tide as moving seems asleep,
    Too full for sound and foam,
When that which drew from out the boundless deep
    Turns again home.

Twilight and evening bell,
    And after that the dark!
And may there be no sadness of farewell,
    When I embark;

For tho' from out our bourne of Time and Place
    The flood may bear me far,
I hope to see my Pilot face to face
    When I have crost the bar.

31 December ∗ Auld Lang Syne ∗ Robert Burns

In terms of its lyrics, there seems to be no reason why the popular setting of Robert Burns's poem 'Auld Lang Syne' should not be sung on any night of the year, but some time soon after its publication the song became associated with Hogmanay, the Scottish term for the final day of the year, and it has remained so ever since. The title of the poem is a Lallans, or Lowland Scots phrase meaning 'old long since' or 'days gone by', and the poem is a straightforward celebration of how much of a pleasure it is to share a friendly drink and pass the time with good company while remembering these 'days gone by'.

Should auld acquaintance be forgot,
    And never brought to mind?
Should auld acquaintance be forgot,
    And auld lang syne!

For auld lang syne, my dear,
For auld lang syne.
We'll tak a cup o' kindness yet,
For auld lang syne.

And surely ye'll be your pint stowp!
    And surely I'll be mine!
And we'll tak a cup o' kindness yet,
    For auld lang syne.

We twa hae run about the braes,
    And pou'd the gowans fine;
But we've wander'd mony a weary fit,
    Sin' auld lang syne.

We twa hae paidl'd in the burn,
    Frae morning sun till dine;
But seas between us braid hae roar'd
    Sin' auld lang syne.

And there's a hand, my trusty fere!
    And gie's a hand o' thine!
And we'll tak a right gude-willie waught,
    For auld lang syne.

For auld lang syne, my dear,
For auld lang syne.
We'll tak a cup o' kindness yet,
For auld lang syne.

Index of First Lines

516

517

Index of Poets and Translators

Acknowledgements

The compiler and publisher would like to thank the following for permission to use copyright material:

Agard, John, 'A Date with Spring' and 'The Hurt Boy and the Birds' from *Get Back Pimple* published by Penguin. All poems published by permission of John Agard c/o the Caroline Sheldon Literary Agency; **Al-Massri, Maram,** 'Knocks on the Door' from *A Red Cherry on a White-tiled Floor,* trans. Khaled Mattawa (Bloodaxe Books, 2004); **Armitage, Simon,** 'The Convergence of the Twain' copyright © Simon Armitage; **Atwood, Margaret,** 'The Moment' reproduced with permission of Curtis Brown Group Ltd, London, on behalf of Margaret Atwood. Copyright © Margaret Atwood 1995; **Belloc, Hilaire,** 'Tarantella' from *Sonnets and Verse* by Hilaire Belloc reprinted by permission of Peters Fraser & Dunlop (www.petersfraserdunlop.com) on behalf of the Estate of Hilaire Belloc, 'Jim, Who Ran Away from His Nurse and Was Eaten by a Lion' from *Cautionary Tales for Children* by Hilaire Belloc reprinted by permission of Peters Fraser & Dunlop (www.petersfraserdunlop.com) on behalf of the Estate of Hilaire Belloc; **Bentley, E.C.,** 'Alfred, Lord Tennyson' and 'Wolfgang Amadeus Mozart' reproduced with permission of Curtis Brown Group Ltd, London, on behalf of The Beneficiary of the Estate of E. C. Bentley © The Beneficiary of the Estate of E. C. Bentley, 2016; **Betjeman, John,** 'Hunter Trials', 'Slough' and 'Christmas' © The Estate of John Betjeman 1955, 1958, 1960, 1962, 1964, 1966, 1970, 1979, 1981, 1982, 2001. Reproduced by permission of Hodder and Stoughton Limited; **Bishop, Elizabeth,** 'Manners' and 'One Art' from *Poems: The Centenery Edtion* by Elizabeth Bishop (Chatto & Windus, 2011) by permission of Penguin Random House; **Bromley, Carole,** 'Goldilocks' was shortlisted for the Manchester Writing for Children Award 2015, performed at the CLiPPA Awards and published in *Let in the Stars* (ed. Mandy Coe). An extract from it was published on the Guardian Children's Books website; **Burton, Tim,** 'The Girl with Many Eyes', reproduced by permission of the author; **Calder, Dave,** 'Silkie,' and 'In The Last Quarter' by permission of the author; **Carter, James,** 'Love You More' from *Time-Travelling Underpants* (Macmillan Children's Books) published by permission of the author; **Causley, Charles,** 'At Nine of the Night' from *I Had A Little cat – Collected Poems For Children* (Macmillan Children's Books), 'Innocents' Song' from *Collected Poems 1951– 2000* (Macmillan) All poems published by permission of David Higham Associates on behalf of the estate of the author; **Coe, Mandy,** 'Slip into Sleep' by permission of the author; **Coelho, Joseph,** 'M.O.R.E.R.A.P.S.' by permission of the author; **Collins, Billy,** 'Walking Across the Atlantic' by Billy Collins taken from *Taking Off Emily Dickinson's Clothes,* published by Picador, London © Billy Collins, 2000; **Cotton, John,** 'A Week to Christmas' by permission of the author; **Cummings, E. E.,** 'in Just-' copyright 1923, 1951© 1991 by the Trustees of E. E. Cummings Trust. Copyright © 1976 by George James Firmage. 'maggie and milly and molly and may' copyright © 1956, 1984, 1991 by the Trustees for the E. E. Cummings Trust, from *Complete Poems: 1904–1962* by E. E. Cummings, edited by George J. Firmage. 'l(a' copyright © 1958, 1986, 1991 by Trustees for the E. E. Cummings Trust. Used by permission of Liveright Publishing Corporation; **Dahl, Roald,** 'The Pig' from *Dirty Beasts* published by Jonathan Cape Ltd & Penguin Books Ltd, 'Little Red Riding Hood and the Wolf' from *Revolting Rhymes* published by Jonathan Cape Ltd & Penguin Books Ltd, 'Down Vith Children!' from *The Witches* published by Jonathan Cape Ltd & Penguin Books Ltd. All poems published by permission of David Higham Associates on behalf of the estate of the author; **de la Mare, Walter,** 'Silver', 'The Listeners', 'Someone' and 'Napoleon' by permission of The Literary Trustees of Walter de la Mare and the Society of Authors as their representative; **Dean, Jan,** 'Three Good Things' and 'Rosa Parks' by permission of the author; **Denton, Graham,** 'Evening Shifts' and 'How Many Moons!' by permission of the author; **Dharker, Imtiaz,**

523